THE COMPOUND

Eli Wellington

Eli Wellington/Dystopian Publishing
Post Office Box 401170
San Francisco, CA 94140
info@dystopianpublishing.com

Publisher's Note: This is a work of fiction. Names, characters, places, and incidents are a product of the author's imagination. Any resemblance to actual people, living or dead, or to businesses, companies, events, institutions, or locales is completely coincidental.

Book Layout © 2015-2022 BookDesignTemplates.com

THE COMPOUND / Eli Wellington. – First Edition.
ISBN 978-1-959656-03-6

This book is dedicated to Jen Nelson

The screen came to life, blinking the time. Seven in the morning. Triden swung his legs over the side of his bed and contemplated a moment before standing to make his way to the bathroom. As he moved, the screen flashed the usual morning message: *"Lucky to Be Alive!"*

His studio apartment mirrored all the others in the Contagion Compound. Cinder block walls, a door to his right, and a bare window to his left. The cement floor was covered with a woven mat, his bed frame simple with a single mattress, crisp white sheets, a felted gray blanket, and a white cased pillow. The screen encompassed most of the wall across from his bed and provided the only color in the room.

"Lucky to Be Alive!" flashed again on a blue background, replacing yellow from the image before.

There was a full-length mirror in addition to the vanity mirror in the bathroom, which many in the Compound chose to cover with a bed sheet. Triden refused to ignore the marks on his body and indulged a curiosity about the dark rash covering his skin. His naked reflection in the mirror became a case study every morning as he looked for any changes. This morning wasn't too bad. Sometimes the marks were so dark they looked like an angry storm raged across his skin. Today, the rash appeared pink and almost happy.

While his body looked volatile, the marks and blemishes did not hurt or itch. Some in the Compound had extreme difficulties with the rash, which sometimes manifested with welts and oozing pestilence that landed them in the infirmary for days. No one wanted to be in the infirmary. It marked anyone as a virus trial participant as Society sought to find a cure. There was no choice; it was your moral responsibility to fight the virus, even if it meant sacrifice.

Triden looked in the mirror, his dark brown hair matted by sleep, a dusky shadow of an overnight beard emerging. His dark green eyes reflected back resignation at his situation. He was one of the lucky ones.

Lucky to be alive for sure, he thought. His parents hadn't been so fortunate.

Stepping inside the shower stall, it didn't take long to bathe. He was used to the tepid water and soaped and rinsed his body quickly. Toweling dry, he stepped to the small metal sink and splashed water on his face. He reached for shaving cream and a razor to remove his morning stubble.

The sink faucet was still dripping. He'd logged a maintenance request every day for the last seventy-six days, and still, no one had come to replace the washer; a simple fix.

Back in the main room, he touched the screen, a menu appeared, and he selected the tool icon and logged the drip. The screen confirmed the entry. Day 77. Jobs were prioritized by urgency and a washer was insignificant enough it kept getting pushed to the bottom of the list. He debated about logging a more pressing issue, however, any misrepresentation or deceit was ill-advised. He'd have more problems than a dripping faucet.

The screen flashed a reminder: *"Please be prepared to depart for the dining commons in 15 minutes."* For now, the screen relayed silent messages. If he failed to leave his studio by 7:30, the voice command would start politely and then make more urgent demands. Any delay would have harsh consequences.

Triden reached for the paper-wrapped package containing fresh clothing for the day. He pulled on the loose, white cotton undergarment designed to minimize friction to his skin. The long bodysuit covered the majority of rashes, with a cutout exposing his genitalia, which were then covered by a pair of cotton shorts that could easily be pulled down as bodily functions required. A long brown monk-style robe layered over the white material. A rope sash secured the garment. Sitting on the side of the bed, he pulled on brown leather work boots and tied the laces. Lastly, Triden put a collared hood over his head before stepping to the door. He held out the underside of his left wrist to expose his personal barcode and waved it over a reflective utility plate and the door slid open.

The time on the screen: 7:28.

The dining area gradually filled with others from Triden's compound block. In the early morning, it was customary not to talk but to eat in quiet meditation to prepare for the day. Triden joined the queue to get the customary protein pucks and hot tea. One was a dry concoction that came in a variety of flavors designed to meet all dietary requirements, and the other an herbal mix. Both varied day by day. Today's puck flavor mimicked corned beef and cabbage, one of his least favorite. The taste had a metallic quality, and he was thankful for the bitter tea to wash away the aftertaste. A large screen flashed overhead.

"Take what you need. Waste not, want not."

There was no restriction on the meal; the only requirement was to finish what was taken.

Triden kept his head down, his hood obscuring most of his face. He valued the quiet time and minimal interactions in the morning. The buffet line was self-serve along a steel railing. The protein pucks were stacked in large, industrial food trays, and the tea was dispensed from metal vats into clear glass mugs, the only items to be returned for cleaning after the meal.

The screen overhead made the first verbal sound of the day.

"Welcome to your day, Contagions. Today is a day to rejoice in how lucky it is to be alive! Please make your way to your posts. Work will commence in 15 minutes."

Others around him were already filing out of the spacious room. Each person placed their glass mug into cleaning trays near the exit. Anyone who filled the last compartment would push the tray onto a conveyor belt to start the cleaning process. The system was automated, and everyone knew their responsibility to keep the line moving forward.

The mugs were whisked away on the right, and to the left of the exit, there were bins filled with take-away lunches to minimize lost time for consuming a mid-day meal. Triden knew the bag was filled with two more protein pucks, likely the same flavor as breakfast, as well as a snack puck designed to mimic some type of fruit he'd never seen or a salty, savory grain known as keyma.

The line began to disperse as soon as the group left the dining building. Dark storm clouds still threatened after the heavy rains the day before. Fall was in the air and marked the turning of seasons. Triden made his way down the road, past the rows of the apartment complex toward the center of the business structures. A few thin trees were planted in an effort to create a connection to nature.

Everyone had a role in the Compound based on assessment tests taken when they were young. They were assigned to tasks optimizing their skills. Triden learned about water sterilization and waste recycling and performed maintenance on the large vats of water processed through a filtration system so the Contagion Compound could be self-sufficient.

Stepping into an alleyway, he made his way past several of the main office buildings where other cloaked citizens were entering for their assigned duties. The Department of Water and Waste was marked with a W&W sign overhead. He opened the door by waving his barcode over a utility plate similar to the one in his apartment. Only those with approved access could enter. The door slid open when a green light flashed acceptance of his code.

A wall lined with hard hats filled the vestibule and Triden lowered his hood and selected one of the helmets before stepping toward the sliding doors leading to the interior of the utility building. Only a handful of citizens worked in the office spaces, and Triden usually worked his shifts alone, overseeing the processing and flow of water, ensuring the heavy equipment hummed without issue.

At the end of the hallway, after a series of offices, Triden entered a metal stairwell that wound down to the bowels of the Compound. His heavy work boots created metallic echoes as he climbed down to the dungeon-like setting where he spent eight hours every day.

He tossed his bagged lunch on a metal table at the bottom of the stairs and picked up a pair of leather work gloves to make it easier to turn the large wheels to shift the water from one vat to the next to complete the purification process. He also selected a tool belt from the wall and secured it over the tie of his robe.

Sounds of flowing water and the hum of machinery vibrated around the chamber and reflections from the water glimmered on the brick ceiling overhead. The first task of the day required navigating the myriad of waterways to look for any issues. Leaking pipes and overheating equipment would be the first sign of potential problems of an infrastructure outdated and cobbled together. Any ticket logged on the screen here would get immediate attention. He knew from experience he was responsible for exploring all potential solutions before resorting to creating a ticket.

The cavernous hallways felt familiar and peaceful as Triden made his rounds. As he walked, he confirmed valves were turned, water was flowing, and systems were in order. He was on the last aisle when he noticed a small trickle of water running down the center of the hallway sloped toward a drain. It did not appear to be coming from the sterilization lines overhead. Curious, Triden followed the flow of water, going upstream to find the source.

As he walked beyond his normal route, he realized the water flow originated outside of his work domain. There was rarely a need to traverse the long waterways bringing sewage and waste to the sterilization plant from all areas of the Compound. Those pipes consisted of three-foot diameter iron pipes lined with hard plastic. They were designed to avoid failure. In the event the plastic failed, the iron was insurance that the pipes needed minimal inspection and maintenance.

Triden followed the trickle of water and meandered through the various twists and turns of pipes transporting fluid to the main sterilization station. Normally he wouldn't have been too concerned with the small sliver of water, but he knew the infrastructure was feeling the strain from years of neglect. The Compound was built quickly around an abandoned hospital to isolate those with the deadly virus P3264 instead of relying on mass terminations, the first reaction to the pandemic.

He turned down another tunnel and pulled out his flashlight. He ventured past the main area that had strong fluorescent lighting overhead. The beam of light sparkled across the small stream of water. His curiosity overrode his impulse to dismiss the trickle as insignificant and propelled him forward.

The pipes overhead split with one extending left, and the second continuing past a walled partition. *That's odd*, Triden thought. At some point, all the tunnels were blocked off with chain-link fence and barbed wire. It was illegal for anyone in the Contagion Compound to leave the radius of the facility. A ten-foot cement wall with barbed wire at the top surrounded the Compound and was meant to provide safety and security for both the Contagions inside and Society on the other side. The virus was deadly. If it didn't kill you outright, it remained as a daily reminder there was no cure, and once contracted, always contagious.

"Take a Life, Give Your Own" was another common screen message; a regular notice reminding Contagions any exposure with anyone outside the Compound could result in death for all involved.

The water seeped through the walled-in partition. It was impossible to know how much was being dammed by the wall. Triden looked for the bolts holding the wall in place. It was evident the partition was secured from the other side. He pushed on the panel to see if he could tell where the mounts were placed. Surprisingly, it wasn't attached, and the wood slipped forward, revealing a few inches of the floor below. The water continued to trickle past his feet. Relieved the barrier had not created a dam, Triden pushed again, and the wood scraped along the hard floor and created an opening wide enough to slip through.

Stepping to the other side, Triden looked back at the wall and could see that the nails hammered into place had rusted through after years of exposure to the elements. The wood showed signs of decay and warping. The dark, damp, musty smell of water seeping through the brick walls and slick moss indicated the tunnel was on the edge of the perimeter and not underneath the myriad of buildings devising the Contagion Compound.

Triden ventured down the canal, continuing to seek the source of the water. The floor was uneven, and there were pools of water in spots, along with rocks, leaves, and branches. The trees within the Compound were thin and reedy with different foliage than the flora in front of him. The wet matted leaves, partially decayed, added their own pungent aroma to the brick cavern. He pushed on, climbing over a pile of bricks and branches. He was mesmerized by his surroundings. How long had he been traversing the path? Five minutes? Ten? Surely there had to be an end. As he contemplated turning back, the light started to shift. A soft illumination ahead, he stepped around a pallet of abandoned bricks and saw the opening to the tunnel. Stepping forward, he was met with rusted rods of steel preventing entrance to anything larger than the leaves and debris at his feet. Reaching out and touching the metal, he looked beyond to the open field and surrounding forest flanking the portal.

He could feel his heart pounding in his chest. To go beyond the bars would be a criminal act. He closed his eyes and took a deep breath. The smell was wonderful. Earthy and rich, it was unlike anything in the Compound. He could hear birds cawing in the distance, and when he opened his eyes, he saw a big black bird in the sky.

A black bird. It was an omen. No good was to come venturing into the woods. Triden took one more deep breath and turned to retrace his steps. A few feet back into the cavern, he stopped. He would try the bars and prove once and for all that walking into the field was not an option. He could always come back and enjoy the view. He would only have to quell the desire for more.

He returned to the partition and shook the first metal rod. It did not budge under pressure.

See, it's solid. His inner voice guided him. Then another internal voice answered, *Try another.*

Each bar was as solid as the prior one, and as he grasped the last one and pulled, he was surprised when the bar shifted slightly, sprinkling powder from the plaster from the arch overhead onto his robe. He brushed it off, thankful it didn't leave a mark on the brown material. He exerted more force and pulled again. More plaster fell, and the bar was freed. Expecting more resistance, Triden fell backward, landing in a pile of decayed leaves and mud. He looked down at his robe. How could he explain the dirt? The W&W facility was clean and spotless.

He knew he should tell his supervisor about the tunnel and the opening and report the water leak, but he wasn't ready to share the information about the portal. It was the closest he'd been to the outside world since he'd been confined to the Compound when he was six. He'd forgotten the lure of nature and what it meant to be outside. Truly outside.

The trickle of liquid was from a rivulet of water left over from the rains the day before. Triden pulled bricks from the abandoned building pallet and stacked enough to divert the flow of water away from the tunnel entrance. He wanted time to think. He also used several bricks to prop the metal rod back in place. He wiped some of the damp leaves over the scraped plaster overhead to disguise the freshly exposed area. If anyone were to find the exit, he hoped it still looked abandoned from years before.

He did not have a watch. The screens around the Compound alerted everyone when it was time to rise, eat, work and even sleep. Everyone was on the same schedule. There was a harmony and balance in the structure. He could tell by the rumbling in his stomach that his breakfast protein puck had served its purpose and it was time for more sustenance.

After he checked the security of the portal, he made his way back through to the maze of tunnels, following the stream of water in reverse to find his way. He carefully replaced the piece of wood and made a mental note as he backtracked so he could retrace his steps when the water was gone. Already his makeshift brick barrier had diverted water flow, and the remaining liquid was drying quickly.

As he reentered the main chamber, he retrieved the protein pucks and quickly consumed them while looking at the mud on his brown cotton robe. There was dirt on his shoes, and faint footprints were a giveaway to where he'd been.

He grabbed a wrench and made his way down the long tunnel.

CHAPTER 2

Sir William Newbiggers was pleased with himself. The president to Society had spent thirty minutes painstakingly maneuvering the strands of his dyed jet-black hair. He reached for the aerosol can of hair spray and released a steady stream across his head. No one was allowed into the interior of his dressing room during the early morning. His personal valet knew not to enter the presidential apartment until he'd rung the buzzer on his nightstand to summon him.

Only the surgeon, sworn to secrecy by his health oath, and Sir William knew he'd undergone scalp reduction surgery twenty years ago. When his balding hairline started to show, Sir William took immediate action. The offending area of his skin was removed and the scalp still producing hair pulled up to allow for the manipulation of the strands Sir William painstakingly combed each morning. When the gray hair started to arrive, he quickly reached for a product to mask those as well. He was 74 years old, and if it weren't for the excessive pounds, he might have been able to pass for a younger man. He wasn't too concerned. He still had many women who sought him out, and many men wanted to be him.

Before he started the meticulous styling of his hair, he'd brushed dark hair dye through his bushy mustache and set a timer to make sure no gray showed on his face. The timer went off as he put down the can of hair spray, and he reached for a damp washcloth and wiped the hair over his lip. He carefully applied foundation to even out his splotchy skin, reddened and lined from too many fried foods and jiggers of aged Scotch.

He looked at his reflection in the mirror. It had taken longer than usual this morning because of the mustache dye, and yet he was pleased with the image reflected back to him. It was time to summon his valet.

An hour later, Sir William emerged from his quarters

dressed in a charcoal wool suit with a red tie speckled with small Society crests. He joined his wife in the large dining room. Lilia, a tall blond woman whose plastic surgery extended her beauty, sat at the opposite end of the table. Her addiction to a youthful appearance was about to cross the line to skin pulled too tight. What started as a slight nip and tuck with a mini-lift fifteen years ago evolved into regular procedures to remove wrinkles, cellulite, and any blemish which marred her appearance. She hid the expenses from Sir William and parsed money from her abundant spending account for clothes, club activities, and Society functions. She barely looked up when he entered the room. His allure had worn off years earlier. She'd gotten what she wanted from their relationship: two children and a hefty allowance. Their daughters had already finished their breakfast and left to meet their tutor.

Years earlier, Lilia had insisted they have a child to solidify her position, and their prenuptial agreement had specified a more generous stipend with a child to support. The bonus was twins. She tried to isolate the girls from their father as much as possible. *How do you raise your children to do as you say, not as you do?*

She wanted more for her girls than marrying for money and security. While she thought she was marrying for love years ago, she also knew she'd been calculating on whom to love. As her mother said, "It's as easy to love a wealthy man as a poor one." Lilia wasn't so sure.

She hoped her girls would see their value without a man in their lives. Maybe she'd be lucky, and they'd opt to spend their time with other women. *Avoid the misery and heartache; men aren't worth the time.*

She'd hardened her heart, however, if she looked too closely, the hurt and pain were still below the surface. *Why wasn't she enough?* She was beautiful, took care of herself both physically and surgically, and William still strayed.

As soon as he was no longer the resident of the Presidential

Palace, she'd make a change. Maybe she should find a woman the next time around.

The two ate in silence, and Lilia was the first to leave the table. There was nothing to say to her husband as she departed to start her day.

The sun was beginning to creep over the horizon as Rose-leen stepped onto the platform of the treehouse that was her home for as long as she could remember. The canopy of the forest looked lush and green, and morning dew glistened on the leaves surrounding her. The air was brisk and cool. Autumn was arriving, and with it, the leaves were turning to crimson, gold, and orange. This was her favorite time of year because the world started to mirror her appearance. She tucked a few loose tendrils of copper strands behind her ear.

Trust the one who walks with us.

She was used to the messages which came to her each morning. They were often cryptic, and yet over time, the meaning usually became clear. She was fairly certain this was a reminder of the community built in the treetops.

Roseleen looked over to the neighboring trees and saw others emerging from their treetop lofts to start their days. The trees provided private homes for each family, while the majority of the Forest Seers' activities were conducted on the ground below.

She wrapped a dark gray woven shawl around her shoulders and welcomed the extra warmth over her leather shirt and pants. She spent most of the year barefoot and loved the feeling of the earth. She connected with the forest in a primal way and could feel its vibrations. As the weather turned colder, she started slipping on leathers to protect her from snow and frost.

She stepped to an opening in the platform and started her descent to the ground. A short ladder took her to the tree branch below. Navigating across and back and forth, she used the branches to lower herself towards the ground. The limbs began to merge into the large base of the tree, and she side-stepped her way to the root system below. The tree was familiar after years of climbing up and down the trunk, and she could practically traverse the limbs blindfolded. She knew every knot and texture in the thick dark bark.

The bird always knows the migration path home.

Another message emerged, and the corresponding image was confusing. It was unlike any bird she'd ever seen. She didn't have time to reflect on the edict and instead made her way to the underground storage area.

Lifting the heavy wooden door, she walked down several steps into the cellar. Shelves containing a variety of wooden bins flanked the walls. Other shelves held pottery filled with perishable items which wouldn't make it through the winter exposed in the cool storage area.

She collected several roots and tubers foraged recently as the weather turned to fall. She also selected several eggs and some strips of dried meat.

As she emerged from the cellar, she thought about how the long dark days of winter would be arriving soon. She treasured these weeks of fall weather before the forest became dormant and the birds moved south.

Her mother, Shira, similar in build to Roseleen, with copper hair streaked with white strands, was stoking a newly lit fire. They smiled and continued their tasks without speaking aloud.

"You slept well, Daughter?"

"Yes, Mother," she relayed silently.

The two women worked in synchrony to prepare the morning meal. Other women were moving around the sheltered forest floor, tending to babies, making additional fires, and cooking. The Forest Seer men were away, hunting for the last kills of the season to ensure the families would be well fed even after the first snowfall.

"He is coming soon, Daughter."

"Yes, Mother, I can feel him. I don't see him, and yet I know he's close."

"Be careful of the other one. Not all want to do good in the world."

"I know. I hope I'll be able to tell them apart."

"You will, darling Daughter. One has a pure soul; the other has allowed evil to take the place of love in his heart."

Roseleen ladled the breakfast meal into several bowls, handed one to her mother, and added a spoon to her own. The remaining two she covered with a towel to be shared with her father and brother upon their return. The two women ate in silence, and Roseleen saw the strange bird in her mind's eye.

"It's so strange. What is it?"

The birds overhead in the trees did not provide an answer.

⁋

Doctor Jayr Lenus pushed open the glass door leading into the Lab for Human Betterment building and inadvertently spilled his morning coffee down the front of his white research coat. He was always battling clumsy traits, which had prevented him from pursuing a career in surgery. With care, he was able to adhere to the rigors of running a sterile and secure lab. He'd been assigned to find a cure for the virus that had killed millions over twenty years ago. The Contagion Compound housed the survivors, and until he found a cure, they were destined to remain confined.

The virus, officially known as Pathogen 3264, had evolved over the years. The Path continued to mutate, and when he found himself getting close to a cure, another variant would be discovered. One trait remained constant: once infected with P3264, patients were always a contagious carrier.

Sometimes, the virus exposure had been ruthless, and a newly infected person would go into convulsions and die in a frothy, writhing seizure. Other times, it was more gradual, with rashes and boils covering the skin and a fever that effectively cooked the infected person from within. The Contagions in the

Compound responded differently. Rashes covered their skin but never triggered the high-temperature fever ending in death. The rashes remained a permanent reminder of their exposure to P3264. No other common denominators had been discovered, except one. Contagion survivors all had an identical DNA blockchain. However, it didn't guarantee survival. Many who had died also carried the blockchain.

Twenty-four years earlier, when the first cases were discovered, there was less known about the virus other than it was highly contagious and incurable. Initially, no one survived, but a group had emerged, resistant to the death sentence served to so many others. The infected faced mass terminations promoted as a humane alternative to death by the virus. Eventually, the surviving patients, all children, were isolated in the Contagion Compound. Advocates fought for their right to live separated from Society.

"Lucky to Be Alive!" became the defining motto, and Society offered a solution in which Contagions could move freely within the Compound, contribute to Society, and live full lives, albeit without children. To date, not one of the now-adult Contagions had produced offspring; with sterilization another blow dealt by the virus.

After a quick stop in the restroom to clean his research coat the best he could, Jayr started to analyze data from the tests he'd left running the night before. A variety of Petri dishes and instrumentation filled the research space, and at first glance, it was impossible to know if there was anything promising from the day before.

Some days were discouraging, while others provided small glimmers of hope. Some days he was inclined to walk away defeated, yet most of the time, he saw his job as one in which he could prevail. He would find the key to the virus. He would solve the puzzle.

He turned the page on the output file and scanned the list.

Null.

Null.

Null.

He sighed. If the rumors he'd been hearing about his research being halted were true, he was racing to find a cure. It was time to try again.

CHAPTER 4

Mallor stood before the red-faced man in the high-backed wooden chair and smiled. He knew the signs of a man at his breaking point. Sweat beaded on the man's face, and his eyes darted around the room, avoiding eye contact.

"We're going to go over this one more time," he said slowly. "Who was your source for the article you published about Sir William?"

The sweat on the man's forehead started running down his temple, and he squirmed. Restraints held his arms and legs in place against the heavy chair.

"I told you, I can't reveal my sources."

"But you can spread lies about our fearless leader?"

"Lies?" The man paused. "Oh, yes, lies. Of course. I see that now. They were lies." He coughed, and a spittle of blood caused him to gag and choke for a moment before continuing. "My source showed me documents which appeared legitimate from inside the Statecraft office."

The man coughed again, and more blood filled his mouth. Mallor could see him piecing together the information. Coughing up blood meant internal bleeding. If it went untreated, the man would die soon. This was Mallor's favorite part. The dawning realization when one of his subjects could see they were powerless. They did not control the outcome. Only Mallor controlled what would happen next.

"So, if they are lies, there is no reason to protect your source. They have humiliated you; they have caused you to lie and spread falsehoods about Society. They do not deserve your protection."

The red-faced man started nodding fervently.

"Yes, that's true. Spreading falsehoods about Society, about the Statecraft."

"Tell me the name of your source."

The man lowered his head and the words were almost indistinguishable. Mallor leaned in close and smiled again. He had the information he sought.

"You've done the right thing." Another thread of blood-filled spittle drooled from the man's mouth. Mallor knew the man would be dead within the hour.

CHAPTER 5

The Barcode was already packed with Contagion residents done with their workday. The bar was like many others peppered around the Compound, for drinking and socializing in the evening.

Triden pushed open the heavy wooden door and entered the room, scanning for his best friend. He lowered the hood of his robe to make it easier for Benjam to spot him in a crowd filled with people in identical attire. Both men and women in the Compound wore the same brown issue clothing with only the white undergarments modified for gender.

A large screen overhead flashed the public messages so familiar to all in the Compound. *"Lucky to Be Alive!"* was replaced with *"Take a Life, Give Your Own."*

Triden wasn't particularly superstitious, but the sign seemed to amplify the risks of his discovery of the opening to the field and forest earlier in the day. He couldn't stop thinking about what was on the other side of the rusted metal bars. The call of the earth was almost enough to make him throw caution to the wind. Yet he couldn't rely on the solution he used today to erase the mud from his clothing, particularly because it hadn't been pleasant; a high price to pay to keep his discovery private and not anything he cared to repeat soon.

Benjam, a tall, muscular thirty-two-year-old man, waved him over to an open area in the U-shaped bar flanked with tables and booths lining the walls. The din in the room drowned out his call and the room buzzed with the chatter of those who worked in silence and were now free to talk.

As soon as Triden joined him, Benjam raised his hood to cover his dark hair, hazel eyes, and skin speckled with freckles.

"I'm not ready to match tonight. How's my favorite sewer rat?"

Triden laughed. Should he tell Benjam about the portal?

They did not keep secrets from each other. He decided he would tell him in time. For now, he wanted to process his next steps on his own.

"Funny. Sewer rat. You heard?" Benjam was the eyes and ears of the Compound and the go-to person for anything "Off Book."

"Of course. It's one of the more entertaining stories making the rounds today. What happened?"

"I was performing maintenance on one of the sewer lines, and it leaked." A small lie to buy him time to sort out a game plan.

"Really? I heard more like gushed." Benjam laughed.

Triden didn't share that it had been intentional and he'd controlled the flow to cover the mud on his robe and boots.

"Let's just say it was disgusting. I had to get my clothes re-issued and permission to shower."

"I suspected that caused your delay tonight."

The bar was self-serve, and Triden picked up a glass mug and drew a pint from one of the three taps facing him on the bar. Similar taps were placed at each table and booth, as well as baskets of protein pucks. He selected the middle tap and filled his mug with a pale amber drink called Weesha. The lighter version called Paleem was Benjam's choice and the third, Gaush, was dark and sludgy—too musty and pungent for Triden's tastes. He reached for a protein puck. The poultry flavor went well with his fermented beverage.

He wasn't surprised the story of his "accident" had spread like wildfire through his quadrant. Most days were routine, so anything different always made it through the gossip vine; another reminder it was best to keep his discovery to himself.

As the screen overhead flashed the turn of the hour, the energy in the room began to shift. It was time for evening matching. Everyone lowered their hoods. Varying shades of skin, light to dark hair, some short and others with long tresses, started to mill around the room. Triden and Benjam stayed on their stools.

People could pair off at any time during the evening and go "On Book." However, the last hour before closing time prompted those who were interested to find a companion. There was an unspoken protocol, and everyone knew the rules.

When deciding to pair up for the evening, both individuals would scan their barcodes on the readers scattered around the room. If they'd paired together anytime in the past seven days, the mating would be denied. If they mated more than five times, the match would also be denied.

The restrictions existed to minimize physical bonding and anything creating desires for a deeper relationship. No one could start a family and triggering any emotions for the desire for children went against the established rules

Triden looked at Benjam. "Going On Book tonight?"

"Yeah, if I can find a match. I think I've hit my limit with most of the people here. I may have to start frequenting an-other bar." He laughed. He was often sought out by both men and women at The Barcode.

Several women approached them and engaged in a brief conversation. Benjam scanned his wrist, and the reader finally approved the third person, a short-haired brunette woman Tri-den had been with last month. There was no room for jealousy or possessiveness within the Compound.

"Have fun. I'm heading home."

Triden didn't want the distraction of companionship to-night. He had a lot on his mind.

Sir William nodded absently as his two main advisers reviewed the daily brief with him. Honestly, he didn't know why they bothered. There were people in place to make sure his wishes were carried out in good order. He stifled a yawn, irritated that he had to endure these daily reports as "protocol." He glanced at his personal screen and drafted a message for all of Society to see.

"When there's a *WILL*, there's a *WAY*!"

He pressed send and looked up.

"What?"

Annabella Connor's expression conveyed he'd missed something requiring his response.

"Sir William, we need direction." Her tone was soothing. "Might I suggest we defer an answer until more information is known?"

He hesitated. "Yes, yes, let's defer on..." His voice tapered off. He wasn't sure if they were still discussing manufacturing or a new topic.

Annabella filled in the blank.

"Good decision, Sir. We'll defer approving the Compound budget until we've completed a thorough study of the infrastructure."

Sir William disliked discussing the Contagions. He knew they served a purpose in making Society run smoothly, but they were tainted and could never be part of Society again. While some would argue they were the strong and resilient ones to have survived P3264, Sir William couldn't see beyond the rashes.

He, too, had watched the broadcasted attempts to find a cure. He'd seen the different ways the pathogen afflicted those infected. He'd lived through the mass hysteria and the extensive terminations, which had been the last-ditch effort to control P3264. While those in the Compound survived, they still had the power to destroy anyone who came into contact with them, intentional or not.

If only this would go away, he thought. *I don't know why we bother.*

Annabella continued, and her words buzzed in his ear while he looked at his personal screen. He typed another message to his followers.

"Go BIG or Go Home." An alert popped up on his screen. He had an interview in fifteen minutes with the Society Communication Office. He would have a full hour to talk to his constituents.

"The SCO interview is soon. Let's finish this later." He liked sounding authoritative and dictating his next steps even though he knew from experience that later would never come. He was done listening to the drone of the morning report.

As he prepared to leave the room, he turned back towards Annabella. "Let The Flodden Club know I'll be playing this afternoon. Tell Mallor I expect him to be there."

Annabella nodded as he exited the room and reached for her personal screen. She typed a quick message to Sir William's confidant and tried to push down the uneasy feeling at the mention of his name.

Roseleen stood at the tree line of the forest and harvested the last of the fall glassenberries from the bushes along the open field. She could see the gray walls of the Compound, originally built years ago to contain those who had committed crimes against Society. As a pathogen impacted numerous citizens, it became a holding place for patients infected with and surviving P3264. The barbed wire was impenetrable, and it was rare to see activity other than the automated conveyors delivering large containers to the entrance for pick up by large Society trucks.

The Power Walker can walk between the worlds.

The Forest Seers' intuition had given them advance notice to retreat from Society before the virus emerged. Those who did not heed the warnings paid a terrible price. Millions were killed by the contaminant and by the hand of those fearful of the plague spreading rampantly. Only ten percent of the population remained, and they were divided between Society and the Contagion Compound. The Seers had escaped without detection and were able to move freely in the forest, hunting and gathering their food, supplemented by the vast storage system they had built upon their transition to nature. They had tools, containers, fuel, and leather to make their day-to-day survival easier. They consciously made a decision to live simply to avoid drawing attention to their elaborate treehouse village deep in the woods. They banished Society screens and other elements of technology that dictated behavior. They connected with each other over meals and collaborated to keep their families safe and thriving. With the removal of Society interference, their intuitive powers became more attuned to nature, and they continued to receive messages from the universal energy they referred to as "The Source." They knew they were safe.

For now.

⌯⌯

Triden stared at the ceiling of his studio apartment, unable to sleep. Restless, he got up and looked at his schedule for the following day. It was basic and routine. His title was Water and Sanitation Engineer, but there wasn't much for him to do. The water purification and sewer systems were mostly automated. He spent his days wandering the mass network of pipes and filtration vats, looking for any malfunctions.

He had taken assessment tests upon arrival at the Compound, and when he was old enough, he'd been assigned to the role because of his deductive and analytical skills. Society denied the funding to replace the outdated and strained systems, so Triden's role was reduced to the oversight of a network he could only patch and protect. He had recommended they reduce the operations by 20% to avoid overtaxing a decaying infrastructure, and fortunately, his supervisor understood the value of his recommendation. The sewage filtration system serviced both the Contagion Compound and Society. While it was agreed the Contagions had a right to be contributing members of Society, new virus laws were enacted with the establishment of the Compound to prescribe isolation and codes of behavior to stop the continued spread of P3264.

The dictum *"Take a Life, Give Your Own"* established the moral responsibility of all. Years earlier, while the Contagions were still children, several boys had tried to leave. Their exposure to others in Society had caused panic and concern for all outside the institution walls when those exposed died horrific deaths upon contact. The three Contagions had been retrieved and publicly executed. The replays of their fate quashed other Contagions' thoughts of leaving the Compound.

Triden knew he would return to the tunnel tomorrow. He

told himself he would look for birds overhead and smell the fresh air and nothing more. As he drifted to sleep with his game plan in place, he knew it was a safe and noble strategy and one which would be difficult to keep.

CHAPTER 8

Sir William glared at the screen before him.

"Annabella!" he bellowed, red-faced and pacing the room in front of his massive desk. A large Society screen filled the far wall. His office controlled the news feed and messaging running along the bottom. The Propaganda Department managed the main screen to convey "the sentiments of the Statecraft" to prevent misuse by the elected officials. The ability to speak freely was coveted and a right granted to members of Society when the Signet of Democracy was established.

Annabella entered the room. Her blond hair was pinned up, and she wore a dark blue dress with gold buttons in two rows down the front. She looked to the screen and saw her husband, Jordon, discussing rights for the Contagions.

"Let's be honest, the infected are people, too. There has to be a way to find a cure. The current administration is sitting idle while thousands suffer in the Compound. It is time for us to control P3264, not let P3264 control us!"

Annabella turned toward the red-faced leader.

"Don't worry, no one is listening to him. Your poll ratings still show support for your efforts."

"Polls! I HATE the polls. Why do I have to be dictated what to do by a poll? It's only a small representation of Society! I don't have to explain myself! I'm the head of the country, dammit!"

Annabella backpedaled. She should have remembered the last time she mentioned polls. Her boss was a fickle man, and it was hard to keep track of his sensitivities. The tallies, while showing a slight majority of support, highlighted he had not maintained the high rating of when he had taken office two years earlier. She would talk with Jordon in the evening. He had told her he would be on screen, but she hadn't connected it would be so soon.

"Sir William," she used a soothing, mothering voice, "you are amazing, and no one can argue you're not doing enough to take care of the Contagion Compound. Here's your chance to message the citizens of Society."

The rotund man in front of her stopped his pacing.

"Yes...the best. Of course."

"And, I can get you some pictures you can post of the Compound to show how well the Contagions live within their own community. They want for nothing. Freedom to move within their world, unlimited food and drink, their own living quarters."

The red rage splotching his face started to clear as Sir William responded; a toddler being consoled by its mother.

"They don't understand."

"I know."

"No one does more for the people of Society."

"I know." Annabella patted his arm.

"Let's send out a message." She handed him the remote keyboard controlling the banner feed on the screen.

"Jordon Connor is a HACK. He's a LOSER. NO ONE does more than I do to help the Contagions."

Sir William entered the text, and seconds later, it scrolled along the bottom of the screen.

"Honestly, Annabella, why haven't you divorced him yet?"

"We have kids, remember?"

For several days Triden made his way through the myriad of tunnels to the abandoned area. He stood and watched the world of nature outside his barred view.

Birds sang overhead, and occasionally he saw a long-eared animal hopping in the field. This morning he looked out and saw a four-legged creature with what looked like wooden bones sprouting from its head standing at the forest edge.

What is that*?!*

It wouldn't hurt to take a closer look. He hadn't seen anyone during his days gazing at the field and forest. He deliberated with himself. The only reason the law existed to restrain Contagions in the Compound was to avoid exposing anyone to P3264. He doubted he'd be able to get close to the strange animal at the edge of the field. Could the virus even be passed to animals? He didn't know.

He quickly removed the rusty rod and placed it to the side. He kept a firm footing, knowing how little effort was needed to dislodge it from its position. He didn't relish the idea of another sewer shower anytime soon.

Triden debated whether he should slip off the heavy, dark robe but decided against it. The white undergarments he wore would show any spot or blemish. The brown material would be more forgiving.

He stepped onto the soft earth outside the Compound, his heart pounding. Droplets of water clung to the grass around his feet, and the material of his robe speckled with darker dots as the dew penetrated the material. It wouldn't take long for the water to dry, and Triden pushed on, watching the interesting animal still standing fifty feet away.

The bone spiked and adorned animal raised its head from grazing and made eye contact with Triden. Both froze. The man was the first to move and delicately advanced to get a closer look, trying not to spook the unusual creature.

He paused twenty feet in front of the large beast. It had a coarse, tan hide and a massive frame. The spikes on its head were impressive, more like wood than bone up close, sprouting and curving overhead. It was an impressive sight to see. The animal was larger than it had first appeared from inside his tunnel perch. The black nostrils flared slightly, the only indication of the animal's concern about his presence.

Triden took another gentle step forward before the majestic animal turned and bounded toward the interior of the woods. He watched as the beast maneuvered between the trees and disappeared into the undergrowth of the forest.

A lightness filled his heart, and Triden realized he was smiling. This was the most magnificent thing to happen to him. He felt happy and joyful about the encounter. The animal erased his trepidation about leaving the Compound. There appeared to be minimal risk, and no one died. All the tension in his body dissipated, and he felt exhausted. Best to get back before anyone questioned his whereabouts.

Triden turned back toward the tunnel entrance and looked up. The Contagion Compound loomed before him. Built on rocks and stone, tall cement walls surrounded the buildings inside. Barbed wire flanked the top of the gray structure; it was the first time Triden saw his home for what it was.

He lived in a prison.

॥॥

Jayr shook his head as he looked at the Petri dishes left to incubate the night before. He'd gone home optimistic he'd isolated a protein resistant to the virus, and yet this morning the samples had no living organism other than P3264. Everything he tried was devoured by the insatiable disease.

Every month, he received 500 updated blood samples from the Compound that he analyzed for variables that would indicate either a mutation or a consistency which could provide insights for finding a cure. He'd reviewed the data so many times he practically had it memorized. There had to be a key somewhere in the information.

Maybe that's the problem...I'm looking for a solution using the same data sets.

The doctor reached for his screen and typed out a memo to his supervisor. He knew he was taking a big risk, but he was determined not to let the pathogen win. He would find a cure.

"Requesting permission to enter the Contagion Compound. I will use established protocols to protect myself from infection. It is a critical juncture in my research to find a cure. I will gather additional samples from a broader cross-section of Contagions to validate with lab samples and to identify any new strains or mutations."

He'd run out of options, and it was time to look for a new key.

CHAPTER 10

Sir William turned to the screen to assess the current news of the day.

"Adam Keeson, a well-known journalist, was found dead in his apartment. He died by apparent suicide. The note left behind apologized for a recent article that was critical of the Statecraft and expressed regret for the use of an unverified source. The implication is the article was fabricated and not true. We will continue to report on this story as information becomes available."

Sir William remembered the defamatory news article he'd asked Mallor to investigate. The president believed any hesitancy on his part would be perceived as weakness. He acted to minimize any negative news about his affairs. He leveraged his presidential banner to proclaim the news as false and dismissed any questions of the appropriateness of his behavior.

Loyalty was critical, and anyone who dared contradict his opinions and policy objectives was taking a risk. Sir William lived by his own code. Any opponent would be destroyed; only loyalists were rewarded. There were no rules Sir William believed he needed to follow. He was charismatic, powerful, and had a knack for finding every loophole of opportunity. Those who opposed him learned too late they'd crossed the wrong person. Sir William squashed any opposition quickly. Mallor had proven to be a loyal and productive member of his inner circle. Sir William didn't worry about the details. Results were important; nothing more mattered.

The news story on the screen changed: another protest related to the Contagions. It annoyed Sir William that this topic showed momentum. Those in Society who opposed the Compound were naive and foolish. How could they not see it was better to keep the Contagions confined? Had they learned nothing from the "Time of Mass Terminations"?

Annabella entered his office as a picture of her husband flashed on the screen. She'd shown the president over and over again she was a loyalist and could be trusted even if her husband voiced opposition. Initially, when they first met, he was not sure of her motives. She was adept at reading public opinion and nullifying any efforts to undermine Sir William's objectives. Her husband was the opposite and had only gotten more vocal, even as his wife met with media channels and openly opposed Jor-dumb's theories. Sir William enjoyed the slur he'd created for Jordon's name.

"We have a Precinct Three honorary dinner tonight. It is anticipated the chancellor of the precinct will announce his next election run tonight. They are looking for you to provide an endorsement." Annabella dropped to the couch, kicked off her shoes, and tucked her feet under herself. She tapped on a personal screen as she spoke with Sir William.

"It looks like there will be about 250 in attendance."

"I want to make sure he supports our efforts for the Compound. It is imperative the Contagions are isolated from Society. We cannot have another rampant spread of the virus plague Society."

"Yes, the chancellor is very aware of the importance of isolating the Contagions. Everyone still remembers the "Time of Mass Terminations." No one wants a repeat. There were too many people lost, and it took years to recover. Only now is Society advancing forward, thanks to you. Another resurgence could mean an economic collapse and could destroy Society as we know it."

"Tell your husband, Annabella, he's still living in the past. There's no cure for the virus. It's a cancer to Society, and it's time we focused our medical attention on new advances for all."

"Are you saying you want to halt the vaccine research for the Contagions?" Apparently, the rumors were true.

"Yes. So much time and money have gone into finding a cure. The Contagions are living full lives in the Compound. With the infected isolated, everyone is safe. Society members must hear the message. It's the best for both Society and the Contagions."

"I understand." Annabella was comfortable with this approach, especially since she and Jordon were planning a way to take over management of the Compound. There was a lot of money to be made in keeping the Compound running. Sir William could hand over the reins of management and not be bothered by the Compound anymore.

Sir William watched the screen, distracted by the story of a Society celebrity. The young actress had been featured lately in a Society theater series.

"Sir William?"

He nodded, not taking his eyes off the monitor.

"I will arrange to promote a humanitarian piece on the Compound to show those in Society that all Contagions are leading full lives. We can dismantle any opposing stories with visuals."

"Yes, yes. That sounds ideal. I don't want to hear anything more about the Contagions."

"To clarify, we'll leave the research intact until after the story has run. Once we perform a poll and see public opinion shifting, we can announce the changes in research efforts."

"Good thinking. Let's tell Society what they want to hear. The money devoted to pointless research will be better spent elsewhere. It's time we focus on the things which make Society stronger."

Annabella uncurled her legs, stood up and slipped on her black stiletto heels.

"Don't worry, Sir William, I'll take care of it."

"That's why I hired you. I trust your loyalty. You will be rewarded."

CHAPTER 11

Triden stepped through the opening and onto the soft ground of the field. He'd been venturing out for snippets of time when he could break away from his maintenance duties. He hadn't seen the majestic animal with the bones on its head since the first day he had stepped beyond the Compound.

There were no guards at the facility since no one tried to venture outside after years of messages promoting moral responsibility. Additionally, all known areas with access to the perimeter had scanners to detect his barcode. There were no secrets if he exited a main doorway. He would be shamed and ostracized for not honoring his role and responsibility for the safety of all. The penalty would land him in disciplinary classes about the virus from the first case to the establishment of the Contagion Compound. It also showed the history of the millions who died during the "Time of Mass Terminations." and finally, it showed the three boys who'd threatened the safety of all and had been executed for exposing innocent members of Society.

There was an exhilaration and thrill at being outside the Compound. He minimized his guilt about venturing beyond the perimeter, knowing that he wasn't putting anyone else at risk.

He loved the smells around him. He touched the leaves of plants, some smooth and others rough like sandpaper. He leaned in to whiff the sweet, haunting smell of the small, delicate flowers beginning to fade as the days turned colder. The forest floor covering was soft, lined with leaves from the foliage above. Looking at the canopy overhead, sunlight sparkled as the wind turned leaves and swayed branches. Birds called to mates and there was a subtle hum of activity around him. A brown animal with a bushy tail scurried along tree branches, unconcerned about Triden's presence many feet below. He could get lost in time watching the creatures crack open tree fruits and dart back and forth among the branches.

Looking overhead once again, he observed the movement of the sun. It shifted enough to give him fair warning to return to the barred tunnel. It didn't take long to retrace his trail and step inside the moss-covered brick tunnel. He carefully replaced the rusted bar and made his way back to the main corridor.

Triden moved within the Compound without issue but it was getting harder to shake a level of dissatisfaction. He was now acutely aware of his limitations which had intensified as he'd expanded his horizon to include the outside world. How had he not seen that the Contagions were being used? Every person in the Compound had a job that supported Society and had reduced them to slave labor.

He understood the need for isolation from the rest of the world because of the infection risk, however, he couldn't understand why the Compound had not been expanded to include the field and forest nearby. The spindly trees planted along the sidewalks within the Compound provided some connection to nature, and occasionally birds would land on the branches. Now having touched the earth, walked on the soil, and smelled the vegetation, he felt the confines of the Compound more severely. They were not afforded basic rights to live in a natural world.

It was later than he realized when he returned. He was thankful he performed his rounds alone. He quickly looped the maze of piping and noted nothing was amiss before climbing the stairs to the upper level. It was time to go to The Barcode and see his best friend.

He arrived and secured their regular table and poured a pint of Weesha while he waited for Benjam. Fifteen minutes later, the young man slid onto the bar stool.

"Sorry about the delay. There's a short in one of the electrical panels and Quad 4 has been without power for the past hour. Finally got it patched together." As a chief engineer and programmer assigned to Compound infrastructure, Benjam was occasionally detained. The sanitation network was not the only outdated equipment.

After several pints of Weesha, Triden was feeling relaxed. He leaned toward Benjam.

"Are you happy?"

Benjam laughed. "Happy? Well, I'm not unhappy. I have everything I need, free-flowing Paleem..." He reached for a protein puck. "Scrumptious meal options," he said with a hint of sarcasm as he snapped the puck in half and handed Triden a side. "Here, eat something. It will make you feel better." He looked at his best friend closely. "Why, what's going on? You haven't seemed like your normal self for a few weeks."

Triden hesitated. He shared everything with Benjam, yet he still felt a wave of anxiety at the thought of anyone discovering he'd been outside the Compound.

The screen overhead flashed, *"Take a Life, Give Your Own."* Triden saw it as an omen to stay quiet.

"Everything's fine, really."

"Sure, Tri? You know I'm here if you need anything. I can hook you up. Extra sheets, towels, a blanket?"

"Thanks. I'm good."

Another message rotated across the screen, reminding all that the pathogen, shortened to The Path, dictated their be-havior. *"Respect The Path and Stay on Your Path."*

Triden pushed down his feelings of guilt about venturing outside the Compound. He hadn't seen anyone, and he ration-alized his actions. No one had been threatened while he was in the woods.

Benjam leaned in. "See the woman on the other side of the bar?" Triden nodded. "I've been On Book with her the max number of times. I rigged one of the barcode scanners to show approval of the match without adding to the count so we can continue to connect. You know what would make me happy?

Removal of the five times rule. I really like her and we shouldn't have to hide our relationship, but we have to make sure we don't draw attention to our Off Book sessions, so we're pairing with others tonight."

Triden was surprised. Benjam seemed so open to spreading his attentions to every woman who showed interest and never spoke about anyone in particular. He looked closer. The woman was beautiful with smooth skin and blue eyes. Her smile was captivating; he could see why his friend was drawn to her beauty.

Benjam slammed his mug on the bar top. "You know what we need? We need to find partners for the evening. Time to go On Book." He started scanning the people in the room. "What's your fancy tonight? Male? Female? You tell me...."

Maybe a physical interlude with someone would take his mind off the feelings of being trapped inside the Compound.

It didn't long for the two men to pair off with others in The Barcode. They scanned their wrists and headed to the door.

"I'll see you tomorrow, Triden. Be happy!"

Triden smiled. "Lucky to be alive!" He turned toward his apartment with his companion for the evening following behind. *Lucky to be alive. Now more than ever before.*

Sir William stared at the stack of square tiles before him and then back to the Quilt cards on his tableau board. The game involved both chance and skill. Players had to quickly deduce the strongest spread on their tableau using their luck of the draw.

Three other players, all cabinet members from the Statecraft, had joined Sir William for the card game at The Flodden Club, a private resort in the capital owned by the president's private corporation. A club dealer who oversaw many of the president's games sat at the head of the table. Two elaborate hourglasses with sand to ensure the game progressed quickly marked time in one-minute increments and were placed to the dealer's right.

Sir William selected three betting tiles worth more than an average Society member's annual wages and casually tossed them to the center of the felt table into a printed area known as "The Bank." Two of the other players followed suit, matching the bid played by Sir William. The fourth player lowered his head and said, "Bow," the customary response when resigning a hand. He transferred his tableau board to his game steward, who cleared the cards and placed them face down on the table next to the dealer, ready for the next deal.

The sands reached the bottom bulb of the hourglass, and the dealer called out the next step of the game.

"Challengers?"

Sir William initiated the payment to The Bank, and the remaining two players had a chance to increase the bid. The player to Sir William's left shifted in his seat and fingered a square tile.

"Player accepts opening."

The next man at the table did not hesitate and picked up two square tiles in front of his playing area and added them to

The Bank.

"Player challenges."

The dealer looked at the two remaining players.

"Please match the challenge or bow out."

Sir William selected two more tiles and tossed them to the center, matching the raised bid. "Challenge accepted."

The man to his left lowered his head and said, "Bow," before handing his tableau board to his game steward to clear.

"Challenger, please show your tableau."

The Cabinet Minister who resided in Precinct Four of the Statecraft of Society lowered his tableau. The dealer called the sequence.

"Yellow primary, green high, orange low."

It was technically a higher hand than Sir William's cards, but he had extra insurance.

"Purple secondary, blue high, green low with red dual."

The two-sided red dual card elevated the color for his cards.

The dealer announced the result. "Winner, Seat One." He picked up a long-handled tool with a crescent shape and deftly collected the square tiles in The Bank and pushed them toward Sir William's game steward. The assistant would count and stack the tiles in increments of five and place them before the designated player.

The game was built on tradition and protocol and was considered a gentleman's game of honor. Each of the men at the table had been initiated into the gameplay as part of their majority training in school. The table was often a place where deals were made beyond the wagers flowing in and out of The Bank.

The next hand was dealt. Protocol required that each player leave their cards facedown until the dealer turned the hourglass.

"Select." The dealer indicated approval to pick up the cards as he turned one of the hourglass vials. While players could take up to a minute to assess their hands, oftentimes, they would bid early to establish a power position at the outset. Players could be seen as weak or slow if they delayed much longer than the first contribution to The Bank.

The second hourglass vial was used when the game speed was accelerated and the sands of the minute timer had not fully sifted through to the lower bulb.

Sir William picked up his cards and assessed his options. His game steward stood behind him. Stewards with readable expressions did not last long at the Quilt table. Considering they received a percentage of the winner's purse for the evening, it was ideal to pair with a winner and stay stoic.

They played for two hours, and only after Sir William had amassed a large collection of stacked tiles did he suggest they stop for a drink and a meal. Mallor had entered the play area and watched silently for a few minutes. His presence was another signal to Sir William to end the betting.

The group moved to an alcove table elaborately set with white linens and a centerpiece with the Society flag displayed among the Statecraft flower. The blood-red rose and ivy arrangement symbolized the long-lasting prosperity of Society. The Statecraft was the political structure to ensure Society continued as it had for the last millennium.

Sir William started. "I brought you here to ask for your loyalty." He paused, looking at each man individually, looking for any sign of disagreement. Fortunately, the three men were attentive and agreeable.

"As you know, I ran on a reform ticket to make changes and..." He paused for effect. "When there's a *WILL* there's a *WAY*. I plan to deliver exactly what the State needs."

The three men nodded approval.

"I have noticed a growing voice of concern in your three precincts related to my policies. I am looking to you to resolve this conflict."

"But Sir William, our constituents are allowed to speak their opinion."

William did not like the interruption, and he continued, "Of course, they can have an opinion. And it needs to match mine. Show me your loyalty and take steps to make sure we all see eye to eye."

Mallor stood in the corner and nodded his approval to Sir William.

"Let's eat. The chef prepared a particularly decadent meal for us. Nothing reconstituted here."

The member from Precinct Four cleared his throat.

"Sir William, if I might have a word."

The president hated this type of interruption. He didn't want to be bothered with State business while enjoying a good meal. He saw Mallor nod, and sighed.

"Yes, what is it?"

"Many in my precinct are voicing concern for the citizens in the Compound. They believe a cure should have been found by now to reintroduce Contagions to Society."

Sir William was bored. *Didn't they realize the Contagions were isolated for a reason?*

"We have to look at the science. This is a virus with no cure once it takes hold. We've all seen the live clinical trials. The results have been so gruesome many people have asked not to broadcast them. We want people to know what P3264 means to Society. As far as I'm concerned, the Contagions are lucky to be alive!"

"But Sir William, citizens in my precinct are starting to protest in the streets."

"Show your strength! Show your loyalty!" Sir William was annoyed. The cabinet members were idiots, losers. Couldn't they see they had a position of power over their constituents? "I'm sure you'll control the masses. I would hate to have to remove you from your assignment."

Sir William pushed his chair back and stood. "This

discussion is over. Control your communities, or I'll control them for you."

Roseleen looked up at the full moon from the platform of the treehouse she shared with her parents and younger brother. She could hear an owl in the distance, cooing a soft hello. The nights were getting crisper; she pulled her gray woven shawl around her shoulders.

The Power Walker can traverse between the worlds.

Some of her premonitions came with a vivid visual image, and others were only an inner voice or a feeling. She'd been getting messages about the Power Walker without any indication of who or what it was for months; she'd stopped questioning what the messages meant.

Her mother emerged from the interior of the treehouse. "Darling Daughter, aren't you cold? Come inside."

"In a moment, Mother."

The older woman sat beside Roseleen. "You received another message?"

The younger woman nodded.

"I don't understand. The message says he can walk between the worlds. Does that mean the earth and the moon?"

"I know from experience all will be revealed. It is not our place to question, only receive. Guidance should be heeded, not ignored. We will know soon enough. The important thing to remember is to be prepared for whatever comes."

"I'm afraid it will threaten our home. I love it here and don't want anything to change."

"Do not fear, Daughter. For one, worry won't change the outcome, and besides, I haven't received any message suggesting we face a risk."

Roseleen tried to shake her uneasy feeling. "Thank you, Mother. I appreciate your insights. I've been seeing death and destruction."

"It could be nothing more than a rebirthing period. The

forest ebbs and flows through the seasons. Winter is almost here. Things will die, and the spring will bring new life. It is the cycle of the woods. Have no fear; we are prepared."

The older woman stood then leaned down to kiss Roseleen on the top of her head. "You have a true gift, Daughter. The universe has chosen you because it knows you can handle the messages you receive. It is not your role to decipher their cryptic meaning; it is only your responsibility to respond when the meanings become clear."

"I don't want to let down anyone. What if I can't decipher the meanings in time?"

"Time is an elusive thing, Daughter. The timing will always be divine in nature. Have faith."

"I'm trying, Mother."

"And, more importantly, have patience."

The older woman returned to the interior of the treehouse. A few minutes later, Roseleen joined her family inside.

◫

"Request Denied."

The doctor read the response from his supervisor.

"Risk too great. We cannot lose you to this deadly disease. P3264 remains highly contagious and can kill you immediately upon contact."

The communication continued, "Or worse, you could experience a slow and painful response if your immune system successfully fights the virus for a few hours. Either scenario will result in your untimely death. Only children with a mutated response survive in the Contagion Compound."

A video started to play on the screen showing a person exposed, their skin turning red and welted as the virus increased their internal temperature and cooked them from the inside out. The virus had evolved. Initially, it had been considered a flu with little risk of complications, and there hadn't been much concern. As time went by, the virus had become more virulent. It also became apparent that once exposed, every person became a carrier who was always contagious.

The government, looking for a way to stop the spread and save the economy, acted quickly and harshly. Those exposed were terminated. It was considered the more humane option for victims of a virus that cooked the hosts, the slow burn consuming their last breath. The doctor still remembered the screams as he had watched helplessly from behind a hospital barrier. It was then that he had decided to shift his focus to research to save as many people as possible.

The doctor sighed. The video was overkill; everyone in Society had seen it numerous times to cement their knowledge of the risks of P3264.

He wasn't particularly surprised by his supervisor's response, but he was frustrated by his exhausted options. He reminded himself it had taken a team of scientists to find cures for other ailments, often over many decades. By comparison, his research was still in the infancy stage.

Reviewing the test data from the past twenty-four years, he tried to see a theme, anything that could provide a hint or clue to unlock the secrets of P3264. How else could he parse the data? He'd sorted by age, ethnicity, sex, and even by precinct.

He had organized the data to construct a progressive chart to display the steady climb of infections and the sudden dip in the curve after the Time of Mass Terminations. The data tapered off to a dwindling line to show the few remaining infected patients who had all been under eighteen when exposed. They were sequestered and moved to the Contagion Compound. No new cases had emerged in twenty-two years, and everyone in the Compound had grown to adulthood and settled into lives of their own.

Absentmindedly, the doctor tapped on different variables

to overlay onto the graph. He'd already looked at the parsed sets; he felt as if he were facing a brick wall and had no thoughts on what to try next.

An overlay showing the sex of each patient showed the virus did not discriminate. Men had a slight uptick compared to women, but not enough to be statistically significant.

Examining age highlighted that the elderly had died more quickly. The more robust immune system of younger patients meant a longer incubation period before the pathogen ultimately prevailed.

Continuing down the list of filter options, the doctor selected precinct. At the onset of the disease, there had been ten precincts. Three of them had been wiped out completely, highlighting that the artificial boundaries did not confine the virus. Another three had been halved in population and the remaining four, with the least amount of exposure, still lost thousands of people.

When the Contagion Compound was established, the precincts were also restructured to create the five which exist today. Precinct Nine, with the largest loss of population, became a mass graveyard with millions of bodies buried without markers. Rich or poor, noteworthy or unknown, no longer had significance, with all accomplishments stripped away by the ravaging disease. The mounds of bodies were covered with ten feet of dirt; skittish survivors were unclear on how long a body could be contagious after death. While there had been no indication of the risk of exposure, people stayed away from the burial site. Years later, grass and trees started to take hold as nature once again showed its perseverance. The rolling hills disguising the piles of bodies below took on a peaceful quality. Society members started to pay tribute to the fallen with pinwheels, including the name of the departed on the paper squares that rotated in the wind. The land was speckled with thousands of pinwheels with relatives and friends finally able to honor the departed.

Society finally moved to a state of acceptance. All the surviving children transferred to the Contagion Compound were orphans; their parents either died of the disease or were in the mass grave of those terminated.

Jayr looked at the death rate, which spiked higher in several precincts. What was the missing denominator? Something had to be consistent to allow the rampant spread.

Twenty-four years ago, the doctor had completed his residency and was trying to find his way in the medical world. He was from the prior Precinct Three, an area minimally impacted. Areas Six, Eight, and Nine were especially hard hit. He had taken over the research nineteen years ago after the first doctors moved on to more rewarding work when a cure had not been readily found. Jayr had made a promise that he wouldn't give up. He would ensure the virus was eradicated. The various mutations over the years had made his work more difficult.

He looked at the precinct overlay. What did he remember about the three areas? Had the residents disregarded the protocols and exposed more people? There was no evidence of different behaviors.

There was something hidden in the data at his fingertips. He rotated through the overlays again and watched the wavy lines of the graph as they switched with each data point. There was nothing evident providing insights for a cure.

Pushing his chair back, he stood. It was time to get new data sets with or without his supervisor's permission.

⁌ ⁍

Triden sprinted across the vast field to the forest edge. The Compound walls were tall, and there were no guards to be concerned about. Barcode scanners tracked resident whereabouts, and loud alarms would sound if anyone strayed into private areas.

Benjam was an electrician and could access the control panels feeding power to the Compound. He had shared the information over drinks at The Barcode. It was for safety reasons that some areas had limited access.

The residents in the Compound had arrived as children. The oldest residents had been fifteen, and the older group was trained to take over the more complex tasks of running the facility to ensure everyone had utilities, food, and shelter. Society members set up the system before anyone had transferred. They still were involved, delivering pallets of protein pucks, kegs of beverages, and clothing. All inside the Compound had tasks to ensure the community ran smoothly. Every night a fresh set of undergarments and robes were delivered to each apartment, wrapped in brown paper. Maintenance was performed by a subset of workers. Triden's role was focused on the water and sewer system. Benjam worked on any outages in the electrical system. Others worked behind the scenes to make sure meal supplements were available, and others assembled components for manufacturing.

There was an infirmary where everyone could go if they weren't feeling well or if their virus symptoms took a turn for the worse. Doctors from Society were available with screen interviews to suggest treatments.

Everyone in the Compound avoided the dreaded hospital. Many wanted to feel "normal" and just endured the symptoms of their malady. Most knew, however, that if they went to the infirmary often, they would be tagged for Lab of Human Betterment testing. The Society research group had been seeking a cure for P3264 for over two decades. In open transparency, they broadcasted the treatment process live on the screens. Triden had stopped watching the horrid experiments. Too many people he knew had died. The Contagions learned early it was better to suffer in silence than subject themselves to research which had not yielded a positive result.

Every time a treatment failed to make advances, Society would broadcast a message: "We will continue to look for a cure. P3264 has shown us it is a powerful pathogen, but we know we will prevail in the end. The best minds are hard at work to find a cure. You have a wonderful life in the Compound and have community together. You are lucky to be alive!"

Triden turned at the forest edge and looked back at the now familiar mass of gray buildings encased with walls and barbed wire. He had come to the Compound as a young boy and only retained a few memories of his mother and father: the soft touch of his mother's hand stroking his head as he drifted to sleep, a soft smile at the corners of her mouth as she gazed at her only son; his father, with eyes similar to his own, with laugh lines showing the age difference between parent and child. When he had trouble falling asleep, he would close his eyes and tap into the memories of his parents. The recollection of his mother's touch and soothing voice would guide him to slumber.

The sun was high in the sky. His daily routine had evolved into taking his bagged lunch of protein pucks and drink outside in the forest. He found a fallen tree he used for a seat and table. Somehow the pucks tasted better outside, although he suspected it was more the enjoyment of the setting versus the flavor appeal of the industrialized nutritional bars.

He looked at the rays of sun smattering through the trees and made a mental note of the placement. He had to return to the Compound when the sun moved the distance of three fingers on the horizon when he held his hand to the sky and used a nearby tree as his reference point. He was grateful to see he had a little more time.

The winter was going to be difficult. The fall weather was already turning colder, and several days of rain had prevented him from venturing into the wooded terrain. Snow would make it all but impossible; there would be no way to disguise his tracks.

Done with his lunch, he moved to the ground and leaned against the large fallen log of the tree he used as his table. He watched the small brown creatures he called "fluffy tails," having no idea what they were. He hadn't seen the "bone crown" beast since the first day he'd ventured outside of the Compound.

He loved this time. It was mesmerizing. A soft breeze cooled the air, and he slid down lower against the log for shelter and drifted to sleep.

Sir William looked out the window of the Presidential Palace at the throng of protesters outside. The chanting was barely audible from the crowd outside the tall iron gate beyond the expanse of green lawn between his office and the street. He could make out several of the large signs stretched across several protesters.

"Contagions are people, too! They have rights!"

"Newbiggers is OLD news."

"We don't need a WILL. We need a WAY!"

The president turned back to his office and looked at Mallor. "I want the streets cleared. This is unacceptable."

"They have a right to state their opinions. They are responding to rumors that the virus research funding is being canceled."

"Don't they realize that without the Compound's efforts they wouldn't have clean water or clothes to wear? It's time to stop wasting money looking for a cure."

"I know, Sir."

"I'm the best president Society has ever had. No one has done more than me to make Society better."

"I found out who authored the anonymous book." Mallor referred to a publication gaining popularity within Society.

Sir William smiled, distracted from the protests outside.

"Really? Was it someone in the Statecraft Central Office like we thought?"

"I've taken care of it. No need to involve you. The author will not be compelled to write a sequel any time soon."

Sir William smiled. "It was all lies. Accusing me of abusing my position in office for personal gain. Trying to taint my name by making up stories about my personal affairs."

Mallor had done his research and knew there was a sound basis for the book, more than Sir William let on. It was important he have insurance when it came to the type of work he performed. He knew more than Newbiggers realized.

The Contagion protests outside only touched the surface of the corruption.

The allegations in the book about a fourteen-year-old girl in a hotel room in Precinct Three, along with the siphoning of Statecraft monies into Sir William's private businesses, and the twenty-year-old boy in Precinct Two, and the excessive gambling at the Quilt table all were true. But the inside knowledge of foreign powers manipulating his voting on tariffs and treaty agreements was most alarming.

The list went on and on. Sir William was a man who saw himself as invincible. Mallor, however, knew it was only a matter of time before the shell game would be revealed. In his line of work, he'd seen it all. He'd be well on the outside and undetectable when the foundation of Sir William's world started to crumble. He'd taken precautions to make sure the trail did not lead to him or his "unconventional" tactics.

Not all is how it appears.

Roseleen gazed at the sleeping man before her. He wore a brown hooded robe and dark leather work boots. She saw some marks on his left wrist, lines etched about an inch in height. While her skin was fair with a smattering of freckles, his was darker, the color of the forest tea she made each morning. His lips curled slightly in a smile as he slept peacefully. The brown hood had fallen backward while he slept, revealing short dark hair which framed his face. It was different than hers, and she wondered what it felt like. She tentatively reached forward, not to disturb him. The strands were soft to the touch. He shifted in sleep, and she carefully pulled her hand away.

"Mama? Is that you?" Triden opened his eyes slightly while sleep dragged his eyelids lower. A shadow of a woman was in front of him.

"Mama? I miss you. I'm so glad you're here."

What a wonderful dream. He hadn't dreamt of his mother for years. He wanted to savor the moment, but sleep retreated and he remembered he was in the forest. He must have drifted off after lunch.

His eyes opened wider and started to focus. Was he still dreaming? A beautiful redhead leaned over him and replaced the image of his mother in his mind.

Fear and panic stabbed him as he scrambled to stand up.

"I'm sorry, I didn't mean to wake you." The woman reached out to calm him.

"DON'T!" he yelled as she touched the sleeve of his robe.

He was on his feet, trying to back away but blocked by the fallen log behind him.

"Don't touch me!" His mind was racing. What had he seen on the screens? Was his robe enough protection? Had he exposed her? Was she going to die?

"It's OK. I didn't mean to scare you. Really, it's fine. Don't worry." She looked confused at his reaction.

"But... but..." He struggled to find the words. "I'm a Contagion. Please, please step away."

"You're a what?"

"You don't know?" *Was that possible?* "I'm a carrier of the virus P3264."

Roseleen smiled. "I'm not worried."

"How can you say that? I may have exposed you. Don't touch me or come any closer."

"What happens?"

"I don't know for sure. I've seen pictures of when the virus takes hold. It's a death sentence."

"Does it happen right away?"

"I think so."

Roseleen held out her hand and smiled. "It looks OK to me."

"My robe must have been enough protection."

"Actually, I touched you while you were sleeping."

Triden grappled with the information.

"Why? Why did you do that?"

"I don't know. I've never seen anyone who looks like you before. I was curious."

Tears welled in Triden's eyes.

"I'm so sorry. I didn't know. I never intended to expose anyone." He deserved his punishment; giving his life for taking another.

Wait a second, I didn't do anything wrong. Triden struggled with shifting emotions. "You should never have touched me. I shouldn't be held responsible if you die."

Of course, I never should have been outside of the Compound. The fault is truly mine.

He took a deep breath, still trying to come to terms with

the gravity of the situation.

"I'm Roseleen..."

How could she be so calm? Did she not understand he was a carrier of a deadly disease and she'd just been exposed?

"And you are...?"

He hesitated. Did he give her his barcode number or his informal name used by friends? Should he identify himself at all?

"Hey, if I'm about to die, I should at least be able to know your name."

"Triden."

"Nice to meet you."

"Show me your hands."

She held out both, palms up.

"Do you see any redness? Any welts? Do you feel a fever coming on?"

"Nope. All looks good, and I feel fine."

"Maybe you should sit down and we'll see if anything changes."

Roseleen perched on the fallen log, and Triden started pacing.

"People develop a red rash and a high fever. The fever gets so hot it practically cooks them alive." Triden winced at the details. "Sorry, I shouldn't have told you."

"How long does it take?"

"Well, in the pictures I've seen, it happens very quickly."

"So, it would have happened by now?"

"I don't know. I'm not a doctor."

"I'm fine. Really."

"How do you know, are you a doctor?"

"No, I just know."

"That sounds crazy."

"That's what everyone says who doesn't understand."

"Understand what?

"I'm an Oracle."

"You're a what?" He'd never heard of such a thing.

"I get messages."

"What kind of messages?"

"Insights, premonitions, information."

"Like what?"

"The message I'm getting right now is... *Embrace the one in front of you to know their truth.*"

Now he knew she really must be crazy.

How could she explain to Triden she knew she would be alright? She'd been sensing his presence for weeks. She knew their paths were going to cross, and she knew it meant a positive change. What exactly? It would be revealed in time. For now, she knew they were destined to meet, and she wasn't to die immediately. She had no fear, only relief they'd finally connected. When he awakened and she saw his eyes, she knew. The only visual element to her messages were his slate green eyes. Triden was the Power Walker.

◍

Jayr felt despair. He'd been blocked by his supervisor, and his research was stalled. If the rumors were true, the countdown clock was ticking, and he didn't have much more time to find a cure. Time to be creative. He wasn't sure it would work, and the consequences might be dire, but he saw no other options.

He stood naked and looked at the items collected on his bed. The most uncomfortable part would come first. He picked up the plastic balloon with various compartments and stepped into the leg holes, and pulled it up. It didn't take long to adjust the sections of the soft bladder, which would collect his bodily fluids for as long as needed. The soft, pliable material molded to his body, and two separate compartments hung between his legs. One would capture solid waste and the other liquid.

Next, he pulled on two knee-high cotton socks before

stepping into a long-sleeved cotton bodysuit to encase his figure. The head guard covered his hair, and only an oval of his face showed, along with his hands. The rest of the garments he would put on after he left the Society perimeter. He packed the items into a black surgery box designed to carry diagnostic equipment. It wouldn't be unusual for the doctor to be toting the large box on wheels.

He tied the laces of his dress shoes, lowered the head covering of the cotton bodysuit, and slipped into his traditional floor-length, white research robe with the Lab of Human Betterment emblem on a pocket covering his heart.

He looked in the full-length mirror on the back of his bedroom door and moved in a circle, watching his reflection. There was a slight bulge under the robe where the cotton hood lay across his back. A hint of the white socks was visible as he walked, but there was no indication of the bladder contraption under his clothes. He doubted anyone would notice the slight abnormalities.

He rolled the large surgery box to the door. One stop at his home office, and he collected his exam bag and a large flat envelope with the Lab of Human Betterment seal. He hoped the address on the outside met the requirements. He would know soon enough.

Leaving his penthouse, he rode the elevator down to the parking garage and he stowed the sturdy box in the back of a white van with the lab seal, placed his exam bag and envelope on the passenger seat, and climbed inside. He saw a neighbor and waved as he started the vehicle. His heart was pounding, and yet he felt excitement as well. This was the first thing he'd done in months that felt productive.

He pulled into traffic and made his way to the driving conduit used by trucks and service vehicles accessing the Contagion Compound daily. Most were flatbed utility vehicles designed to carry cargo containers from the Compound to Society. Clothes and uniforms were manufactured on-site at the

Compound. There was also a laundry facility that washed and folded Society linens within the Compound, and the doctor followed the truck filled with soiled items for cleaning.

He'd never been to the Compound. However, in his research, he'd read about the protocols used to interact with infected patients from years earlier, and the supplies were still accessible in the storage room located down the hall from his lab.

The traffic began to thin as he moved further away from the populace of Society. Wide-open fields flanked the road, and the truck rumbled forward. In the distance, he could see the gray cement complex.

How depressing, he thought as he moved closer. The colorful world he left behind seemed to be consumed by an overcast pale light. Clouds overhead spotted the sky, and the feeling of isolation was palpable.

He followed the utility truck into the Compound. He watched as the vehicle maneuvered to an automated assembly line, backing up and linking the container on the flatbed to the track which carried the large vessel to the interior of the Compound. The receptacle disappeared through the vast portal, and a few moments later, a different container emerged and fed onto the flatbed. The driver took a few minutes to secure the bin before his return to Society. The doctor watched as several trucks entered the large parking area and exchanged their large containers for commodities produced inside the Compound.

He parked the medical van at the perimeter of the lot to ensure he did not disrupt the flow of the vehicles. He still needed to finish dressing in the protocol gear. Stepping inside the back of the van, he opened the surgical case. He slipped off his dress shoes and slid on industrial boots designed to encase his feet and protect him from exposure. Next, he slipped on a heavy leather ankle-length robe. The leather was stiff and dusty from years in the storage closet. The doctor sneezed a few times as dust particles floated free in the confines of the van.

The most daunting piece of the outfit was the headgear. A large leather cover with two glass lenses for visibility slid over his head. A long protrusion contained an air filtration system. He'd checked the filter before he left his home, and it worked perfectly, even after years of neglect. Leather strands secured the pieces together; the doctor could only imagine what the sight of him would convey to the inhabitants inside the Compound. Before stepping outside of the van, he pulled on leather gloves, made with a soft waxed kid leather to give him as much dexterity as possible without exposing him to the virus.

Retrieving his exam bag and the official document outlining the purpose for his visit, Jayr looked for an entrance. The cargo bay terminals were unmanned, and there was only automated activity as containers were moved in and out of the Compound, swapping commodities.

He looked around, at a loss as to where to go. High above the parking area was a tower built into the side of the wall with glass windows on the three sides facing the parking area. No one appeared to be inside. His trip could be over before he got started. He stood in the open expanse of the lot.

"Hello?" His voice sounded muffled and small coming from inside the mask. Even trying again with a full yell, he wasn't making much of a commotion. He walked the perimeter of the vast lot, looking for some type of entry. As he returned to the area under the tower, he saw the post was now occupied, and he waved his arms to get the attention of the person above.

"You are at a restricted site; please retreat," a metallic-sounding voice boomed over a loudspeaker.

The doctor waved the envelope in his hand and yelled, unclear if anyone would be able to hear him.

"I have official business on site."

The person above hesitated, and then he heard a loud buzzer. A panel in the wall slid open, revealing an enclosed chamber indiscernible when closed tight. He stepped inside and the wall closed, confining him in the enclosed cube.

His heart was racing again. Unclear whether or not he was being let in or contained, the doctor took a few deep breaths to steady his nerves. He was having trouble with visibility through the mask eyes. The placement didn't conform to his own features and he could hear his breathing reverberate through the extension as the air purifier hummed quietly.

Once the door sealed to the outside, a rumble started, and the interior wall slid open, revealing a second vestibule. Two Contagions were inside behind an enclosed space; they greeted him with curiosity.

"State your business."

The doctor fumbled with the envelope as he looked for a way to hand it to the closest person. His hands were shaking slightly. He hoped he appeared as official as possible.

They indicated he should put it into a canister which he picked up from a table.

"Insert it into the tube, please."

The doctor did as he was told and watched the canister get sucked up a pipeline attached to a tube on the other side of the glassed partition.

"I'm a doctor from Society. I've been instructed to come and get additional data samples to aid in my research." He paused. "I'm trying to find a cure or antidote for The Path."

The two men looked nervous and the doctor realized they were not accustomed to interacting with anyone from outside their world.

"I'm here to help you. It's all there in the document."

They opened the canister and retrieved the envelope inside. They scanned the contents and then conferred with each other. The doctor could not hear what they were saying, their voices muffled behind the barrier.

"I'm sorry, we did not know you were coming. We are not prepared."

The letter outlined the doctor's goals. He wanted to meet with a cross-sample of the residents, both men and women, who ranged in ages from the oldest to youngest in the Compound. He needed to acquire enough information to expand his data and to compare the new samples with the ones already available to him at his lab.

The young man spoke again, and the doctor recognized his accent. This was someone who'd been from Precinct Nine, which had been decimated by the virus. Located in the northern domain of Society, they had a distinct dialect retained even while in the Compound. Most living in Precinct Nine had been terminated and it was a dialect he hadn't heard in a long time. It felt oddly familiar and tickled the recesses of his memory.

The two Contagions looked at the doctor's outfit.

"Are you sure your clothing will protect you from us?

"It's the standard-issue protocol," he replied, although he wasn't sure. The suit hadn't been used in a long time, and while the leather was waxed and he was covered from head to toe, there were many unknowns about P3264. How much had it mutated over the years? Obviously, the residents of the Compound were leading productive lives. Had the more powerful strain been eradicated? There were so many unknowns reinforcing Jayr's resolve to be there.

He looked at the two men. The second person spoke, and he heard another dialect almost forgotten from years past. Precinct Seven.

"We will put together the group of people for you to interview, but it will take time. Everyone here has work to contribute to the successful running of the Compound and Society. We will have to stagger your interviews through the shift assignments. Is this acceptable to you?"

The doctor nodded affirmatively, the protrusion of his

mask slicing the air.

"Please return in three days at this time. We will set up an interview space to protect you."

"I do need contact with everyone. It's important I can retrieve blood and urine samples to assist with my research."

The two men huddled once again.

"We will have someone from the infirmary collect the samples you need. They will assist from this side of the barrier."

"Thank you."

"Remember, our motto is *'Take a Life, Give Your Own.'* Participants need to be assured their lives are not at risk."

"I understand. I waive my rights as it relates to sacrifice. I am here because I believe I am sufficiently protected. If I am wrong and anything happens to me, please do not terminate anyone in the study."

The two Contagions conferred again. "That is not our protocol."

"Please, give me your assurance no one will suffer if they agree to meet with me."

"We will include the information as part of the selection process. We will ask for volunteers and make sure they know they are exempt from punishment."

"Thank you again. This is critical for me to move forward with my work."

"See you next week."

"Yes." The tense anxiety on whether or not he would be accepted at the Compound dissipated. He was thankful they hadn't questioned his documents.

The doctor turned toward the exit and saw the screen overhead.

"Lucky to Be Alive!"

Yes, lucky indeed, he thought as he stepped back into the expansive lot and walked to the van.

〖11〗

The customary morning message on his apartment screen was replaced with an alert message.

"Contagion 36MA46RA23, please report to the infirmary for research study participation. Your supervisor has been informed of your delay this morning."

The message triggered fear as Triden read it. A previous memo had solicited volunteers, which had likely been ignored by all residents, and now participants were being randomly selected.

That can't be good.

No one wanted to be sent to the infirmary. Not everyone returned.

Triden was comfortable in his world. The rashes covering his body were tolerable. He did not have the intense heat or itching that tortured some Contagions. The rashes became part of his body's blueprint. *Why didn't they select someone with more acute symptoms?*

Today was an important day. He had promised Roseleen he would meet her at the log in the forest. He hadn't slept well, tossing and turning, unsure if he would find her dead or alive. She'd agreed to stay by the fallen tree for an hour after he'd departed the day before; Triden's best guess on how long it would take for The Path to ravage her body.

He had hesitated at leaving her and only left at her insistence. He'd stayed as long as he could, his nap already extending his time in the woods beyond a safe period out of the Compound. Finally, he'd returned, slipped inside, and with mixed emotions secured the metal bar. *How could she be so sure?*

Triden had no way to get her a message if he was detained in the infirmary.

He scanned his left wrist to exit his quarters and ran into Benjam in the hallway.

"Did you get summoned to the infirmary?" Triden whispered, trying to respect the quiet of the morning.

Benjam shook his head. Negative. He leaned in closer and whispered, "That can't be good." His response mirrored Triden's thoughts.

In the dining area, Triden picked up his bagged lunch and two protein pucks and headed toward the infirmary. Better to face his demons head-on and hope he would be able to leave in time to meet Roseleen.

He couldn't stop thinking of her. She was beautiful with flowing copper hair and gray eyes. She was also the first person he remembered meeting who wasn't a Contagion confined to the Compound. If she'd survived contact with him, she must have the same mutation as those confined in the Compound because P3264 had no mercy as it consumed most of those exposed.

Triden didn't understand why he and the others in the Compound had survived the virulent disease. Were there others he could have contact with and not expose them? So many questions plagued him since they met and he had no answers.

Entering the infirmary, he saw someone wearing the oddest clothes: a heavy tan leather cloak and a mask encompassing the entire head, with round glass disks to provide visibility. A long extension protruded forward, and there was a slight hum coming from what he assumed was an air filter inside.

A temporary barrier was set up separating the stranger from Triden and the others in the infirmary room.

"I'm Contagion 36MA46RA23, reporting for research participation."

He was ushered to a seat facing the leather-cloaked individual.

"Hello, I'm Jayr Lenus, a doctor from Society. I've been seeking a cure or vaccine for P3264 since its onset."

Triden nodded.

"I'm gathering new data samples to compare for mutations from the strains already identified. This information will also validate the work already completed. Are you willing to participate?"

Triden nodded, knowing he was being asked, and yet there really was no choice. He'd been selected. It would be impossible to get an exception. That's not how things worked in the Compound.

"Great."

The doctor proceeded to ask a variety of questions.

"How old were you when you were exposed?"

"Six."

"How old are you now?"

Triden wasn't sure, exactly.

"Around thirty."

"Which precinct did you live in?

"Nine."

"Can you walk me through a normal day here...from when you wake to when you sleep?"

Triden answered the last question and yet omitted his most cherished daily activity, venturing outside the Compound. It was illegal and punishable. It occurred to him he could be terminated, particularly if anyone learned of his interaction yesterday with Roseleen, and he fidgeted in his seat.

He looked at the screen overhead and noted the time. One hour before he was supposed to meet Roseleen at the log.

He turned his attention back to the doctor. "Is that everything?"

"I will be returning regularly to gather additional information. Before you go, we need to collect fluid samples."

Triden complied and sighed with relief as he exited the infirmary. Only a standard examination without detainment. He was thankful he could slip undetected into the underground of the Compound. No one was interested in seeing how the water and sewer systems operated. The screen on the outside of the building showed time had slipped by faster than he'd expected. He had to be careful above ground not to run quickly or it would draw attention to his actions. He walked methodically toward the W&W building. Once entering, he walked past his supervisor's office, stopping briefly to report his arrival before entering the stairwell to the systems underground.

Picking up his tool belt and gloves, he made his way toward the secret passageway. He was running late and was fearful of what he might find.

Sprinting to the forest, he tucked in between the trees and quickly made his way to the fallen trunk. His worst fears were confirmed. There she was, lying next to the fallen tree, her body lifeless. Guilt and shame washed over him. He'd taken a life. He would do the honorable thing and give his own.

CHAPTER 16

Sir William sat at the Quilt table with his game steward patiently perched on a tall stool behind him. He'd amassed the bulk of the betting tiles after three hours of play, and yet he wasn't ready to return to the Presidential Palace. He still had to crush the two opponents at the table. The chancellor from Precinct Two dropped out early, his betting tiles lost to The Bank. The remaining cabinet members from Precincts Three and Five were playing well but still suffered losses with cards not strong enough to beat the ones on William's game tableau.

The dealer called out the winner.

"Player 1 takes the round."

Sir William watched as the dealer pushed the square tiles from The Bank into his playing area. His game steward handed Sir William a clean tableau board and started sorting the tiles into stacks of five.

He didn't like to lose. He played to win, and he'd make everyone stay for hours to turn the tables. He didn't know the cabinet members from the precincts were coached by Mallor to throw their hands throughout the course of play to ensure Sir William left triumphant.

Do it for Society. If he's happy, Society is happy.

The cabinet members, all vying for time with the president and a commitment of Society resources for their precincts, played along, making sure it wasn't too obvious they were coddling the president in exchange for his favors, for his support.

After an additional thirty minutes, both of the remaining cabinet members lost the sufficient number of tiles to appease Sir William's gambling addiction, and the men moved to the dining table to discuss Society affairs.

Sir William was in a jovial mood after cashing out an amount equal to his hefty annual salary. He begrudgingly tipped the dealer and his game steward the minimally acceptable amount.

A decadent meal arrived, and plates were set before the four men. It didn't take long for the precinct representatives to share their thoughts with Sir William.

"Precinct Three is seeing a growing number of protesters in favor of promoting a better life for the Contagions. We'd like to have the assurance of the Statecraft you'll send troops to avoid rioting."

"And, Sir William, Precinct Two is hoping you can do something about the public lands to the north. It would be advantageous if we could harvest wood from the forests. The population is booming, and we are short on housing."

"Yes, and Precinct Five is expanding its manufacturing capabilities and would like support imposing tariffs on foreign competitors to ensure our products are deemed desirable."

Sir William wished he could enjoy his meal without all the tedious comments. He'd run for office to enhance his business holdings but never expected to win. During the rallies and campaigning, he'd used his own facilities to host events and house the security detail assigned to protect him, which added millions to his balance sheet. It was only when he'd acquired the office did he begin to understand the full power of his role. He loved being in the most powerful position of Society; however, he bored easily at the mundane requests made daily by those around him.

He had assumed the role of Chancellor of the Signet decades earlier when his main focus had been building his empire. As the Chancellor, he was primarily responsible for documenting Society policies. He'd taken on the duties to ensure that the rules and regulations favored his business ventures. He'd been able to rezone and push through building permits enabling the growth of Newbiggers properties. The role was perceived as mostly administrative, and he'd been able to delegate policies that didn't directly impact him for others to resolve. No one identified the potential conflict of interest until the recent publication of the anonymous book.

Daily, he tried to avoid most of his duties, happy to hand off the day-to-day tasks to Mallor, Annabella, and others of his inner circle. He was happiest when he could attend political rallies that allowed him to speak to the constituents of Society. He'd relayed phrases to energize his supporters.

With a *WILL*, there's a *WAY*!

Go BIG or Go Home!

He rambled on, touting his expertise and what he had accomplished, and routinely belittled his competition, often giving them disparaging nicknames like the one he'd given Jordon Connor. He loved to hear cheers from the crowd as he waved and postured. He easily ignored those protesting outside the large gatherings, convincing himself the people inside were the majority and the ones outside only represented a small fraction of citizens of Society.

He looked at the men at the lunch table.

"Tell Mallor and Annabella we've discussed this and for them to help you with the details." He waved off any other comments from the precinct cabinet members and took a big bite of his steak.

▌

Annabella and her husband, Jordon, sat in their living room in front of a blazing fire. Jordon was removing a cork from a rare vintage of wine, and his wife held out her glass to be refilled. They'd already consumed one bottle.

"I wish you could have seen his face when he saw you on the screen!" Annabella squealed. "He's such a manipulable idiot."

"Now, now, dear. It's not nice to talk so disparagingly about our fearless leader."

"Fearless? Ha!"

The two laughed together again, and Jordon accidentally sloshed part of his newly poured glass of wine onto the rug.

"Dear, can you get me a towel?"

"Don't worry about it, Jordie. The maid comes tomorrow."

"Bella, I think I'm drunk."

"I know I am! We have lots to celebrate! I got that bloated pig to sign the amendment we needed to assign jurisdiction of the education system over to the Department of Society Wherewithal, which opens it up for privatization. Our corporation can present a bid for all five precincts, and no one will be able to trace it back to either one of us."

"Bella, you're brilliant!" Jordon smiled. "I have to admit, when you first told me you were going to be Executive Advisor to Sir William, I thought you were crazy."

"He can't be bothered with details, and it's easy to convince him it's his idea most of the time, too."

"Here's to my brilliant wife." Jordon raised his glass before taking another drink.

"Having you as a talking head for the alternative party keeps us protected from both sides."

"I didn't think it was possible, but you were right!"

"His followers only see what they want to see. William's their savior, providing solutions to all their woes. And his detractors see you as their ally, fighting for their rights. No one seems to care we're married."

Jordon laughed. "Nothing like a few well-placed 'off the record' statements to press members indicating our marriage is off the rails to gain more sympathy. As soon as William is no longer in office, we can 'patch up our affairs' and be a committed couple once again."

"You know what the best part is, Jordie?"

"No, Bella, tell me."

"Whoever wins the next election, one of us will be assigned as the executive advisor, and we can still work the system from within."

"After we secure the schools, let's privatize the Contagion Compound. It's been part of Society's burden for far too long."

"Jordie, I almost forgot! Today another opportunity came up! Precinct Two wants to harvest wood from the public lands. We can get that contract, too."

"I love it!" Jordon took another gulp of wine.

"The Contagions are a powerful resource for us all. Expanding their output to trade items will increase our economic stronghold. And the best part? We only need to provide shelter, food, and water, which means we can undercut the production costs of other countries. Society will be the most dominant country in the world with us at the helm. No one can stop us!"

The couple clinked their wine glasses again and drank to their future.

Triden looked at Roseleen, her beautiful still body laid out before him next to the fallen log. He didn't know where she'd come from in the forest and didn't know what to do. She deserved more than abandonment in the woods. He stepped closer and observed her creamy skin with its smattering of freckles. Her copper hair flowed around her face, and she looked serene, eyes closed and quiet.

At least she didn't cook from the inside out. He'd seen too many gruesome images of how the virus consumed its victims.

Wait... He paused. *She looks fine...* He didn't see any red splotches on her face or hands, the visible parts of her body. Triden pulled the sleeve of his robe down over his hand and tentatively reached out and touched her.

"Roseleen?" He gently shook her shoulder.

She jolted upright.

"Oh...hey, Triden." She blinked a few times. "I can't believe I fell asleep."

Triden could feel the tension in his body dissipate. There were no words for how grateful he was that she was alive.

"You... you..."

"Scared you? I'm sorry. I got here early and it was so peaceful and quiet, I must have drifted off."

"How... how..."

"Am I OK? I told you yesterday I'm fine."

"Yes, but every person who comes into contact with a Contagion is exposed. No one has had immunity and they have all died."

"You didn't die."

"There are those of us who survived, but we have the marks of the disease." He pulled up his sleeve to show the red rash.

"I'm fine, really. Look." She pushed up her own sleeves.

"See... nothing amiss." She stood, and Triden instinctively stepped backward. She stepped toward him and slowly engulfed him in her arms. She could feel his hesitation and nervous agitation as she closed her arms around his back. She held him for a minute before he raised his own arms and returned the embrace.

It felt magical. Triden didn't want to let go. To be touched freely in an open space. No scanning of barcodes, no monitoring, no limitations on contact.

Tears filled his eyes.

"I don't want to hurt you."

"It's alright. I know it's fine." Roseleen hesitated. *Should she tell him more about her visions? Would he understand?*

In due time. Change is in the air... Her inner guidance gave her the answer.

"I brought you something." She reached into her leather bag and pulled out a package. She unfolded the layers surrounding an odd-looking wafer with filling. It looked nothing like the protein pucks stashed in his lunch bag.

"Try it. It's a root bread with boar meat." She handed him the package.

He sniffed at the food and smelled an aroma he couldn't place. The meat smelled smokey and the root bread was smooth in his hand with a faint aroma of its own.

He took a bite and started to chew. The flavors merged and triggered hunger pangs. He took another bite, chewing slowly, trying to savor each morsel. The flavors were both rich and delicate; nothing compared to the dry harshness of the protein pucks. This was moist and decadent. He was torn between devouring it quickly and savoring it slowly.

"Do you like it?"

He nodded an affirmative. "What is boar?"

"It's a small pig-like animal."

"And what are root vegetables?"

"They grow underground. We forage for the wild roots

around our home. The cresswood root works well for making a dough we cook over a fire to make flatbread."

Triden saw a bushy tail scurry up a tree behind Roseleen.

"What's that?" He pointed at the furry creature.

"A squirrel."

"Does a boar have bones sprouting from its head?"

Roseleen paused for a moment, and then her face lit up.

"You saw a stag?"

"I don't know. It had four legs, a tan body, and branches of bones on its head."

"You saw a male deer. Also called a stag. They're magnificent, aren't they?

"Yes. I only saw him once."

"The boar is smaller than a stag and hefty. I'll point it out to you if I see one."

Triden smiled. He wanted to see her again. Learn about her world. He didn't want to leave.

He turned toward the northern tree and held up his hand to the familiar measuring point.

"I have to go. Can I meet with you again tomorrow?"

Roseleen nodded.

"Be safe, Triden."

"Lucky to be alive, Roseleen."

Yes, change is in the air, she thought as she watched him turn toward the field and the Compound beyond.

Mallor stepped inside The Flodden Club and showed a membership card to the desk attendant. Only elites in Society could afford the hefty initiation fee and annual dues to join. Sir William sponsored him and waived the buy-in on Mallor's behalf as partial payment for services rendered.

He found Sir William finishing lunch with three of the precinct cabinet members.

"Sir, if I could have a word, please."

The other men pushed their chairs back and said hasty goodbyes. They'd gotten what they came for and the meal was a formality. Sir William would leave with money credited to his club account, and the precinct members got approval for their area's initiatives.

After the three departed, Mallor sat in one of the chairs. He reached for an uneaten pastry and took a bite. He enjoyed the tasty treat.

"Your recent detractor is writing a retraction. He sees now how he fabricated a story."

Mallor did not tell Sir William his tactics for acquiring the promise from the vocal critic. He'd enjoyed watching the man squirm in his seat, fear transparent on his face, with a racing heartbeat, a nervous tic by his temple, and pale skin dotted with sweat. Mallor loved the power in his interrogation room. He controlled everything. He dictated the action and the result.

He especially loved when someone tried to put up a fight. He had no respect for the whimpering, cowering men who released their bowels and told him what he wanted before he'd even started. The adversary had proven himself to be an interesting subject. It had taken three hours to convince him what he'd reported was based on disgruntled Society employees of the Statecraft and that rumors of Sir William's dalliances with a variety of call girls, a stripper, and a young boy were un-founded. Mallor also convinced the author the call girls had not been a gift from the neighboring country trying to influence a weak and self-centered leader as outlined in the publication.

"I can always count on you to do a job well done." Sir William waved toward the three empty seats at the table. "These idiots, on the other hand, keep bothering me to sign a variety of documents. I don't understand why I have to be involved with precinct business. They should manage it themselves."

"That's not how the Signet is written. There is a balance of power with checks and balances in place. You are the checkmark."

Sir William sighed. "It might be time to change the Signet. Can't we amend it or something? Or better yet, let's create a new position and have an appointee take care of it."

Mallor looked at the rotund man.

Could he really be that stupid?

"Sir William, as the President of Society, it is your leadership which is demanded. If you seek reelection, you need to show by example, not delegate. Give away too much of your power, and there will be no reason for anyone to vote for you at the polls."

Sir William nodded, realization finally dawning on his pudgy face that he'd proposed handing over the reins of his position to an appointed figurehead. He absentmindedly stroked his thick mustache.

Mallor thought it best to change the subject before Sir William became despondent and pouty.

"How did it go at the Quilt table today?"

"Very good. Precinct Two caved quickly; he really doesn't know the odds of the game. It took longer to defeat Precincts Three and Five. They are better players."

Mallor didn't let on to Sir William that hands were folded

or misplayed to ensure the money on the table flowed to the president. Everyone knew to get business done with Sir William, the easiest way was to line his pockets.

Where does he think the money comes from? The precinct cabinet members' salaries? No one in the cabinet had enough personal funding to drop thousands at the Quilt table each week.

Sir William maintained his business ventures when he assumed the role of president by appointing his son from a previous marriage to the Executive Board. Even still, there was a fine line between presidential benefit and mandatory state business.

Several in Society tried to hold him accountable to emoluments laws, and yet an apathy among most residents allowed Sir William to continue his practices without scrutiny. Society citizens were too consumed with their own affairs to be concerned about the president. He promised a better life for his followers, and they held firm to the belief he would deliver. If he could make things better for himself, clearly, he could make everything better for them, too.

Mallor learned never to underestimate the ability of personal motivations to cloud a person's judgment. Self-preservation prevailed every time. He'd witnessed it over and over during his interrogations. Everyone could be broken.

CHAPTER 19

The doctor unpacked the samples he'd collected at the Compound. It surprised him how easily he'd been able to get inside to meet with a cross-section of the residents and gather information.

The Compound was very different than Society. He observed large screens peppered throughout the common areas, all flashing affirmations, as well as safety precautions. *"Lucky to Be Alive!"* rotated to *"Take a Life, Give Your Own,"* and then *"Together We Prosper," "Give for Tomorrow,"* and others he couldn't remember.

Network screens were abundant throughout Society and the communications were very different. They played advertisements, blasted out a thread of the president's ramblings on a scrolling banner, and shared live broadcasts of Signet meetings and updates on policy. There was also a view for alternative news providing additional insights outside those of the leaders of Society. The ability to speak freely was a cornerstone of Society, even when the opinions varied from the majority of others.

The most disturbing images at the Contagion Compound were the gruesome replays of early attempts to find a cure. He thought back to some of the more horrific reactions leaving patients writhing in pain and frothing at the mouth. They had stopped broadcasting the trials, but the Compound still looped the older editions.

While inside the Compound, he observed a community tightly structured in protocol and behavior. He looked at the vials and the barcodes assigned to each person. The letter and number sequences did not give him a visual sense of his research subjects, and he spent the next hour cross-referencing barcodes to the individual names of the participants.

Everyone at the Compound had a first name they used

socially in the evenings. Their barcodes were used to scan in and out of locations and, as the doctor discovered, it was also used to pair with others.

There were no last names. Most of the infected he met said their first name was the name they remembered from their parents. Others had selected their own with the help of older residents who provided them with a list of potential options that ensured that everyone had a unique moniker. The doctor realized how much of the Contagions' personal identity had been stripped from them when they arrived at the facility.

The doctor transferred the name "Triden" onto the vial in his hand. It was helpful to know there was no other person in the Compound who shared his name. When he probed into the barcode and naming convention, he asked why the barcodes were needed.

The question perplexed the residents.

"My name won't get me into my home. My barcode opens doors."

"I can only pair with someone based on barcode scanning."

For a man who spent his days slicing data sets and looking for variables, he was surprised at how little the Compound residents questioned their world's structure. None of them appeared agitated or upset with their situations. Most greeted him and said goodbye with what appeared to be the Compound catchphrase: *"Lucky to Be Alive!"* He learned the response phrase was *"Today and Tomorrow!"*

The doctor didn't know if he should be relieved or outraged about the circumstances at the Compound. Everyone appeared well adjusted and content. He looked down at the vial in his hand.

Triden.

There was something different about the young man. He'd been fidgety. It was subtle, but the doctor was trained to detect symptoms. He noticed the younger man kept glancing at the screen overhead.

The doctor acknowledged he'd taken the participants at the Compound out of their normal routine. Triden's behavior may be nothing more than someone reacting negatively to the change in his daily ritual.

The doctor would have a chance to observe more when he returned the following week. This was the most excited he'd been with his research in a long time. He may not find a cure, but at least he wasn't sitting idle resifting prior data sets. Even if the vials yielded no new information, at least he would know he was using the best data available for his research.

He moved to the separator and started to spin the samples to remove the plasma from the cells. He would be able to review the antibodies present and compare them to blood samples from those who previously succumbed from the illness.

The process took time and he walked to the cafeteria to get lunch while he waited. He hoped to have definitive findings before his supervisor learned of his deceit.

Better to ask for forgiveness than permission.

Normally he never would have operated outside of Society protocols, much like the Contagions living within their residence structure, but he was a desperate man looking for any options to warm the cold case.

※

Roseleen climbed up the deck platform of her family's treehouse.

"Mother!"

The older woman emerged from the interior of the house perched among the tree limbs.

"I met him! His name is Triden!"

Her mother smiled and hugged her daughter.

"This is wonderful news! We've both detected he was

near."

"How will I know how to proceed? I'm scared I won't be able to understand the messages."

"There's no need to question. The messages will be clear in time. You'll be guided in the same way you've been informed to expect his arrival."

"He doesn't know his power."

"I'm not surprised, Daughter. You both are newly stepping into your purpose in the world. Come, sit with me." The two sat side by side on a bench molded into the tree limb. "What is the message you are receiving now?"

"Most recently, '*The bird always knows the migration path home.*' Does it mean anything to you?"

The older woman nodded, "No, dear, I don't know, except all will be revealed in time."

"I don't know how much I should tell him. Will he think I'm crazy because I receive messages?"

"In good time, Daughter. You've just met, and until he knows you better, he probably won't understand."

"What if he doesn't believe me?"

"Daughter, you worry too much."

There's always a fork in the road.

The destination is more important than the path.

Embrace the one in front of you to know their truth.

Roseleen had hugged Triden earlier because of his innocence and hesitation. She hadn't thought about how he might pull away from her, with his fear of infecting her still a lingering concern.

He was unlike anyone she'd ever met. Most of her family had copper hair, ivory skin, and many had freckles like the ones across the bridge of her nose and cheeks. Triden's skin was darker, and his green eyes conveyed more than he realized. His skin was soft and smooth, even covered with patches of the P3264 rash.

When she had hugged him, she saw his reality. He was a

man trapped inside a compound who'd found a way to escape to the woods undetected. He took pride in the work he did, even though he was often bored. He didn't have the words to convey his frustration at not being more challenged daily. Roseleen suspected he would yearn for simpler days when he learned of his upcoming role.

"Mother, it's too early for him to leave his world behind."

"I know. For now, enjoy getting to know him."

Time would guide them both.

Sir William's young wife, Lilia, thirty years his junior, snapped her fingers to get the attention of the attendant standing on the sidelines by the door of the large dining room. As the servant approached, she waved her hand to indicate the dishes should be cleared. She'd only eaten half of what was on her plate, and yet she knew in order to keep her figure, she'd likely already eaten too much.

The household staff member retrieved her plate.

"Can I get you anything else? Tea, perhaps?"

"No, this was more than enough. Tell the chef the servings are still too large."

"Of course. Anything else, ma'am?"

"No, be gone. I can't stand to look at food anymore." She stood and returned to her office.

She'd been surrounded by school children all morning. She was regretting her choice to make her work as the Top Lady of Society centered around education. She hated how every child wanted to touch her with their tiny sticky fingers. She had assumed they would be cute and quiet, and she wouldn't have to be near them. Instead, they ran around her, squealing with laughter, getting their hands into everything. That morning, a man in her protection patrol had caught a vase before it toppled and broke.

Sitting at her office desk, she rubbed her temples, trying to will her headache away. The smooth skin defied her age, secretly lifted and tucked regularly to remove any wrinkle or blemish.

Thank God her tub of lard husband hadn't tried to enter her bedroom recently. She'd heard rumors of a porn star consorting with her husband at a local hotel. All the better, let someone else deal with his groping hands and fumbling efforts.

She looked out the window at the expanse of lawn, wishing she'd cleared her calendar completely. She would only have a few minutes with the young man who delivered her daily mail. The young clerk pushed a cart by her office door, and she beckoned him inside. Her security patrol remained outside the office since there was no other way to leave than through the same door used to enter.

"Drop your trousers." The order didn't surprise the young man, and he swiftly dropped his pants to the floor. He was ready for her. She carefully lifted up her designer skirt.

"Be careful and don't rip my skirt this time. I have a meeting in a few minutes."

He pulled down her panties, entered her from behind, and thrust a few times before ejaculating inside her.

Why are men so quick? She'd hardly gotten started. It really wasn't about having an orgasm. It was her little secret that she could have any man she wanted. Her husband had betrayed their vows within a week of their marriage, and she was astute enough to know men like Sir William didn't play by Society rules. There was no reason she had too either. She didn't know the boy's name. She had noticed his erection the first day he'd delivered her mail. He'd smirked at her, challenging her to make a move. She'd recently read a book by an anonymous author outlining Sir William's infidelities, and she wanted to even the score. She dictated when and how. She didn't want to look at the young man, so she always made him stand behind her. She'd hoped after repeated encounters he would have developed a little more control. She liked to believe she was the reason he had no lasting power. It stroked her ego to make him orgasm so quickly.

Fuck you, William, you nasty, arrogant prick.

CHAPTER 21

Triden looked down at Roseleen's fingers intertwined with his own. He was still processing that she was resistant to The Path and he could touch her with no harm. Yet, his fears lingered in the back of his mind. There might be the possibility of a delayed reaction, and one of the days, he'd come to meet her and see she'd started developing the rash as well.

"Don't worry, I'm fine."

"How do you do that? It's like you can read my mind."

"I have eyes." Roseleen smiled. "I can tell when you worry. It's written all over your face."

He'd never been one to censor his emotions, and his hood hid his face, keeping his reactions private. There was no room for emotions in the Compound. Everyone knew how to act and where to be at any given time. Everyone adhered to the guiding principles, and if there were any complaints, it was met with the standard response.

Lucky to Be Alive!

Today and Tomorrow.

He'd stopped wishing for things to be different in his life a long time ago. Back before he'd found the tunnel showing him a new world. Before he'd met Roseleen.

No one had defected from the Compound for years. Or, at least no one Triden knew about. There'd been the three boys who'd tried to run away after being transferred to the facility. Shortly thereafter, the message was received.

Take a Life, Give Your Own.

The lifeless bodies of the three boys, along with their unidentified victims, were flashed across the screen.

It was a moral mandate to follow the rules. It was a matter of life or death. Or so he'd thought before he met Roseleen.

He had many questions without answers. He didn't dare tell Benjam or anyone else about the portal to the outside. He couldn't risk exposing Roseleen to anyone else in the Compound. There could be a different mutation of the virus she could not stave off.

He looked at the sun shimmering through the tree leaves. Soon the days would be cloudy and snow would fall. How was he going to survive inside the Compound after experiencing snippets of freedom every day? The snow would force him to the interior of the Compound and it would keep Roseleen at the forest edge. Any tracks crossing the field would betray them both.

"You're worrying about something again."

"Yes, snow."

Roseleen didn't have to probe. She'd already thought of the implications of the changing seasons.

"Does anyone get to leave the Compound?"

"Only research participants. Recently a doctor from Society came to take blood samples. He's the only person I know from the outside. All communications with Society are normally done over the screens."

"There has to be a way."

"You should have seen how the doctor was dressed. He was covered from head to toe in thick leather clothing. Even his head was covered with a mask."

"I've seen trucks in the south parking lot. They come every day to drop off things and retrieve other items."

"They're picking up clean laundry and other items we manufacture. And I'm sure they're dropping off food and beverages. We don't produce any food items inside the Compound."

"I almost forgot; I was so excited to see you. I brought you a treat!" Roseleen retrieved a leather-wrapped packet from her satchel and handed it to him.

Triden unwrapped the parcel, and inside he found a blue cake-like cookie.

"I made it using the last of the glassenberries. I hope you like it."

He bit into the circular disk and smiled. It was sweet and the texture was soft and velvety on his tongue. He was so accustomed to the dry, flaky texture of the protein pucks, he didn't know food could have such a wonderful quality. He resisted the urge to pop the entire cookie into his mouth and instead ate it slowly, savoring every bite.

He looked at Roseleen with a grin. "You're spoiling me. I don't know if I'm going to be able to eat protein pucks if you keep feeding me things like this. Here, try one." Triden rummaged in the paper bag containing his daily rations of pucks and tea. Today's flavor was cresswood, an earthy grain harvested in the north. It wasn't too bad compared to some of the other flavors.

Roseleen snapped off a piece and took a bite. She grimaced at the taste. "Ugh! Are they all this bad?"

"Believe it or not, this is one of the better ones."

"I'm sorry you have to endure this. I'll bring you a better lunch tomorrow."

"You don't have to keep feeding me, really."

"I hope you don't mind; I'm not going to finish it."

"No, I don't need to torture you." He laughed and took the remaining bites from her and dropped the pieces inside his lunch bag. He'd finish it later. For now, he wanted to savor the aftertaste of the cookie.

"I think it's the best thing I've ever tasted."

"I'm glad you like it. I'll bring you another one tomorrow."

Triden looked up at the sun and sighed.

"I should get back. It's a good thing I work alone, but there's still a risk someone could be looking for me."

He stood up to leave and hesitated. He wanted to hug her, but his concerns about physical contact between them made him hesitate. He looked down at the ground.

She reached out and took his hand.

"It's alright, really." She stepped toward him and kissed him on the cheek. He responded by wrapping his arms around her. He didn't want to let go. Her hair smelled of wildflowers, so different from the industrial soap supplied to the residents of the Compound, designed to minimize the redness of rashes the Contagions dealt with every day.

"I'll see you tomorrow."

"Can't wait. Be safe."

"I will be. I'm lucky to be alive." He smiled when he saw her reaction. She was beginning to understand the differences between their two worlds.

Roseleen watched him walk toward the field between the forest and the Compound. Her life included him now and she dreaded any day she didn't see him.

She turned and started to make her way through the trees. A large boulder indicated it was time to turn. Further down the path, she stepped over another fallen log and came to the river's edge, and turned again, following the water as it flowed west. She loved the sound. As the river meandered alongside her, she stepped back into the dense layer of trees by the water's edge and twisted and turned among the trees. The ground was soft and earthy. Some moss was visible on one side of the tree trunks as she moved deeper into the canopy of leaves. The treetop village was about twenty minutes away from the field by foot. They selected the site for the seclusion in the woods: a retreat and oasis away from Society. The Forest Seers heeded the universal messages and retreated from Society before their actions would have been fully monitored and restricted.

Universal guidance provided insights on how to build the treehouses, what to bring, and what to leave behind. Tools and materials were meticulously stored in underground storage bunkers. Other bunkers were devoted to food storage; many in their community harvested and hunted food before snowfall to prepare for winter. When they were confined to the tree-houses, they would knit and sew clothes and make repairs to tools or other items needing attention.

Roseleen made the last turn and walked toward her family's home. She climbed the tree limbs to the platform. Stepping inside, she slipped out of her woven wrap and the leather coat underneath and hung them on wooden pegs by the entrance. The large room was partitioned into private areas for her parents, her brother, and her own space. There was also a communal area with a large circular braided rug made by Roseleen's mother. In the center of the treehouse, there was a heater warming the interior. No one was home, all away tending to the last of the daily tasks leading up to the first snow. She opened her harvest bag and did a quick inventory of the food she'd foraged that morning before meeting Triden. Root vegetables, berries, and several tree fruits were likely the last items she'd be able to find before the frost.

The communal kitchen was below the collection of tree-houses. Thirty families had heeded the messages and established the Forest Seer community. They worked together for the good of all and leveraged the skills and strengths of each member. They were democratic and, when there was uncertainty on the best course of action, the Seers would share the messages they received with the group and interpret them together. Everyone respected the messages and occasional accompanying visions. They survived and thrived by recognizing the importance of the information.

When living in Society, many had been scorned for listening to "the voices in their heads," and they learned to keep quiet except with those of like minds. Moving to the forest enabled everyone to be open and there were no judgments related to their abilities.

Roseleen opened the curtain partitioning her area of the space, and stepped inside. Her chair, made from branches curved and bent to create armrests and the chair back, was in the corner by the foot of her bed. A large slice of a tree trunk served as the seat. She loved the chair and would read one of the many books included with their items from Society. Her bed frame was also a tangle of wooden branches, and the mattress was filled with dry grass from the open field. The tree had an aroma which evoked a feeling of security; she was safe in her home, high in the limbs of the tree. She pulled the curtain closed, reached into her pocket, and pulled out a small white stone she had found that morning. It was unlike the dark gray boulders dotting the landscape or the smaller rocks found at the river's edge. She placed it on the shelf over her bed.

As she extended her hand, she saw a small patch of red on her arm. The rash was small, red, and angry-looking.

How can that be? A wave of fright washed over her as she looked at the rash and considered the unknown of what it meant.

You are on your path.

The message didn't quell her fears. It only reminded her of how little she knew.

⫍⊪⫎

Triden slipped into the tunnel and secured the metal bar. He looked out to the meadow and realized he was creating a path in the field. The long grasses were being matted in place, and a subtle line meandered toward the trees on the other side. He made a mental note to vary his trajectory to the forest even though he realized the walled community didn't provide much view of the field. Regardless, he treasured his ability to escape the Compound for brief periods and didn't want to jeopardize his freedom.

He ate the last of his protein pucks now that the taste of the glassenberry cookie was gone. He no longer thought of it as food, only sustenance to survive. He washed it down with the bitter beverage included in his sack meal.

Picking up his abandoned tool belt, he made his way to corridor seven and reviewed the filtration system. He worked quickly, checking the gears and machinery humming around him. He noticed a slight leak at one of the pipe joints, another reminder the system was in need of more extensive maintenance. He could bandage the system, but it wouldn't hold forever. He made a mental note to stop by his supervisor's desk on his way out.

He looked at the screen in the main cavern of the basement housing the W&W equipment. Fifteen more minutes until his workday was finished. He stowed the tools in a locker and made his way to the metal stairs to climb to the upper level of the building. He knew his manager had no clout to repair the infrastructure.

The supervisor looked tired as he knocked on the open door to get his attention. He would keep the conversation short; as long as he conveyed the potential risk, he felt he'd done his job.

Leaving work, he went to meet Benjam. The Barcode was already heaving with energy as Contagions mingled and maneuvered around the room with mugs of fermented cider and tried to decipher who was who in their identical robes. They met at their usual section of the bar; Benjam was already there, holding a stool for him. Triden slid onto the seat and filled a mug with Weesha.

"What's going on with you?" Benjam leaned in. "Have you been Off Book?"

"What? No." Triden shook his head. Off Book indicated two Contagions were meeting up even after they had scanned together five times. As he thought about it, he smiled. Roseleen was certainly Off Book, but they hadn't been intimate, so technically, his answer was true. He liked the idea of being with her. She was unlike anyone he'd ever met and he loved touching her.

"What about you? Any additional encounters with the woman you pointed out recently?"

Benjam smiled. "Yes, but don't say anything. We've managed to have additional time together. I hate the secrecy. I wish there was a way to remove the mandatory limitations. Why shouldn't we be able to find love with the one we want?"

"Indeed." For the first time in his life, Triden understood the desire to settle with one person. "You have my support, for what it's worth."

"Society set the rules, but they don't know what it's like to live here. We should be able to make our own decisions."

"I agree, but I don't know how to get a message to Society. There's no direct communication through our screens."

"That needs to change."

"I don't know how."

"Let's drink. At least that's one thing we can control."

The two men filled their glasses and toasted.

"Lucky to be alive!"

"Today and tomorrow."

Find a cure! Find a cure! Find a cure! Contagions are people of Society, too!

The muffled chants drifted to the presidential chamber. Sir William faced the mirror performing his morning routine, meticulously maneuvering each strand of hair into place and spraying it down with precision. He noticed some gray roots emerging and dabbed a bit of hair color from a tube using a cotton swab. He set the timer to avoid leaving the color in too long and highlighting the color job with a variance in hue.

"Mallor!" the president yelled into the screen on his personal device, and the younger man with weasel-like features and bald head appeared. Even at the early hour, he looked dressed and alert.

"Yes, Sir William?"

"Those protesters are outside again. I don't like it. You know my stance on the Compound. This is unacceptable."

"We can clear them if they are a threat to the safety and well-being of Society."

The president shook his head. "They aren't a menace. They're just loud. Isn't there a volume ordinance we can use to clear the streets?"

Mallor paused and repeated, "We can clear them if they are a threat to the safety and well-being of Society." He paused, watching for the man on the screen to assess what he was saying.

"Aaah, yes. A threat. Hold on." He pressed a button on his screen.

"Annabella!" It didn't take long for her image to appear, and Sir William merged her into the conversation with Mallor.

"We need to clear the streets. The protesters are a threat to the well-being of Society." William parroted the phrasing of his fix-it man.

Annabella nodded. "I see, Sir William. Have you thought of the opportunity before you?"

Sir William looked puzzled, and she continued.

"You have the chance to show your strength and leadership."

"Yes, yes, of course. I am a strong leader. No one is stronger than me in leading Society."

"That's right, Sir William."

Mallor was looking off-camera with a muted microphone. Annabella took the opportunity.

"Do you have a copy of The Signet? Why don't we clear the protesters and you can give a speech to Society in front of the Presidential Palace? What better building to convey your position and power than your residence?"

Sir William started nodding excitedly.

"Yes, a rally of sorts. I can see it now. Society will applaud me for taking care of this threat, this nuisance outside."

Annabella shook her head.

"Sir William, if we're going to clear the streets, it's unlikely we can amass enough people for a rally."

The president pouted. He hated giving speeches to a screen. He loved hearing crowds chanting his name.

"Think how strong you'll look holding a copy of The Signet. You will convey the proclamation of those who started Society; the people who saw a way to greatness and established our history. You can be remembered with the same greatness. This is your chance to reinforce to Society you are a leader and you believe in The Signet. You are their Savior."

"Yes, yes... exactly! Mallor, how long will it take for you to clear the protesters?"

"I've already put in the order, Sir. The Guard should arrive within 20 minutes. Does that give you enough time?"

Annabella chimed in. "That is fine. However, I ask we wait a little longer to get him dressed and ready. Sir, I'm ten minutes away. I'll meet you at your chambers. Mallor, I'll give you the OK when we're ready. I trust it will only take a few minutes once we give the approval?"

"Yes. From the footage I've received, it should be quick." He did not mention that the protesters were unarmed, with no way to fight off the Guard. It would be an easy task.

※

Forty-five minutes later, the streets were cleared by the Guard using pepper spray and smoke bombs. The crowd dispersed quickly, and those delayed by the effects of the smoke and spray were shoved into unmarked vans and driven off-site.

The president, along with his son, Annabella, and Mallor, walked across the lawn, Protection Services agents flanking the group. A nondescript intern set up a transportable screen, and Sir William stiffly held up a leather-bound copy of The Signet. No one noticed it was upside down, a fact only discovered later during the multiple replays of Sir William's speech.

"Citizens of Society. Time is of the essence. This is not the time to protest; this is a time to look at the great society we live in. Our economy is strong! We have secured our borders and set up protections to avoid the spread of P3264. Thanks to the timely response of our emergency teams and those on the front lines, we stopped the mass terminations and isolated the Contagions in their own safe space. They are lucky to be alive!"

Sir William paused. This was the point in the rallies when people would cheer, and he waited briefly before realizing the viewers on the screen could not be heard.

"With my direction and approval, there are many working around the clock to find a cure for the contagion. P3264 has shown us it is a deadly adversary not to be taken lightly. For the good of all in Society, it is imperative the Contagions are not exposed to the clean members of Society. It is in their best interests to keep them confined to the Compound. In their sanctuary, they have a life! They can contribute to Society! They are alive! When we are apart, we thrive!"

He waited again, listening for applause before remembering the flatness of addressing the screen before him.

"Um, er... Nobody is better at being a leader for Society than me! When there's a *WILL*, there's a *WAY*!" He pumped The Signet up and down in the air for emphasis.

Stepping down from the podium, he handed the leather-bound copy of the governing treatise to Annabella and walked back to the Presidential Palace. Annabella tucked the book into her designer purse.

"Thank God it's quiet again. Those misguided fools protesting the treatment of Contagions. Those in the Compound have a good life. They could be dead."

"We will prepare additional statements to send to all the precincts. It's important your message is heard throughout Society."

Back inside the Presidential Palace, Mallor dismissed himself from the meeting.

"I'm going to the detention center to get more information about the rioters."

"Rioting? I didn't know they were rioting. I just thought they were being loud."

"Remember, Sir William? We cleared the street because of the potential threat. You proactively avoided violence by eliminating any issues immediately."

"Of course." The portly man waved his hand dismissively at Mallor. "Go. Let me know what you find out."

Once the door shut, Annabella curled onto the couch, her legs tucked underneath her as she looked at the screen dominating the office wall.

"It looks like a favorable response, yet some of the news channels are questioning your tactics to use chemicals and smoke to clear the streets."

"How else were we supposed to get rid of them?"

"Don't worry. You came out of the Palace as a man of power. You are the leader of Society."

Annabella gave Sir William a moment to bask in the praise. It would soften him for her additional requests.

"You showed yourself as a man of faith devoted to the covenant of Society. The Signet is the true testament for all the precincts." She retrieved the text from her bag and placed it on the low table before her.

"Any updates on the school program? I'd like to meet with our consultant and make sure the schools are prepared for the next session."

Sir William was distracted.

"It wasn't too windy, was it? He looked in a mirror and patted down his dark hair. The helmet of hair spray kept all but one or two stray hairs in place.

"You looked powerful." Annabella viewed the screen and grimaced. The replays of Sir William's speech showed The Signet upside down.

How can you be such an idiot? How hard is it to hold a stupid book?! She made a mental note to add to a long list of items to monitor whenever Sir William had a press engagement. She was also always on the lookout for his latest dalliance at any function or rally. The president didn't seem aware of the risk of having someone so close to him in a public setting. Decorum and decency were not in his vocabulary.

Annabella had insider knowledge of details of Sir William's past. The president showed a talent for building up an empire, declaring bankruptcy, paying pennies on the dollar of his debt, and retaining the assets.

It was genius, and Annabella wished she'd thought of it. Instead, she and Jordon were planning a different way to secure their wealth. It was already taking shape, and it wouldn't be long before they'd privatized the school districts and then the activities of the Contagion Compound. She was about to have the best of both worlds; a steady position within Sir William's closest circle and private businesses to tap into the resources of the Contagion Compound. She was not under the same magnifying glass as the Newbiggers family, and she saw value in staying in the shadows. She and Jordon could reap the rewards without the need to explain their company's acquisitions. She was completely content to leave Sir William in the spotlight. She only had to be a good handler and surrogate mother to keep the president on track.

CHAPTER 23

Roseleen stretched and turned in bed. The sun was rising on the horizon, and the soft muted hues were visible from her window. She looked at her right arm and sighed in relief. The red rash which had bloomed on her arm yesterday was reduced to a faint pink shadow this morning. She must have come into contact with an urushiol plant when she was foraging for the last bits of fall bounty. The plant leaves were known for their toxicity. Triden's concern about infecting her was making her hypersensitive to any abnormality she observed on her own skin.

Nurture yourself in nature.

She pulled on a simple woven robe and made her way down the trunk of the treehouse. To the south of her home, there was a shower enclosure. Large bladders of water were warmed by the solar generator, and she stepped underneath and enjoyed the flow of warm water. When the weather was warmer, she often opted to bathe at the river's edge. With the cooler air, the heated water felt luxurious. She was careful not to aggravate the diminishing rash.

Returning to her room, she dressed quickly in the leather pants and shirt designed to protect her in the woods. The community was proficient at tanning hides of animals collected for food. Recently, they'd been drying the meat to extend the storage life for the winter. This was her favorite time of year, with the winding down of external activities and the Forest Seers coming together for the winter months. They would share stories from their past and connect. They also fostered their skills, tapped into their internal guidance systems, and discussed the visions for their future. At night, they would light lamps and play games, and sing. Laughter filled the darkness.

This year, she felt a sense of sadness as winter approached. This was the first year she knew Triden, and even though they'd only known each other a short time, it felt like he'd been with her always. She did not want to be separated from him during the snowy months.

She'd awakened early, and the other Forest Seers were slowly emerging from their treehouses. She hoped for more time to reflect, to meditate, and to tap into The Source for messages before the magic of the morning disappeared. She quickly wrapped a few more glassenberry cookies along with some boar jerky to share with Triden.

She looked up and saw her mother descending from their loft above.

"Good morning, Daughter."

"It is a beautiful day." She paused. "Mother, have you received any insights about Triden?"

"No, dear. I've been getting other messages I want to share with the Council."

"Anything of concern?"

"Not yet. As you know, it's cryptic. I'm looking for the Council's perspective."

The Council was a group of the top Seers in the community. Anyone who was unsure of the meaning of a guided message could bring it to the group. It was considered a duty and a responsibility of all Seers to seek additional insights instead of solely relying on their own intuition.

"Have you thought about approaching the Council, Daughter?"

"It's a consideration for when I have more information."

"There's nothing trivial about finding the Power Walker, even if we don't know his role."

"There's nothing new to share."

"Additional messages will come with time. Patience, Daughter, patience."

Roseleen smiled. Patience was not her strong suit, and she was getting nervous about the first snowfall. The air was brisk and cool, with snow arriving any day.

[◌◌◌]

The doctor retrieved the samples from the separator and started logging data. He felt renewed energy, knowing he held the most accurate snapshot of P3264. He could compare the data sets, and even if everything was identical, at least he felt productive. The Path had swept through the precincts, and at first, people had responded slowly to exposure, but the virus mutated as if it learned from its carriers. As a person's immune system worked to destroy the virus, it ultimately killed the host. Before much was known about P3264, the common symptoms were a fever with a dry cough which cleared after a few days. Like other viruses, the exposed people were contagious and passed the virus to those around them. However, it didn't take long to discover that P3264 was unique; anyone infected was permanently contagious.

Mass hysteria had swept through the precincts, and walls were erected to block off the exposed Contagions from the healthy people in Society. As the virus adapted, it mutated and killed those not already terminated by Society. Some children emerged as the only survivors, and a public outcry against killing children resulted in the creation of the Contagion Compound.

The doctor finished uploading the raw data and grouped the findings into a new heading so he could distinguish the Society provided data sets with the new samples. He added the collection date as well so he could continue to parse data as he obtained more samples.

Next, he created a report, put the cumulative data sets side by side, and scrolled through the sort criteria, looking for insights.

The number of male and female samples were identical by design. The ages varied since the Contagions had grown up since being housed separately. Regrettably, there were no identifiers for the samples from the Society. He had queried his supervisor years ago and was told the Contagion blood samples didn't need cataloging since they all were from the Compound. Jayr had stopped requesting more sample details when he was accused of being difficult. He had learned to work with the information he was given.

"Clearly not a group of scientists gathering data." Jayr noted the gaps in the information.

He tapped the screen and removed the Society data set from this comparison. He wanted to look at the new information as a stand-alone group.

Average age: twenty-eight.

Sex: split evenly with 30 males and 30 females.

He referred to the first data sets. He only received blood samples for 500 of the Contagions even though thousands had been sequestered in the large, gray buildings.

Opening his communication tab, he wrote his supervisor.

"I'm looking for data variances and I have limited blood samples. Are there additional queries I can reference?"

He had collected 60 samples earlier in the day. He hoped there was sufficient DNA data to cross-reference with the first data set. He wrote a quick algorithm to compare sample properties and identify potential matches between the data groups.

He watched as the algorithm processed, cross-referencing hundreds of blood samples. Several minutes later, the result showed a zero percent match.

Am I really that unlucky? Jayr reviewed his algorithm and validated it was correct. He entered the query again to confirm the original findings. Still no match.

He tapped a question onto the screen and learned 26,271 Contagions lived within the Compound. Most of them worked on the assembly lines producing a wide array of goods for trade and use within Society.

If all Contagions were exposed to the virus and the mutations matched, would it matter if he didn't have more samples?

He looked up from his desk and realized the sky was dark outside his window. He'd been processing the data for hours and he could feel stiffness settling into his body. He stood and stretched, urging the aches and pains to ease.

The data analysis would have to wait until morning. He turned off the lights as he exited the lab. He knew there was something hidden in the data. He just hadn't found it yet.

CHAPTER 24

Sir William looked across the long dining table at his wife. Their twin daughters sat on either side of their mother. Several chairs separated the Newbiggers women from him.

"Lilia, I've been told it would be helpful if you could attend the Society Signet dinner next week."

"That doesn't fit with our arrangement, William." Lilia never used his title when addressing him. She knew who he was, the son of a commoner who embellished his heritage as a titled patron of Society. She'd been astute enough to learn about William when they started dating.

"I know, but this is important. It's Society business related to the Statecraft. It's been too long since we've been seen together. The news coverage is beginning to talk about your absence from events."

"What are you going to give me?"

"I was hoping you would donate your time for the benefit of Society."

"I want you to make a public statement about my Be Kind program."

Sir William sighed. "You mean the one for children?"

"You know what I'm talking about. Don't minimize my efforts."

"Of course not." William had stopped using endearments when addressing his wife. They seemed to annoy her more than spending time with him. Their marriage started well. For a full seventy-two hours, he'd looked only at her. And then she caught him in the coat closet with the young attending clerk. He told her the young blond was only looking for his claim ticket.

"Really, by unzipping your pants?"

William had pushed the young girl aside and chased after his new wife. To his surprise, she hadn't been angry but calculating.

"You're going to give me a child, William. And then we'll put this incident behind us."

Thirteen months later, the two welcomed twins to the world, and Lilia closed her bedroom door to her husband. She focused on raising her children and minimized their interactions with their father.

As Sir William's political aspirations grew, he believed it was better to give Lilia what she wanted and stay married. The smear of divorce during a critical campaign cycle wouldn't look good. He was running as a solid Society citizen, upholding core values of commitment and purity. Besides, people loved Lilia. Women wanted to be her, and he knew many men wanted to sleep with her.

Lilia used this information to renegotiate her prenuptial agreement when William was sworn in as president. She could have walked away, a well-taken-care-of woman with no need to stay in their sham of a marriage. She knew William's financial picture was a reckless flow of money out of his accounts, which contradicted his posturing as being one of the wealthiest men in Society. She found a way to funnel funds herself and would be paid first if there was any liquidation of his assets. She also insisted the family home in Precinct Four be free of debt and held in her name only. Even if William decided to declare bankruptcy again, her own assets were protected. If they parted, she would be worth the bulk of the Newbiggers portfolio, even if most of it was heavily leveraged.

"You will promote Be Kind, and I will leave promptly after dinner. You are welcome to stay as long as you'd like, but you have to announce I'm leaving because I have a commitment in the morning at Precinct Three."

"Agreed." He was getting off easy this week. Oftentimes, she refused to negotiate.

Lilia smiled. She would get some extra support for her foundation. Many news agencies in Society scoffed at her Be Kind program, often saying her husband could benefit from it because of his vulgar remarks.

No one knew she had a disabled brother who had blossomed due to the efforts of her Be Kind Foundation. She'd hidden his existence. She valued her role as the Top Lady of Society and her brother deserved privacy. Even William did not know about her sibling.

"Can you wear the red dress, Lilia?"

"No." She knew William liked it and thought about burning it. The young girl she'd been when she first met William at a dinner party had quickly become jaded during their two years of dating. She had received many apologies, flowers, chocolates, and jewelry to beg her forgiveness for whatever dalliance occurred in the moment. She'd lost her innocence and her respect for men, considering them too weak and too influenced by their bodily needs. Reinforced by William's constant need for affirmation, she saw most men as pliable to her whims.

Life would be so much easier if she didn't like the finer things and didn't have an addiction to plastic surgery. Fortunately, the Signet dinner wouldn't last more than a few hours.

CHAPTER 25

The doctor encrypted his work before leaving for the evening. While he was the only virologist assigned to finding a cure for The Path, other lab participants had access to the data files. He hid the data since he'd acquired it outside normal protocols. He also didn't want to jeopardize his ability to gather more samples. It surprised him how easily he'd infiltrated the Compound, and yet, after being there, he had learned it was a system in which rules and authority were not questioned.

As a member of Society, he arrived in a position of power. As a doctor with documentation, he displayed further credibility. He realized the inhabitants were innocents unaware of the mechanisms, graft, and corruption which existed within Society.

He was not a political man, more interested in performing tests to better humanity, and yet even he was not immune to the minutia which flowed across the screen.

"When there's a WILL, there's a WAY" flashed on the screen, echoing his sentiments.

A news feed of Sir William holding an upside-down copy of The Signet ran before him.

"With my direction and approval, there are many working around the clock to find a cure for the Contagions."

The doctor laughed; he worked alone. He'd never met Sir William or received any directives from him. It was rumored the president had a penchant for Quilt and was probably gambling away the Society coffers.

"P3264 has shown us it is a deadly adversary not to be taken lightly. For the good of all in Society, it is imperative the Contagions are not exposed to the clean members of Society."

At least he'd said something truthful. The virus had mutated and changed from the initial discovery. The doctor would be looking for further mutations in the samples he'd collected.

"It is in their best interests to keep them confined to the Compound. In their sanctuary, they have a life! They can contribute to Society! They are alive! When we are apart, we thrive!"

The doctor cringed. Too many in Society were willing to keep the Contagions isolated, with no desire to find a cure. The doctor's life mission was to reintroduce the Compound residents back into Society, no longer labeled with the stigma of Contagion.

He'd taken extreme care when processing the blood samples because of the risk of infection. The original data sets were processed, logged, and the physical blood samples destroyed to remove any threat of exposure. Then the data was cross-tabulated to allow for research queries. His supervisor had provided samples when he was assigned as the virologist in the Lab of Human Betterment. He had received additional specimens when the virus mutated. With no registered changes to the virus for the past decade, no additional queries had been provided.

He made an impromptu decision to revisit the Compound the next day. He wanted to expand his new data set. With enough blood samples, he would find an overlap. He was too tired to do the math in his head as he walked down the hall of the Lab of Human Betterment building. With over 26,000 residents in the Compound, finding a match to one of the Society samples could take a while, yet he only needed one to shine light on the current state of P3264.

Hope flared again. He would find a cure. Failure was not an option.

Triden and Roseleen sat side by side at the fallen log in the forest. She unwrapped their lunch. Triden went straight for the glassenberry cookie, and she laughed.

"Don't you want your sandwich first?"

He reached over and took the boar-filled packet, sandwich in one hand and cookie in the other.

"Both are amazing. I'm finding it harder and harder to eat the Compound's protein pucks."

"Ick...I understand. Whatever that was yesterday, it wasn't food." To Roseleen's palette, the puck tasted like metallic cardboard.

After they'd finished eating, Triden tentatively reached out and took her hand.

"I... I..." he struggled to find the words to tell her how he felt.

She turned toward him and, with complete ease, wrapped her arms around him. He marveled at her ability to touch so freely. His whole life, his ability to touch was dictated by protocol and scanning barcodes to make a match. Even though Benjam and others in the Compound had managed to go Off Book, he never had. His closest relationships were not physical. Benjam was his best friend, and yet he hadn't felt comfortable enough to tell him about venturing outside.

Being with Roseleen amplified how alone he felt in the Compound. Social interactions in the evening did not establish true intimacy. It was a new emotion for him, and he wasn't sure how to proceed.

He pulled back and looked into her eyes. They were beautiful, gray in color, and showed knowledge of a world he did not know. She smiled.

He started again.

"I... I..." Words failed him again, and he finished the sentence, "want to thank you for lunch." Internally, he knew it wasn't what he was trying to say. He wanted to tell her he thought of her all the time. He loved the feel of her touch and was scared about the coming winter isolating them.

She gazed into his eyes as if she'd heard his internal dialog.

Instead of answering, she leaned in and kissed him on the mouth. He returned the kiss. He was feeling bolder about physically connecting with her. She removed her woven shawl, an invitation for him to continue. Soon they were undressing each other.

Triden hesitated once his outer robe was removed.

"I have rashes on my body from the virus. I'm afraid of what will happen if you touch them directly."

"I understand. It will be fine. I want to be with you."

"I want to be with you, too, but we can't risk it."

Love has no boundaries.

"Remember when I told you I was an Oracle?"

"Yes. That's your people, correct?"

"No. I'm a Forest Seer."

"What's an Oracle then?"

"It's my power in the world."

Triden looked confused, and Roseleen continued.

"I get messages from an energy we call The Source."

"What kind of messages?"

"Information about the future. I've known we were going to meet. This is how I know we can touch."

The Power Walker can traverse the worlds.

"I don't understand."

"Trust me when I say it's alright."

They kissed again, long and slow, and Triden eased her onto the ground. He wanted to feel her skin next to his. She smelled like flowers and the woods as he nuzzled her neck. He inhaled, wanting to remember every minute with her.

Roseleen reached for the drawstring of his cotton undergarment, and he struggled with the urge to continue and fear of her reaction when she would see his body naked: a network of red splotches covered his arms, torso, and legs.

He pulled back and stood. Roseleen extended her hand, urging him to return to her side.

"It's OK. I think you're beautiful."

He stepped out of the cotton bodysuit, revealing his skin covered with a patchwork of red.

Roseleen stood and reached toward him. She moved her hand across his chest as if her hand could soothe away the crimson color.

"Does it hurt?"

"No." Triden looked down. "It doesn't repel you?"

She stepped closer. "No, it's part of who you are."

"It's ugly. I'm marked by my curse."

"You are not ugly, Triden. You are beautiful."

He was not used to hearing such an endearment. *Him? Beautiful?* His whole life, he'd heard how the virus contaminated him and made him less human than those in Society. He was a threat to the very well-being of those outside the Compound. He still didn't know why Roseleen was the exception.

She kissed his mouth and then his neck. She moved lower and kissed the red skin over his heart.

He couldn't wait any longer. He lowered her to the ground. Both of them reacted with pent-up urgency; the days sitting next to each other, laughing together and getting to know each other, to culminate with an act they had both fantasized about for days.

With the last of their clothing removed, he moved his hands over her soft skin. He hesitated, looking for her sign of approval. Their eyes met, and she nodded. He entered her, and together, they started to move in rhythm, and Roseleen wrapped her legs around him, urging him closer.

This wasn't like any of his On Book encounters within the Compound. He touched her body, delicate and soft beneath him. He wanted their union to last forever, but his body betrayed him, and he shuddered inside her. He could feel her response and realized he was not alone, both of them accepting the inevitability of the encounter between them.

They lay entwined and quiet, savoring the feel of skin on

skin. The connection between them was strong and poignant.

The bushy-tailed creatures skittered from branch to branch above them. Roseleen had called them squirrels. Birds called overhead, as if to announce their actions.

Today was the best day of his life.

Lucky to be alive!

Today more than any other day.

CHAPTER 26

Mallor loved his secret dungeon. It was where he did his best work. He enjoyed watching the fear in his targets when the reality of what was going to happen spread across their faces. He moved slowly and deliberately, teasing out every ounce of fear from the person strapped in the chair.

Let the game of cat and mouse begin. The cat was going to win, but there was no reason the mouse wasn't good for some play beforehand.

The protester cleared from the street outside the Presidential Palace was restrained by leather straps binding his wrists and ankles to the heavy wooden chair. The chair was positioned over a drain in the cement floor.

"I have rights!" the protester asserted, eyes darting from Mallor to the wall of instruments adorning the adjacent surface. A single light hung over the chair, casting lines of shadows across the protester's face.

Mallor pulled on a floor-length black coat, rubberized and waterproof. He wore a pair of knee-high rubber boots, and he took time to pull on two thick surgical gloves, which allowed for dexterity and yet protected him from any fluids emerging over the course of the next few hours.

"You gave up your rights when you started protesting."

"What? What do you mean? I'm a member of Society. I'm entitled to voice my opinion."

"Not when your opinion threatens the health of Society. You are a terrorist. A menace."

The protester squirmed in the chair. "You have no right!"

"That's where you're wrong. I have every right to protect Society, and you have been identified as a menace. Do you understand?"

"No. No, I don't. I'm entitled to speak my mind."

"Yes. That is true...until what you say becomes a security

threat. Do you understand?"

"You're fucking nuts. Let me go!"

"All in good time." Mallor reached for a tool on the wall. "Let's get started. Do you understand?"

He could hear the sound of urine making its way to the floor drain.

"How disappointing. We've barely gotten started, and you've already pissed yourself."

The Society Signet dinner was boring Lilia. She was wearing a full-length black velvet gown with a strand of pearls hanging down the open back of her dress. Sir William had managed to fit into the military-style double-breasted suit with insignias marking his position in Society. The fabric pulled taut across his belly, which had expanded since he'd taken office. They walked together to the main atrium to meet dinner attendees. As they emerged in the public area, cameras flashed, documenting their arrival. Sir William reached for Lilia's hand, and she smiled toward the camera and subtly moved away from his grasp by sidestepping towards one of the precinct cabinet wives.

She rarely ate at these functions. The food was decadent, but she followed a strict regimen of exercise and diet, and the thick sauces and overly sweet desserts did not tempt her. She hadn't spent all the time and money on her body to mirror her husband's indulgences.

She looked past the table to the screen on the dining room wall. The time displayed in the lower corner ticked by slowly.

It was customary for Sir William to sit at the head of the long table. She was seated to his right, and the dignitary being honored this evening sat directly across from her and at Sir William's left. The additional dinner guests were placed in husband-and-wife rotations around the remaining chairs. Those considered less influential were seated at the opposite end of the table. However, being in the room with Sir William indicated some level of influence in Society.

She turned to Annabella, thankful the other woman seemed to understand her husband. He needed a good handler.

It must be a thankless role to play nurse maid to the ever-changing whims of William.

"It's good to see you, Annabella. Keeping my husband out of trouble, I assume?" The two women had an unspoken understanding. *Don't fuck my husband, and you can stay.*

Annabella had never shown an ounce of physical interest in William. Still, Lilia had heard the rumors of the shaky marriage of the Adviser and her husband, Jordon. The woman's husband was not present at the elaborate dinner; another sign of trouble at home.

Lilia scanned the rest of the couples dotted around the table. *Are any of them happy? Or are they all trapped in the confines of Society protocol to advance publicly?*

The time displayed on the screen inched closer to an acceptable getaway. She kicked William under the table to get his attention.

"Dear, don't you have something to say to everyone?"

"Can't it wait, my sweet?"

"I think not."

William fidgeted in his seat and then stood, rising with a crystal glass in hand. Tapping the side with a knife, he quieted the gathering in front of him.

"My wife and I would like to thank you for your attendance this evening. The Signet Dinner is a long-held tradition of bringing Society precincts together and forging forward with our common goals. When we survive, we thrive!"

William shifted his weight from foot to foot, which made him appear inebriated even though he'd only consumed one drink. His addictions focused on food, sex, and gambling at the Quilt table.

"This week, we made tremendous gains. Tremendous. Bigger than big...I met with each of the precinct ministry directors, and we've agreed the precincts are entitled to direct their own cabinets. These steps have been taken to ensure that the nuances of each precinct's needs are addressed specifically. Meanwhile, we also agreed there are assets in Society to benefit us all. As such, we're going to harvest wood from the surrounding forest."

Several dinner attendees clapped tentatively, unsure if they should applaud the announcement or wait for additional information. The smattering of clapping stopped as William continued.

"The forests have long been preserved as sacred and public lands, and yet as Society grows, it is time to replace outdated protocols with prosperity promoting plans. We are squandering our resources by ignoring them. The visual of the trees bordering Society do us no good. By harvesting the trees, all will benefit in Society. We can build new homes, new office buildings, and increase manufacturing."

William cleared his throat and continued.

"Starting next week, we will begin gathering wood and making expansions!"

He paused, waiting for the applause of approval. The dinner guests picked up on the cue and clapped.

Lilia kicked William again and glared at him. She didn't care about the forest. He'd promised her he'd announce the work she was doing for the Be Kind Foundation.

William raised his glass again. "Drink with me as we celebrate a new era for Society!"

Instead of drinking, he returned his glass to the table as he sat down and picked up his utensils.

Lilia leaned in, "You promised you'd promote my Be Kind

Foundation if I came tonight."

"Did I, dear?" William feigned ignorance. "You didn't hold my hand when we entered the dining hall, so I consider our agreement invalidated."

"Holding your hand wasn't part of the arrangement." Lilia turned and smiled toward the other diners, pushed her chair back, and raised her own glass.

"If I could have your attention, please!" The chatter quieted, and she paused a moment before continuing.

"Sir William is too modest to tell you himself, but he made a pledge yesterday. He's donating money to support the Be Kind Foundation school program. Our children deserve the best education Society has to offer. Classrooms have been neglected, and in keeping with his "No new taxes pledge" for the citizens in the Statecraft, he has graciously donated money out of his own funds to ensure every child in Society is provided with a new screen and supplies to excel in their studies."

Lilia continued. She could hear William choke on his latest bite.

"And there's more. It's not only for the precincts. We're also updating the apartments at the Contagion Compound. The infrastructure has been ignored for way too long."

Lilia smiled. She knew how much William hated the Contagions, seeing them as tainted, impure citizens. It was a spur-of-the-moment decision aimed at getting back at him for ignoring their agreement.

She knew her husband well and loved seeing his face turn red with rage. It served him right for going against her. It was always important to have backup insurance when dealing with William. She reached into her clutch purse and pulled out a check.

"Please join me as we memorialize this wonderful bequest with William's signature!"

Lilia placed the check before William and handed him a pen she'd extracted from her clutch.

"Just sign here, dear. All the members of Society thank you for your tremendous donation." Lilia watched as he scrawled his name, horrified at being disgraced in front of the crowd if he didn't sign.

"Of course, the Be Kind Foundation welcomes any support from those attending tonight. With your patronage, we can *'make tomorrow even better than today!'* Thank you."

William leaned in and snarled into his wife's ear.

"That check won't clear. You got too greedy, dear. There's not enough in the account to cover the amount."

Lilia smiled.

"Oh, but that's where you're wrong. I took the liberty of calling The Flodden Club, and they transferred your Quilt winnings to my account. The check is for show since the money has already been moved. The club was so gracious and helpful since we're both members. Apparently, you've been doing very well. I'm sure you can win back the amount soon."

With the check and pen in hand, she strode out of the hall.

Benjam smiled when he saw Triden at The Barcode.

"Tri, what's going on with you?"

"Nothing." Triden selected a mug, pulled the lever of the tap, and watched the amber liquid fill the glass container.

"All I know is you've been different lately."

Triden wanted to share how he'd met Roseleen outside the Compound, but as he glanced around The Barcode, it was already filling with a variety of Contagions, and he did not trust that their conversation would be private. How would Benjam react to him being outside the Compound walls?

"I'm lucky to be alive!" Triden couldn't resist quoting the Compound motto.

"It's more than that. I can't put my finger on it."

"I know I've been different lately. Let's say I've found a way to be happy."

"I'll drink to that!" Benjam clicked his glass, and the two laughed.

"Hey, I met your doctor friend."

"You went to the infirmary?"

"I got selected to participate in the same study. Seems harmless; he only took a blood sample and asked me a few questions."

"You never know. I worry about being taken away." Triden sighed. "Too many have never come back from the infirmary. Let's hope it doesn't happen to us."

"Here, here... I'll drink to that!"

The doctor looked at the specimen case on the seat of the van and smiled. He'd managed to retrieve eighty more samples during his latest visit. He knew statistically it would be unlikely there was a match. Cross-referencing the samples he retrieved to the initial batches wouldn't take long. With over 26,000 residents in the Compound, he would keep going back until he found a duplicate.

The leather outfit, along with the head mask, had proved effective in protecting him from exposure to The Path. He was feeling bolder in his data-gathering mission.

Each visit would allow him to expand his sample size. He hadn't taken time to talk in-depth with any of the Contagions today, but he had observed they were obedient and cooperative. Some appeared nervous, possibly because of his strange attire. He quickly deduced they thought they'd been singled out for more than a blood sample. Most looked relieved when he informed them they could return to work.

At the Lab of Human Betterment, he inserted the vials into the separator to divide the plasma from the blood cells. The machine was designed to catalog data, and it wouldn't take long before he knew if there was a match between the sample groups.

"Dammit!" No overlap. The doctor rarely let emotions take hold in the lab. He needed to focus and understood his emotions clouded scientific judgment. Wanting a desired outcome could taint findings if he started to manipulate results to prove a hypothesis.

He shouldn't have been surprised. He'd have to take many more samples to statistically improve his chances of a match. He merged the data set with the ones from his prior visit and reviewed the cross-tabulations.

It didn't take long to select data points to create a historic heat map of the virus's spread through Society, and the doctor watched the few red dots of the first infected turn into a swarm of red spreading rampantly from one precinct to the next. Oddly, Precinct One had minimal cases while Precinct Nine was overrun with red dots. The doctor looked for information on the Contagion population, hoping to identify their locations prior to being moved to the Compound. Scrolling through the data, he recognized the information pertained only to those who died. There was no specific information for survivors. He switched to the Compound reports and looked for precinct data. The only information he could find was the date when the resident arrived at the Compound and their aptitude testing results.

That's odd. The doctor sifted through the data points again. *Why wasn't there more information in their medical files?*

He'd been evaluating the blood samples provided by Society and thought it was a complete data set, believing that only five hundred children survived P3264. He was surprised to learn that over twenty-six thousand Contagions lived within the walls of the enclosure. It was a significant group resistant to P3264. It gave him hope. There had to be a common denominator linking them as survivors.

Why aren't more people concerned about the Contagions? Perhaps it was easier to pretend the history of Society didn't include mass terminations and segregation of twenty-six thousand people.

He played the heat map simulation again and watched as a few dots amassed to a pool of red. He hit replay again. What was he missing?

[•]

Roseleen selected a few extra cookies for Triden and encased the sandwich and treats in a leather wrapper. She'd been foraging for the last bits of the fall bounty and stored everything in the food bunker.

Intentions will show the motive and the means.

Turning a blind eye does not erase the past.

The key holder can unlock the door.

She bound through the forest, jumping over branches and

winding toward her meeting place with Triden. There was a lightness in her step, buoyed by the excitement of seeing him. She felt pulled towards him, a natural connection she didn't question. The messages assured her she was on her path.

Love is a stronger bond than leather.

Your internal compass shows all directions.

You will continue to be tested.

She'd been getting a flood of messages lately, and most of them didn't make sense. Her mother had suggested meeting with the Forest Seer Council to compare the messages being received by others.

No one is exempt from learning in this lifetime.

There's always a fork in the road.

Plan ahead to ease the way.

Most of the snippets did not have imagery, keeping their meaning in the dark.

She saw Triden was already perched at the log, and she waved.

"You got here early!"

"I couldn't wait to see you." He took her into his arms and kissed her.

"I've missed you."

She sat on the log, pulled out the leather packet of food, and handed him a sandwich, reserving the cookies for after their meal.

CHAPTER 28

Mallor stepped up to the Quilt table.

"Sorry to interrupt, but there's important business for Sir William. He's needed for a few minutes, and then the game can resume." He escorted Sir William to the hallway.

"Sir, I'd like to talk with the cabinet minister of Precinct Two without you in the room. Do you mind spending some time in the men's room?"

"I don't know why you interrupted our game. Can't you talk with him later?" Sir William was agitated as he was down half of his betting tiles.

"This might be the perfect timing to break the table trend and start your winning streak. You know what they say about Quilt: Once you're on a slippery slope, it's hard to climb back up."

"Good point. I'll be back in ten minutes." William strode down the hall, and Mallor stepped into the Quilt room.

"Minister, may I have a word?"

The sandy-haired, middle-aged man with ruddy skin looked nervous as they stepped toward the dining alcove.

"You know you're supposed to be losing, right? You've been amassing tiles. I thought we agreed you would donate significantly at the table today."

"Yes, but how could I know he was going to bow when I only had an orange corridor with green high? I heavily weighted The Bank, not knowing it would come back to me."

"Just make sure the table favors him during the next rounds."

"Of course. But I also have to be careful he doesn't suspect I'm bowing my hands intentionally." The cabinet minister looked nervous. "I never thought it would be so hard to lose at Quilt. I'm playing the weakest combinations I can, and Sir William seems to miss opportunities with his own cards."

"I don't care how you do it. Make sure he leaves this room happy."

The Minister wiped his forehead with the handkerchief from his lapel pocket. "I'm doing the best I can."

"Try harder. It's not like it's your money you're losing. How hard can it be?"

The two men stepped back to the Quilt table.

"Gentlemen, enjoy the rest of your game." Mallor turned and walked to the door.

CHAPTER 29

Precinct Nine.

Precinct Nine.

Precinct Nine.

The doctor scanned the list of his new study participants. During his last visit, he'd asked everyone if they remembered their prior precinct. With the exception of three individuals, they'd all answered Precinct Nine.

He watched the heat map one more time. Precinct Nine had been consumed by red dots; only the children survived. The abandoned area of Society was now a mass graveyard, and today pinwheels spun on the rolling hills formed over the burial grounds of Memorial Park.

The doctor knew he didn't have enough data to establish a statistical baseline, and yet... He removed the Society samples to look at the most current information.

He pushed down the nagging feeling he was trying to manipulate his findings for a result to give him an emotional win. He'd gone out on a limb to gather the data and wanted to be successful, the result making it worth the risk.

He closed the data table displayed on his screen and accessed the archives. Time to look specifically at Precinct Nine to identify any significant variable. Hours later, he felt tired and overwhelmed. He'd been reading about weather patterns, census data, even the favorite foods of the residents.

Jayr propped his elbows on the lab table and lowered his head into his hands. He tried to clear his mind. There was something he was missing.

Food, exercise, temperature, rituals, chemicals, and so many other variables along with location could be factors. He stood up and vowed to start fresh in the morning.

Lilia slipped into the cloth dressing gown in her doctor's office. She thought it odd to change into a robe when she was being consulted for a procedure to her face. She suspected the surgeon would make other suggestions for her. Sculpting a little here, nipping a little there.

She told her staff she would be receiving an annual physical. Her security patrol was bound to secrecy, so even if one of them figured out exactly which doctor she was seeing, it would never be shared.

She sat on the edge of the examination table and looked at the images on the wall. She prided herself on finding the best surgeon who understood the importance of patient-doctor confidentiality.

She was about to turn fifty, and yet the reflection in the mirror defied her years. She'd lost track of the number of procedures and obsessively looked at her skin each day. She'd seen too many women make mistakes with their procedures, and the results became freakish. Dr. Emery understood the nuances of going under the knife to create an illusion and an enhancement that left the observer to wonder what exercise or diet routine she'd adopted. Her goal was that no one would ever consider she'd taken surgical steps.

She would announce she was being detained at the hospital for a week to monitor a thyroid issue. She would be healing from the incision and manipulation of her skin to retain her youthful appearance without raising suspicions.

The door opened, and a tall, slender man entered.

"Good afternoon, Mrs. Newbiggers. Let's review what we're going to do tomorrow morning. He pulled up a picture of her face on the screen and used a stylus to indicate the steps of the procedure.

"This could be done using local anesthetic; however, this might be a good time to consider some body work as well."

The surgeon knew her well.

⫿⫿

Together we are stronger.
Future actions can undo the past.
Make tomorrow better than today.
Roseleen smiled with the simple messages of the morning. She knew she was receiving them because of her growing feelings for Triden. Already she couldn't imagine life without him.

Fallen trees mark a shift in time.
Return to the flock to be home again.
Share the secrets.
They cuddled together, wrapped in the blanket she'd brought with her from the treehouse.

"How can I be sure I won't infect you at some point?"

After years of programming about exposing others and causing death, Triden still had fears about the ravages of the disease.

Roseleen hesitated. While receiving predictive messages was accepted and commonplace with the Seers, she knew many before her were ostracized for their abilities. They'd been called witches, and some were burned at the stake when they warned of an approaching calamity to befall Society. They learned to only trust those with the same abilities and to keep quiet when receiving messages.

She realized the two battled their own fears. Triden worried about infecting her, and her concern was he wouldn't understand the voices she heard. The thought stabbed at her heart, and anxiety that their budding connection would be nipped before it started rose inside her. She closed her eyes and listened.

Those who see their imperfections hesitate to judge others.
She opened her eyes. Triden was looking at her patiently.

"You can tell me anything."

She saw a man who wasn't able to see his own greatness. He was modest and still not confident of his place in the world. She knew he was trapped in the Compound. She didn't know what his mission would be yet, but she knew he had strength. Her first messages had told her. He was the Power Walker.

"Remember how I told you I'm an Oracle?"

Triden nodded.

"From as early as I can remember, I get messages."

"From your family?"

"I don't really know from where." She hesitated. "You're going to think I'm crazy."

"No. No, I'm not. Trust me."

"I receive messages in the form of a voice in my head. Sometimes I get images, too."

She could see Triden processing the information, but she didn't see any aversion to what she'd told him.

"So, what do you hear?"

"It's just a phrase or an idea. Usually, I don't know what they mean until something happens."

"They're predictive of the future?"

"Sometimes, yes. That's how we knew to leave Society and make our home in the woods."

"Are you a mind reader?"

She understood why he was asking. The messages gave her assurance she would be alright when they touched. From his perspective, it could appear as if she'd read his mind about his apprehension.

"Sometimes I wish, but no, no, I'm not a mind reader. Like now, I wish I could read your mind. Do you think I'm crazy?"

"No... not at all. You're the most generous and amazing person I know."

"Yes, but I could be completely insane, too!" She laughed.

"You're not."

"I knew about you before we met." *Had she told him too*

much?

"Really, how did you know it was me?"

"I saw your eyes."

"Not my whole face?"

"No, the images are more a flash of insight. They're not usually visual. They capture an essence."

"What was the message you received?"

"The Power Walker can traverse the worlds."

"Wow." He was silent for a minute, absorbing the information. "Any idea what it means?"

"No, not yet, except you are the Power Walker."

"I can barely walk beyond the Compound. I only venture a limited distance so I can easily slip back inside undetected. How am I going to manage to walk the world?"

"You said you are part of a research study, right?"

"Yes."

"Maybe they'll find a cure, and you'll be able to move freely in Society?"

"That's a dream I don't dare have. It's already unfathomable that I won't be able to see you during the winter. I can't risk crossing the snow."

She kissed him, grateful he'd only been inquisitive about what she told him, not judgmental.

"Have you gotten any other messages about me?"

"Well, I don't need a voice to tell me you're a great kisser, and I love being with you."

"I love being with you, too." Triden hesitated. "It's more than that, though. I love you."

"I love you, too." She nuzzled next to him, relieved and grateful he hadn't judged her. He hadn't run away with fear about her abilities.

Those who see their imperfections hesitate to judge others.

She didn't see Triden the way he saw himself. He saw The Path as a reason to be contained, a reason to be small. She knew big things were ahead. All would be revealed in time.

◫

The doctor learned how to slip in and out of the bladder contraption quickly, grateful it was disposable and fresh each time. After stepping into the cotton bodysuit, he folded the heavy leather cloak and placed it inside the surgical trunk. He tested the air purifier in the mask and it hummed quietly. He removed and rinsed the filter and reinserted it. He was reminded he could be a bit clumsy as he spilled his coffee again. Focused intently on his research, the coffee was usually an afterthought. Most days, he'd pick up his mug to find a cold film of cream skimming the top. He'd long ago given up the need for the coffee to be fresh, interested more in the effects of caffeine to keep him alert.

He added the knee-high boots to the container and closed the lid. Walking down the hallway, he passed several colleagues now accustomed to him toting around the large device box.

"Research going alright?"

"Yes, making strides," was his standard response.

"Great! Contagions are people, too."

The doctor was aware of the growing political divide in Society. Many had dismissed the Contagions years ago as second-rate citizens, their infections demoting them to the Compound, contaminated and isolated from the rest of Society without any interaction between the groups.

The Contagions' strong immune systems protected them, and yet they still harbored a virus that could kill anyone living in Society. The Contagions were their very own suicide bomb if they came into contact with anyone outside the Compound. Many Society members feared the Contagions. They were afraid of what they perceived as a power over them, a weapon that could be activated at any time.

The doctor climbed into the white lab van and eased into traffic. He was learning more about the Contagions during each visit. He found them as a whole to be a naive and gentle group. Driven by a moral obligation to protect themselves and Society, they lived within a code of ethics without question, and the consequences of breaking the law were deeply understood.

Tucked in the far corner of the large parking lot, the doctor opened the black box and changed into the leather coat, boots, and mask. Large delivery trucks continued to flow into and exit the parking lot. No one gave him any notice as he walked to the wall discretely hiding the entrance. He knew the protocol. A loud buzzer would sound, and a light would flash, indicating the solid exterior wall was moving. He stepped into the vestibule and watched the large metal panel close again. He turned toward the back and waited for the other side to slide open, allowing him to walk into a large, partitioned area. He was greeted by the two Contagions who had worked the entryway each time he visited. They accepted his odd attire as normal, understanding the importance of an uninfected person taking precautions. They still stood far from the doctor, and they'd never made direct contact. Jayr had learned to stay socially distanced from them. Inadvertently, during one of his first visits, he'd stepped too close, and the Contagion leapt back, horrified at the potential contact, even with the doctor encased in leather from head to toe.

"Take a Life, Give Your Own" rotated on the screens throughout the Compound. The doctor was horrified by the footage of people being consumed by P3264.

The screen changed to *"Lucky to Be Alive!"*

The doctor discovered the phrase was used as both a welcome and departing statement within the Compound.

Jayr settled into a chair facing the large partition and pulled out his screen to take notes. He asked to visit with several participants from his first data set. The goal was to get a sense of their days in the Compound and what they remembered before they arrived.

He recognized the tall man with green eyes as he slid into the chair facing him.

"Remind me of your name again."

"Triden."

"Thank you."

"I take it your parents died of P3264?"

"They were part of the mass terminations. I do not know if they contracted P3264 or not."

"Is there a reason you are not sure?"

"They seemed fine in the morning when they left our home. They never returned."

The doctor nodded. He long suspected the terminations extended beyond confirmed cases out of fear. Decisions were made to protect the healthy part of Society. Anyone suspected of having contact with someone with P3264 was often tossed into the infected group as a precaution.

"What do you do here?"

"Initially, I worked in the laundry room, putting sheets through the folding machines. Some stay here for delivery to Contagion quarters. Others are picked up by trucks outside the Compound for Society."

"How long did you do that?"

"About three years."

"And then?"

"Everyone here took aptitude tests. It was discovered I'm good at fixing things."

"So, they moved you out of laundry?"

"Yes, they taught me how to run and maintain the W&W facilities."

"W&W?" The doctor was not familiar with the acronym.

"Water and Waste. We purify the water supply and process the waste matter for sanitary disposal."

"Do you like it?"

"Most days." Triden smiled. He loved it particularly now he'd discovered his chance for freedom every day.

"And the days you don't?"

"I'm aware the infrastructure is breaking down. I keep putting in requisitions to my supervisor for additional maintenance, but it's always denied. The bad days are the ones when there's a sewer leak. Water isn't so bad."

"What's your morning like?"

Triden told the doctor about the daily delivery of fresh undergarments and robes to his studio apartment, how he woke to the screen flashing the news of the day, and messages regarding social responsibility. He told the doctor about the silent, meditative breakfasts of protein pucks and bitter tea.

"Then you work? Five days a week?"

"No, seven."

The doctor was shocked.

"You don't have any time off?"

"Yes, of course, we do. Every evening we socialize at our regional hangout."

"Tell me about it."

"I go to The Barcode and drink with friends. Most nights, we go On Book with someone." Triden hadn't paired with anyone since he'd met Roseleen.

"On Book?"

"We can have private sessions with others up to five times. We scan our barcodes to be placed On Book."

"Why only five times?"

Triden decided it was better not to mention some residents went Off Book.

"To minimize the risk of attachment."

"Why is that important?" The doctor leaned closer to the partition, curious about the answer. He realized after he moved forward, he'd potentially antagonized Triden, but the man didn't flinch, understanding the barrier and his bizarre clothing protected both of them.

"No one is able to have children. The concern is, if we start getting close to someone, it will cause us to want something we can't have." As Triden stated the words, he realized it was true. He'd been with Roseleen multiple times, and he regretted they would never have children.

"What do you mean?"

"We're all sterile. One of the results of being infected with the virus."

"Everyone?"

"Yes, no children have been born within the Compound."

The doctor tried not to react, then realized the bizarre mask hid his visual responses. It saddened him hearing about life in the Compound. Seven-day work weeks, limited engagements with other residents, and no children. What kind of life was it?

"Does it bother you?"

"This is all I know." Even as he said the words, Triden realized that was no longer true. His world had changed dramatically since venturing outside of the Compound.

"Are you part of a team?"

"I'm part of the W&W Department, but I work alone."

"Really, it only takes one to manage the facility?"

"There's not much to do. The facilities run twenty-four hours a day, and it's all automated. My role is to monitor the equipment and look for issues. Most days are noneventful."

Triden knew the system was outdated and strained, processing more water and sewage than it was designed to do. He was taking a chance of a large failure occurring while he was outside the Compound walls.

He pushed the worry from his mind. He'd been monitoring the system for years, and nothing major had happened yet. The last incident was of his own making; Benjam still called him sewer rat.

The doctor put down his portable screen.

"I'm looking for any insights to help me find a cure for the virus. Do you mind if I look at your skin?"

Triden was used to the red rash covering his body. He turned up the sleeve of his robe and pushed up the cotton garment to show the red splotches. He couldn't remember a time without the rashes that marked him as an outcast from Society.

"Do you ever notice any changes?"

"Some days it seems darker than others." He looked at his arm. "It looks pretty mild today."

Jayr had examined many of the Contagions and found the rashes varied. Maybe the rash could provide insights. The doctor made a notation.

CHAPTER 30

Annabella and Jordon reviewed the incorporation documents to make sure nothing revealed they were the sole owners of Alpine Excavations, Inc. They had successfully buried the ownership identity with several layers of corporations, each with undisclosed Boards.

Annabella, in her role within the Presidential Palace, had met several foreign dignitaries interested in the old-growth timber from the public lands of Society. The business entity would secure the rights to remove trees from the forest, and the nominal lease for land access would be more than covered by the large checks foreign interests would pay for the coveted lumber.

"Do you have the documents for Sir William to sign?"

"Yes, right here." She tapped her shoulder bag which contained an executive order folder with the details outlined on the interior pages. "I've told him he's supporting Society for years to come. For him to be reelected, the economy has to remain strong. I've convinced him this is one of the ways to prop up the stock market."

"Do you think he'll have any questions about it?"

"No, I'm going to talk with him as he's heading to The Flodden Club. He'll be distracted and focused on getting to the table. Also, I've been planting seeds about the forest for several months now."

Jordon laughed. "Planting seeds; I love the pun. Did you intend it, dear?"

"Of course!" She kissed him. "We're going to be richer than rich! I added a clause that compensates us if the contract is terminated before five years. The bulk of trees will be cleared by then, and someone else can manage the reforestation after we've taken the profit."

"I knew there was a reason I married you. I love the way

you think, Bella."

"This is a big opportunity which has gone untapped for far too long."

Jordon kissed her again. "Any chance you have time to celebrate with me?" He slipped his hands under her sweater and pulled her closer.

"Hmmm..." She leaned toward him and pressed her body against his. "Tonight, Jordie, I promise. We'll have a lot to celebrate without being rushed."

At the Presidential Palace, Annabella arranged for the press circuit to be onsite to see Sir William sign the executive orders and display his signature scrawled along the bottom. He loved the pomp and circumstance involved with signing documents. It would be broadcast for all to see. The hand-signed folder remained a tribute to the Founders of Society and was put into the Statecraft Archives to mark history for perpetuity.

She checked the time. Sir William was due at The Flodden Club at noon, and the press would be set up at 11:30. It was the perfect amount of time to usher him in, make a brief statement, and whisk the president away for his Quilt game.

The document and fountain pen rested on the tabletop facing several rows of folding chairs assembled for the press.

Annabella stepped into the interior offices next to the presidential office suite. She knocked once and entered Sir William's office.

"Annabella, thank goodness you're here. What do you think? Striped or Signet crests?" He held up two different ties for her to pick.

"Crests. What happened to the one you were wearing?"

"Oh, it ripped." Sir William didn't tell her he'd used it to tie his blond intern's wrists together before he pushed her on top of his desk and yanked off her panties. He thought back to the incident. The intern had pretended she wasn't interested and had tried to wiggle free which made the game play even more fun. She was lucky to have him show interest in her. She wasn't as pretty as his wife, and she'd never have the chance to be with someone of his stature if she hadn't been an intern at the Presidential Palace. Lilia hadn't let him in her bed for years. *What else was he supposed to do?* He had needs. He had desires, and so many people wanted a piece of him. *Who was he to deprive them?* It didn't matter to him the young girl had left his office crying. Obviously, she was overwhelmed with gratitude.

"Do you need help, Sir William?"

"Yes, please." He liked being pampered.

He turned up his collar and put the tie around his neck. He stepped forward, and Annabella adjusted the lengths, twisted the fabric together, and pushed the tie into place. Then she folded down his collar and smoothed his coat jacket.

"Your zipper is down, Sir William."

He glanced down. "What would I do without you, Annabella?"

"Well, we can't have you in front of the press anything less than camera ready."

"Are they here?"

"Yes. Before we go outside, let me tell you what you'll be signing. There are three executive orders. One is the promise you made to Precinct Two related to trade. There's the one for leasing forest lands, and the third is a funding bill for the P3264 research." She intentionally glossed over the details of the forest lease.

Sir William looked agitated.

"Why do we keep spending money looking for a nonexistent cure? At what point do we accept the Contagions are always going to be a blight on Society? They have a good home. They are free to move around the Compound and socialize, with ample food and drink provided by Society. They are *lucky to be alive!*"

She knew Sir William had been on the task force to move

the infected children to the Compound when he was the Chancellor of the Signet within the Statecraft. He had been applauded for his efforts to eliminate the mass terminations and sequester the young children.

"We have to face facts. The Contagions will never be reintroduced into Society. We should stop funding the research. It's time."

Annabella knew how much Sir William disliked the protests to free the Contagions. He saw them as a negative mark on his presidency, and instead, he wanted to focus on the health of the economy.

"I can remove that one if you'd like."

"Yes, it's time to end the research."

"You look perfect. Let's go." Annabella tucked the Compound folder into her bag, out of sight.

Sir William walked with her to the door. He practiced his smile as he went. He didn't know much about the documents he was about to sign, but he'd been assured they were good steps to promote his reelection agenda.

"Have you made arrangements for election rallies across all of the precincts? I want to connect with the people."

"Yes, Sir William. We've booked the venues, and I'll have your schedule tomorrow."

Today she and Jordon would secure the lease rights to the forest. Soon they would take over the management of the Contagion Compound. She had convinced Sir William it was a social service that Society no longer needed to support. Republic Corporation would take over, and they would benefit through the management.

She led Sir William to the temporary desk set up for the signing and smiled for the cameras as she stood behind him. He picked up the fountain pen and scrawled a large signature across the page before displaying the open document for the press photos.

One and two; both were signed, and Annabella sighed with

relief. She hadn't anticipated any real issue with the order; however, until the ink had been applied to the paper, it could have been derailed.

Once the timber clearing had started, she'd slip a revised executive order for the Compound into the batch of orders to sign.

Sir William had been in his role for two years, and Annabella and Jordon had successfully maneuvered the forest rights to Alpine Holdings. It wouldn't take long to make the other changes they envisioned.

She tapped her screen and messaged her husband.

"Signed. Celebration tonight."

He replied quickly.

"The first of many."

She enjoyed working for a man with a Quilt addiction and no desire to perform the role he was assigned. His love of the spotlight made him the perfect candidate to project a presidential image to Society. She was happy to remain behind the scenes and pull the puppet strings.

Ego will betray those with overconfidence.

Take time to be truthful to go down the right path.

Those who can see beyond the view in front of them know they have options.

Roseleen sat next to Triden by the fallen log.

"We live in treehouses with a communal area on the ground."

"You don't live in Society? I thought everyone lived in Society or in the Compound."

"We used to, many years ago, before we moved to the forest."

"I know why I was taken out of Society. Why did you leave?"

"We saw what was happening and didn't want to be a part of it."

"You're lucky. I wish my parents had been able to leave."

"What happened to them?"

"I can't be sure, but I believe they were part of the mass terminations to stop the spread of The Path."

"How did you survive?"

"I was one of the children who showed resistance to the virus. I still have it, but it didn't kill me."

"They terminated people to eliminate the virus and stop the spread?"

"Yes, initially. However, there was a large outcry over killing children, so the cabinet members of the Department of Human Betterment moved us to the Compound."

"So young. Who took care of you?"

"The Compound was filled with children from babies to teenagers. I think the oldest were fifteen; they took care of the younger ones."

"Is there anyone from Society overseeing the Compound?"

"There's no need. Everyone has grown up and has a job to do. With daily shipments of food, our needs are met. Everyone knows they are safe inside the Compound." Triden hoped she wouldn't notice the irony since he was outside of the large complex.

"What do you do in there?"

"I'm a Water and Waste Engineer."

"Do you like it?" Roseleen didn't know what his job entailed. She knew he was confined to the Compound except for the stolen moments they shared near the forest edge.

"I've never really thought about it until recently. It's what people expect me to do. No one questions their duties the Compound."

"I find it fascinating."

"I find you fascinating." Triden leaned over and kissed her. *Plan ahead to ease the way.*

The latest message gave Roseleen comfort.

]•[

Three large flatbed trucks rumbled down the road outside of Society and snorted to a stop, emitting a large cloud of exhaust next to a newly constructed trailer. The drivers had received orders to start collecting logs from the forest. A job was a job, and they didn't question their cargo as long as they were getting paid.

Each log was long and large, with a minimum of a six-foot circumference. They had been stripped of limbs, and the bark showed stubbled nubs where branches had protruded previously. After checking in with the foreman, the trucks pulled forward alongside a crane and were loaded with the logs anchored in place with large canvas straps ratcheted down to avoid an errant log rolling off the truck.

As soon as the trucks departed, another series of diesel

burping vehicles belched into the lot and filled up. It didn't take long before the area around the temporary trailer was cleared of growth. Saws could be heard toothing their way through the thick trunks of the trees. Loggers announced the toppling of the magnificent timber that had been growing for over a hundred years undisturbed. Truck after truck of logs made their way back towards Society to be dispersed to the highest bidder.

The woods cry in pain.

Roseleen sat up with a start. Something had changed. She didn't know what, except it involved the forest around her.

She turned to Triden.

"I have to go. Something's wrong."

"Can I help?" His face reflected his concern.

"I don't know what it is yet. I have to get home."

Triden wished he could follow her, but he didn't dare risk exposing her community.

"I'll be here tomorrow." He wished they had a way to communicate beyond their secluded meeting spot by the fallen tree.

"I love you." She held his gaze. The words felt important to say with the uncertainty she was facing.

"I love you, too." Triden gave her a quick hug and watched her sprint away into the depths of the woods.

Roseleen ran, jumping and weaving her way through the trees and alongside the river.

The woods cry in pain.

The message was getting stronger and louder in her mind.

She rounded the last stretch to the treehouse she called home and saw her mother in the communal area. Other Forest Seers were beginning to congregate as well.

"You hear it, too?" she asked as she joined the growing group.

"Yes. I got a few hints of a message this morning, but now it's very clear and getting louder."

"What do we do?"

Voices hummed around them, and it was decided small groups would fan out and look for signs of what was causing the alarm.

Roseleen joined her father and brother to head East.

The woods cry in pain.

They wove through the woods for an hour, unsure what they were looking for.

The words started to throb inside her head. They must be getting closer to the cause.

Her father held up his hand, a silent signal to stop. The three halted and listened. They could hear shouts and the sound of metal machinery. They slowed and started moving forward with silent footsteps, a skill honed while hunting.

The three stopped short when they saw a clearing that only days before had been full of glorious old-growth trees.

Tears filled Roseleen's eyes, and she felt a tug at her heart. *Why would they be removing the trees? This is sacred ground.*

A massive pile of branches and pine needles were being stacked as workers stripped the trunks bare. The logs were lifted by a crane and swung around and stacked, waiting for the next step in the process.

She looked at her father and brother, a headache radiating through her head. She could see the scene impacted them as well.

Her father put up his hand and moved it in a circle, indicating they should retrace their steps and retreat back into the forest depths.

None of them spoke until they no longer heard the loggers and machinery.

"This explains more about the messages the Council has been collecting recently."

Boundaries are being redefined.

Roseleen had naively thought the message pertained to

her growing relationship with Triden and a blurring of the boundary between the Forest Seers and the Contagion Compound. It never occurred to her the forest would be the boundary in question.

"Let's get back to the Communion. We need to let the others know what we've found."

Roseleen kept pace with her father and brother as they traversed through the woods. She was used to moving through the trees, navigating the root systems, fallen twigs, branches, and the soft, uneven earth beneath her feet.

There was an uneasy adrenaline propelling them forward. Their treehouse village had been built in an area deep within the wooded terrain to avoid detection. They had moved from Society well in advance of the individual tracking they had seen was coming.

The image of the barcode etched onto Triden's wrist reminded her again he was not free to roam without detection.

Her heart ached at the sight of all the severed stumps protruding from the ground. The trees formed a community of their own, and the Forest Seers felt a strong connection to the earth around them. While they hunted animals for survival, there was an order in nature to support a lively ecosystem, and the trees stood as stewards of the land. Squirrels harvested acorns, birds nested in branches, and even the Forest Seers had found a way to integrate themselves within the limbs.

The three made good time, spurred on by urgency, and entered the open communal space below the treehouses perched above. The other observation teams had returned to the camp when it was evident the internal voice was getting fainter the further they had ventured forth. The volume of the message had helped guide Roseleen and her family.

Everyone merged to the center and huddled around Roseleen, her father, and her brother.

"What did you find?"

"Loggers. They've already cleared several acres of old-growth trees near the road to Society."

"I thought this was protected land not to be destroyed," a neighbor probed.

"It appears something has changed."

The Forest Seers had chosen to retreat into the woods because its protected status ensured their safety and minimized their detection.

"Let's monitor the activity every day. Maybe they are only cutting a small section."

"What if they keep cutting?" Anxiety and fear could be felt throughout the tribe.

"We're survivors. We have taken proactive steps in the past to ensure our livelihood. We can do it again. Don't worry yet. We don't have enough information. The Source will guide us."

▓▌▐

"Do you mind if I ask you some questions?" Triden faced the doctor again. It was strange talking to a masked person who he'd never seen, but their prior conversations had started to create a bond between the two. He could get a glimpse of two brown eyes behind the glass disks. The leather cloak and mask concealed everything else.

"Sure. What do you want to know?"

"Are you close to finding a cure?"

"I hope so. It's impossible to tell because variables change."

"Variables?"

"Yes. The virus has mutated multiple times. We had promising results, but then the next data sample we received showed resistance to the vaccine we'd developed."

"Is that why you're collecting more samples?"

"Yes. I'm still looking for something to indicate why everyone here survived. Why does the virus kill so many and leave others untouched?"

"I wouldn't say I'm untouched. I have rashes all over my skin."

The doctor nodded. "Of course, I'm sorry. I didn't mean to imply you weren't impacted. You survived and are here."

"What's it like out there? What is your life like?"

"Well..." *Where to begin?*

"Most of my time is spent in the lab."

"Do you have a family?"

"No. Like you, I lost my parents in the mass terminations."

"You weren't infected?"

"I was away at medical school in Precinct Four, which wasn't heavily impacted."

"Were you able to say goodbye to them?"

The doctor paused. These were memories he'd tried to bury.

"No. They reached out while I was rushing to class. I didn't answer. I didn't know what was happening. No one did. It was decided so quickly as a way to stop the virus."

"Is that why you're looking for a cure?"

"Yes. No one should die from P3264. No one."

"And you haven't had children?"

"My work keeps me busy. I haven't thought about starting a family."

"No one here can have children."

"I remember. We talked about it during my last visit."

"What's it like outside? When you drive here?"

"Society is very congested. Lots of people and vehicles. It takes a while to maneuver through the streets. Once I'm outside of the precinct, there is lots of open land with tall grasses. As I get closer, there are more trees. There's a large forest to the north."

"You're lucky."

"You don't think you are?"

"*Lucky to Be Alive!*" flashed on the screen behind the young man.

"Yes, of course, I'm lucky to be alive. But I'm aware of my limitations. I'm not part of Society. This is my home and where I'll be for the rest of my life."

"I understand your hesitation, but trust me. I'm working to ensure you'll be able to leave here one day and return to Society."

"Do they even want us there?"

"Why do you ask? Of course. Everyone wants to find a cure for the virus."

Triden pulled up his left sleeve and showed the doctor the barcode on his wrist. "I'll always be a Contagion in their eyes."

"When I find a cure, you'll be a survivor." The doctor hesitated. "I mean, you're a survivor now; you'll be free of the virus and won't be labeled a Contagion anymore."

"How can you be sure?"

"It's what I've based my life's work on; finding a cure to return everyone to Society."

"Sometimes I wonder."

"Wonder what?"

"If we're better off staying here."

"How can you ask that?"

"Because we'll still be seen as pariahs."

"No. No, you won't."

"We are the offspring of people who were killed for spreading a disease. We survived, but we kill people if we come into contact with them. Won't people still be afraid? Aren't you afraid?"

"I'm looking for a cure, and I'll die trying."

"Why would you do that for us?"

"I took an oath when I became a doctor to help people. I have a chance to help you, to help everyone here."

"Look at how you're dressed. I don't even know what you look like because you've taken so many precautions to be safe and not get infected."

"I'm following Society protocols."

"I know, and I appreciate you're at risk to be here to get more insights."

"I'm working my hardest to get you out of here."

"If you find a cure, are you going to be comfortable standing next to me without the protocol outfit?"

"Absolutely. The cure will make it possible to reintroduce you to Society. You'll be free in the world."

"Free in the world. I don't remember ever being free. Do you feel free?"

The doctor paused. "I guess so. I have freedom in my movements. But I do have demands and social protocols to follow. I'm committed to my research, and I spend most of my waking hours in the lab."

"So, what you're saying is we're both prisoners within our roles in the world."

"Not really. I can always quit and find something else to do."

"Would you do that?"

"Believe me, I've thought about it. Late nights when nothing seems to be right and I'm feeling helpless. Life would be so much easier if I just quit."

"Why haven't you?"

"Because I know if I give up, nothing will happen. I want my parents' death not to be in vain. I want to find a cure to protect everyone in the future. I don't want The Path to win."

Triden nodded.

The doctor didn't know why he'd been so open. Maybe it was the isolation of spending hours in his lab making him crave a conversation like this one. Maybe it was the anonymity of being cloaked and unidentifiable. "I can't make any promises, but I'm doing the best I can to make it possible for you to get out of here."

"We see the research in real-time on the screens."

"That's from the initial team. It was decided it was better to not broadcast our failures."

"Really? How old is it?"

"I was still in medical school when the terminations happened and the surviving children were sent to the Compound. I joined the research project after I graduated. They stopped the visual broadcasts before I joined. That was about fifteen years ago."

Triden did the math. They were seeing footage from over a decade ago as if it were happening now.

"I guess they keep showing the images so we understand the risks?"

"I don't know why they're still showing you the research loops."

"I've seen it for as long as I can remember."

The doctor nodded. "I'll see if I can find out more about it for you."

"You started research nineteen years ago?"

"Yes, I inherited the initial project and found a vaccine that proved promising. But the virus keeps mutating."

"The mutations occurred within the Compound?"

"Yes. The additional blood samples showed an irregularity which didn't exist at first."

"No one in Society is contracting the virus since we've been contained here?"

"Correct. There have been no new cases since the mass terminations and the transfer of the infected children." The doctor refrained from using the word "contagion."

"Did the virus only mutate once?"

"No, it's mutated multiple times. But nothing recently." Jayr shook his head. "Give me some time and I'll know more."

You will continue to be tested.

Lessons will repeat until the message is received.

No one is exempt from learning in this lifetime.

Roseleen looked up at the sky. The sun was almost overhead.

"I'm going to meet Triden."

"Don't be gone long, Daughter. Now more than ever, it's important we stay close."

"I understand, Mother. He'll worry if I don't meet him."

She stopped at the communal kitchen and hastily packed a few items for their lunch; boar sandwiches, glassenberry cookies, and a few pieces of fruit. She hated the thought of Triden eating the dreadful protein pucks. Even now, she cringed at the memory of the taste. She didn't know how anyone could call the cardboard disks food.

She positioned her satchel strap across her body and started sprinting through the forest. She barely noticed her surroundings, the river churning to her left, other forest animals navigating their way. She was out of breath as she neared the fallen log and saw Triden pacing back and forth.

"I'm sorry I'm late." She knew he still worried about infecting her. Especially after being intimate, he feared something would change and take it all away from him.

He took her into his arms and hugged her tight. "I'm glad you're here."

It didn't take long to fill him in on the logging activities witnessed earlier.

"Do you know anything about it?"

"No. The logs aren't coming to the Compound as far as I know."

"It looks like they're just starting. We don't know how many trees they plan to remove."

She didn't feel hungry but pulled the food pouch out of her satchel anyway and handed it to Triden.

"You spoil me. Are you sure there's enough to share?"

"Yes. We plan for the winter, and we've stored plenty to get us through the snowy months.

"I need to get back. I'll see you tomorrow."

They kissed, and Triden turned in the direction of the Compound.

"I hope one day we'll have more time together."

"Me, too, Rosey. Me, too." She liked how he'd shortened her name. It felt special.

CHAPTER 32

Annabella read the information on her personal screen. The first shipment of logs had reached the processing plant and been sliced into planks. The quality of the wood was stellar, and the diameter had surprised her. She hung up with the site supervisor. She had been assured the initial income estimates were conservative and Alpine Management would reap an even larger profit when selling in the open market.

She turned to Jordon. "We have lots to celebrate!"

"You know what this means?"

"We're going to be rich!"

"We're already rich, Bella. We're going to be extravagant!"

Annabella sidled up to her husband. "I love it when you talk finances."

"Well, then you're gonna love this." Jordon tapped on the tabletop screen and did a quick calculation. "We let everyone know the wood is top quality, and we set a premium price. Then we limit the supply to create a bidding war and push the price up even more. We control the flow of lumber into the market, and we keep the price at a premium." He turned the screen toward her. "This is what I expect we can deliver the first year."

"Do we keep cutting or wait?"

"We keep cutting to optimize our labor and store the processed wood in a warehouse. No one needs to know we're holding back to sway the market."

"I'm meeting with Sir William later today. He was out late last night at a campaign rally and then stared at the screens for hours looking for news reports of his performance. He won't likely be coherent until noon. I've booked a room for him at the Quilt Club for later. The players will have dinner with him. I've made sure we have representation at the table to provide additional support for privatizing the Contagion Compound."

Jordon smiled. "I love it when you talk Sir William manipulations to me."

"He'd throw all of Society under a bus if it would improve his ratings."

"Hmmm. Let me see what I can do with the news report tonight. I've been asked to appear to give my perspective on the financial markets."

"Sir William hates you. Make sure you say something in direct contrast to privatizing the Compound. He'll agree to the terms with our player at the Quilt game tonight just to spite you."

"Done. I'll make sure I drop a tidbit into my interview today."

"Oh, and mention something about his hair being a toupee, too."

"Is it?"

"No, but it makes him crazy when people accuse him of not having his own hair."

"I love you more every day, Bella. You see all the angles."

[Ⅲ]

Sir William loathed the daily cabinet meetings. He looked down at his screen and scanned the various news reports looking for coverage of his campaign rally. He loved standing before a cheering crowd. He could say anything he wanted and kept changing the narrative to find something to spark the crowd. He'd casually tossed out "When there's a *WILL*, there's a *WAY*" last year, and the audience had roared.

Any misalignment with his vision or voice would irretrievably demote someone out of his inner circle. Unsuspecting aides had vanished because they hadn't kept up with Sir William's whimsical policy changes. What would have been perceived as loyalty one day was blasphemous the next.

Sir William thrived on chaos. He reveled in manipulating those around him and dismissed his detractors with ridicule and lies. He glanced up and nodded, feigning interest in what was being said. Focusing again on the screen, he tapped out a message for the scrolling banner along the bottom. He flipped to another news source and saw Annabella's husband.

You piece of shit, Jor-dumb. He smiled. He enjoyed his slur on Jordon's name. He couldn't believe Annabella was still married to the worthless hack.

"The Contagions are part of Society even if they live separately. It is our social responsibility to take care of them."

Sir William snorted. "Jor-dumb knows nothing."

"Your tax dollars go to feeding them, making sure they receive the proper medical attention and lead rich and fulfilling lives within the Compound."

Sir William tapped out a message quickly and watched for it to feed underneath Jor-dumb's image. The red text scrolled.

"The Contagions are contributing members of society. We do not take care of them; they take care of themselves!"

The reporter interviewing Jordon read the scrolling banner on his screen. "How would you like to respond to the president's statement?"

"I'd ask Sir William if his toupee is glued on too tight." Jordon paused to let Sir William take in the statement. "I mean, seriously, have you seen his hair?"

The reporter laughed. "I have."

Sir William stood up, agitated, before he remembered where he was. "I have urgent business I need to attend to. Please go on without me." Retreating behind the closed doors of his office, he flipped to the news report on the large screen attached to the north wall.

"Really, in all seriousness," Jordon was saying, "there's still no cure. That's on Sir William's watch. He was the key Ministry member who coordinated the initial setup of the Compound. He's responsible."

Sir William tapped out his reply,

"The top virologists in Society are dedicated to finding a cure..."

Sir William knew he shouldn't get into a pissing match with Jor-dumb on a live feed, but he was seething. *I did what everyone was afraid to do. I made sure Society was safe from them,* he thought. He banged out a reply and watched it feed across the bottom of the screen.

"The Contagions support Society. They contribute to our manufacturing initiatives..."

"ANNABELLA!" Sir William yelled loud enough to be heard down the hall. It didn't take long for her to enter the room.

"Your idiot husband is on the news again."

"We barely talk, Sir William. We live under the same roof for the benefit of our children."

"He's critical of the Contagion Compound."

"Would you like me to put together a task force to generate a report? If you publish an update, you can control the narrative."

"Yes, yes. I control the narrative. The Contagions are contributing to Society. They are isolated from anyone they could contaminate with the virus."

"They are lucky to be alive..." He tapped the message into the screen feed. "Society hasn't left them behind..."

Jordon looked at the camera and replied to the feed.

"If that's true, Sir William, why isn't the Contagion Compound represented in Society with a member in your cabinet? They are of legal age and should have a voice within Society."

Sir William pounded the top of his desk. "Annabella, get the report done immediately! Be sure it shows the needs of Society and the Contagions are very different and why a representative wouldn't fit in our cabinet sessions. Too much time would be taken for something which doesn't need discussion. The Compound runs smoothly."

"You raise a good point, Sir William. The Compound does run smoothly, and it's time to ensure that the Ministry isn't pulled into future discussions about the Contagions. If you move the management outside of the Office of Human Betterment you can eliminate oversight from within. You could even announce research funding is being stopped and removed from the budget."

"There's no one qualified at the Compound to take on the research."

"Do they need a cure if they are living full lives within the Compound?"

Annabella watched him absently processing what she was saying as he paced behind his desk.

"Yes, I want to remove the Contagions from the reelection narrative, with their protests and criticisms of my contributions to Society."

"Your idea makes a lot of sense."

"My idea?"

"Yes, your idea to carve the Contagion Compound management out of the Department of Human Betterment. I will arrange for a private management company to oversee the transition and ongoing daily activities. The changes will not disrupt any of the maintenance, manufacturing, and labor contributions the Contagions are providing to Society today."

He stopped pacing. "Yes, yes, everything stays the same, and by appointing a management firm, it takes the topic out of the election dialog. Pull it together immediately."

Annabella left the large office and smiled. Everything was falling into place nicely. First, the leasehold on the forest lands and now the chance to privatize the Compound management. She was sure it would prove itself a profitable venture for her and Jordon.

CHAPTER 33

There's always a fork in the road.

The message from The Source wasn't providing much insight yet. Roseleen and her brother, Adin, had traversed the forest to monitor the logging activities. It was shocking and distressing to see how rapidly the trees were being excavated from the land. There did not appear to be an end in sight. Each day the two approached cautiously so as not to be detected, and each day they saw more destruction. It pained Roseleen to see the stubbled trunks, sawdust, and broken branches.

"What do you think?"

Her older brother looked distressed as well. "I don't think they're going to stop until every tree is cut down."

"Why would they destroy the forest? It doesn't make sense. These are protected lands."

"Have you heard anything from The Source?"

"Only 'You will continue to be tested.' This is a lesson I could do without."

Adin nodded. "Me too, Little Sister, me too."

Their new daily routine was to assess the progress and report their findings to the Forest Seers. Occasionally their father went with them. They all agreed the logging wasn't ending soon.

"We have the upcoming winter working to our advantage. I doubt they'll try cut down trees with snow on the ground."

Take time and be truthful to be led down the right path.

The community was abuzz with speculation, everyone comparing their insights from The Source.

No one is exempt from learning in this lifetime.

Were the messages a sign they would have to leave their home? Where would they go? Roseleen's father tried to soothe the anxiety permeating throughout their encampment.

"We will know how to proceed soon. Please stay calm. We

block the messages from The Source if we are stressed."

As she made her way to meet Triden, Roseleen could feel anguish in the woods. The root systems of the trees were connected, and she was empathetic with the natural world around her. She didn't know how it worked exactly, but she knew she was part of a larger web where everything was interconnected, and if someone took the time, they could receive insights like the messages the Forest Seers obtained from The Source.

Triden hadn't arrived, and she sat next to the fallen log to wait. Matted leaves and brush covered the ground after their weeks of congregation. She closed her eyes to tap into The Source. *What message should I hear today?*

It didn't take long to get a response.

Fallen trees mark a shift in time.

She didn't know what it meant, but it didn't sound promising.

The forest is a safe haven.

The second message felt more reassuring. She looked up as she heard Triden's footsteps approaching. She was glad to see him. She missed him when they weren't together.

They hugged when he arrived and then sat, leaning against the fallen tree trunk, eating the lunch Roseleen had packed for them.

"Sure you don't want one of these?" Triden held up his lunch bag containing the protein pucks, and Roseleen grimaced.

"Sorry, those are really bad. I don't care what flavor you have today."

"I know, I'm finding them harder and harder to eat after all the food you bring me. I feel bad I can't give you something in return."

"It's OK. I'm thankful you're getting real food."

"I've been getting additional messages from The Source."

"Anything to share?"

"I keep hearing 'the two-faced woman betrays both sides.'"

Triden took her hand in his. "What do you think it means?"

"I'm not sure yet. I should know in time."

"I find it comforting to know you have an internal compass."

She had always heard messages from The Source and it felt natural, nothing to question or fear. She was surrounded by others like her, and yet, when meeting Triden, she'd gotten shy about her abilities.

He smiled. "You don't have to worry about what you tell me, ever."

"I worry we may have to move and I'll never see you again."

"I worry about the upcoming snow. That's going to present a problem."

"I've been thinking about that, too. I can show you how we walk in the woods without leaving a trail."

"Show me." Triden's voice mirrored his hopefulness.

Roseleen stood and walked before the young man.

"Start toe, then heel instead of heel, toe. It minimizes the pressure on the ground."

The two laughed together as they circled the log.

"Do you think it will work?"

"Luckily, the first snow never lasts long. We'll have a few days to experiment before the ground is covered for the season."

"I don't know what I'm going to do without you." Triden leaned in and kissed her.

Roseleen laughed. "I bet you don't know how you're going to survive on protein pucks alone."

"Don't tease me. It's already bad enough I won't see you. Missing your lunches is going to be equally as bad."

"Equally?" Together they laughed again. Triden knew he was going to miss her a lot more than the food.

"Mallor, I need to you take care of something for me." Sir William had summoned the bald man to his office.

"My intern is telling me she's going to go public with our physical interlude unless I pay her to be quiet."

"Tell me what happened. I need to know how to advise you."

Sir William recounted the afternoon he'd tied his intern's hands together and pushed her over the side of his desk.

"So, you did have relations with her?"

"Yes. But she says it wasn't consensual. She's lying."

"Lying or not, you did tie her hands together. That's not going to go over well if this leaks out."

"Lilia will kill me."

"We have your reelection to consider. We can go one of two ways with this. Do you want me to pay her to be quiet or use my influence to persuade her to keep her story to herself?"

"Pay her. This way, she'll look bad if she comes forward."

"Consider it taken care of." Mallor moved to the door of the presidential office and turned back to face Sir William. "One more thing. Fire her."

"Do I have to?" whined William. "She would be fun to play with again."

"Sir, if she's saying it wasn't consensual, I doubt very much there's going to be a repeat. It would also destroy her story. Get rid of her and make sure you state it is performance-related. If for any reason this story comes to light, you'll already have a foundation built as to why she might fabricate this story."

"But it's true."

Mallor shook his head. Sir William wasn't the brightest person.

"As of now, nothing happened. Understand?"

Sir William pouted.

"Do you understand, Sir William?"

"Yes. It's unfortunate. She was a lot of fun."

"Can I ask you to be careful in your selection next time if you decide to take on a playtime friend?"

"This is why I have you."

"Yes, sir. But at least try to make it easier on yourself. How many checks do you want to write?"

Sir William didn't tell Mallor he'd been doing well at the Quilt table. Ever since he'd taken office, his skills at the table went unmatched. He was a true leader. No one could manage Society better and it was showing through his card playing as well. He'd cut Lilia off from access to the Quilt Club funds and had amassed quite a nest egg. He was thinking about buying a resort in the south to get away from the cold and snow of winter.

"Just make sure she doesn't talk for the easiest outcome for all."

"Of course, Sir William. Anything else?"

The president dismissed his confidant and looked at the various news feeds playing on the large screen in his office.

The first report was on his latest rally, lots of people cheering, and he looked regal at the pedestal. The next news outlet covered it but used a wider shot, and it was evident not all the seats behind him were full. His staffers had assured him the empty seats were to protect him. While he was at the lectern, it would be hard for his protection team to ensure his safety. *Bad reporting*, he mused. News coverage by another agency panned the stadium seats not filled. *Why would they do that*?

He drew large crowds. People flocked to see him. The news agencies were manipulating information to make him look bad. He tapped out a message for the scrolling banner. "Don't listen to the fabricated news; listen to your favorite president."

He sat for a minute and then continued.

"I would like to thank my intern..." What was her name again?

"ANNABELLA!"

He waited with no response.

"ANNABELLA! I NEED YOU!" When she didn't appear, he bellowed into the hall. The workers at desks outside his office all looked up from their work.

"Sir William, she's on the news right now promoting you."

He didn't realize Annabella was going to be talking with the media today. He didn't like not knowing where she was.

"Of course, of course." He paused. "Can you tell me my intern's name?"

"Yes, you mean Syra Bain?

"Yes, that's her name." He stepped back inside his office and composed his message.

"I would like to thank my intern, Syra Bain, for her dedication and support of my presidency. Unfortunately, she was unable to fulfill the requirements of the role, and I've had to let her go. I'm sure she'll make a great addition to a candle shop or something."

He was sad to have her leave. He'd find someone else to fulfill his needs. Maybe even his wife.

⫟⫟

The doctor looked at the data again. No antibodies were isolated in one of the blood samples. He looked at the donor's name. Triden.

How is that possible?

He cross-referenced other blood samples looking for a match. He still wanted to find correlations of the disease in the patients he'd been interviewing. He was getting a glimpse into life in the Compound and his participants were interesting.

Most hadn't had a parent in their lives for more than a few years. The older Contagions had become surrogate adults.

None of them had been exposed to the rigors of life in Society. They all did work within the Compound without complaint. It was as if everyone had embraced their motto: *"Lucky to Be Alive!"*

The doctor wasn't feeling very lucky at the moment. Trying to match current blood samples to prior data sets wasn't yielding a meaningful result. And now, to discover Triden did not have antibodies in his blood sample, how could the doctor explain the latest mutation?

Triden had the rashes left behind after being exposed to P3264. Were there others who no longer needed antibodies to the pathogen?

The doctor scanned the data again.

No antibodies. Did this mean the residents had achieved herd immunity?

Jayr ruled it out. Every other blood sample still included antibodies. What made Triden different?

Society had managed to stamp out the virus outside of the Compound. No new cases had been detected, yet there was always a risk the virus could reemerge at any time.

If only he could find a match to the Society provided samples. He wanted insights into whether the antibodies had been present in the past and now were not detectable. He would risk another trip to the Compound to collect more data. He wondered if he could rely on the Contagions to pull blood in his absence. The more blood samples he could gather, the higher probability he could match someone to the prior data sets.

To validate the new findings, he looked at the first collection of data samples. The blood samples had been gathered when the first people were sent to the Compound.

Every single sample showed antibodies. Each person in the data set had been exposed to P3264.

How long would it take to find a statistically valid match?

He knew the answer before he'd asked the question. *Too long.*

Jayr's supervisor was pressing him for results. Rumors were persistent the research was to be canceled soon.

The doctor turned on the portable screen and replayed the interviews he'd had with Triden; both his first visit, when they discussed the details of his daily life, and the second interview, which had taken a personal turn.

Instinctively, he knew Triden held the answer he was seeking. He turned off the replay and tapped the screen again to reserve the medical van. It was worth the risk to visit the Compound again.

CHAPTER 35

Triden looked forward to his visit with the doctor. It was strange to feel a connection to someone he wouldn't be able to recognize sitting across from him without protective gear. He appreciated how honest the doctor had been about his own past. They had both lost parents because of The Path.

Triden entered the infirmary observation room and saw the doctor's familiar leather garb. He was behind a partition that provided extra protection.

"I didn't expect you again until next week." He sat in the chair facing the visitor.

"I found something interesting with my research." The doctor hesitated. *How much should he share with Triden?*

"I'm going to ask you some questions. I know we've covered many of them already. I'm looking to confirm information." Triden nodded.

The doctor quickly reviewed Triden's history before coming to the Compound. He was an only child whose parents had died because of P3264.

"Do you have any medical records from that time?"

Triden looked perplexed. "I don't know."

"I'm trying to trace your exposure to the virus, and I'm looking for potential mutations."

"We were brought to the Compound and shown where we would live and assigned a mentor."

"Who is your mentor?"

"My best friend, Benjam."

"Tell me about him."

"He's about three years older than me. He showed me how to survive here." Triden shared what it was like when he had arrived. Young and scared, with no parents, Benjam had eased the transition.

"Were you checked by a doctor?"

"Not that I remember."

"You didn't have a blood sample taken when you arrived?"

"I don't think so. But I was young and I don't remember much. It was a traumatic time."

"I can imagine."

"Have you had exams since you've been here?"

Triden paused. "Not often."

"Do the symptoms of the virus require attention?"

"The virus seems to be under control. I don't notice much other than the rashes."

"Any other symptoms?" The doctor made some notations as Triden continued.

"I only come if I have a fever."

"How often is that?"

"Very rare. I try to avoid the infirmary."

"Why is that?"

"Because it's not unusual for someone to come to the infirmary and never be seen again. The sick were the first to be selected for testing."

The doctor made a mental note. They hadn't performed any tests directly on Contagions for years. Would the fear of being a test subject remain after so long?

"You don't seem afraid of meeting with me."

"I was terrified the first time I met you. I didn't know why I had been selected. After I met you and was able to go back to my apartment, my fears faded. There wasn't anything scary about the process."

"I'm glad you're comfortable."

"I'm curious, really."

"What do you want to know?"

"What about Society? What is it like?"

"Very modern. Many buildings in the precincts were destroyed when the cause of the virus was unclear. There were those who thought a building could remain contaminated if it had housed someone known to have been exposed to P3264.

"Is that true?"

"No. So much destruction with no reason."

"Society used to have ten precincts, so many people died now there are only five. The precincts were given new boundaries and names.

"What about where I was born?"

"You lived in Precinct Nine. Mostly working-class people. It's now a cemetery."

"My parents are buried there?"

"No one knows for sure, but it is the primary location for the mass graves. It's a beautiful memorial."

"I don't think we see the same thing on our screens as you do in Society."

"From what I've seen, you are correct. Your messages are Compound specific."

"What are the messages you see?"

"The Society president, a man named Sir William Newbiggers, has a communication banner he uses to send messages throughout Society. There are also news agencies that cover the affairs of the Statecraft."

"We don't see his banner?"

"It appears not. What are the other residents like here?"

"Everyone understands the moral guidelines of staying in the Compound."

"Where do the residents work?"

"Most in the Compound center. There are four housing quadrants sectioned around it. Except for my work. I'm underground in the water and sewer corridors."

"Corridors?"

"Yes, I make sure the equipment is running efficiently and smoothly."

Triden's story mirrored many of the other Contagion's reports. Everyone awakened at the same time, filtered into the dining hall for a quiet meal, picked up a packaged lunch, and convened in a quadrant bar in the evening. They could socialize On Book or stay solo and return to their quarters. This repeated every day.

There was no variance in the day-to-day activities of the Contagions. They were a controlled study group, and yet there was something he was missing. Jayr was determined to find it.

CHAPTER 36

"Here's the management study. I've scheduled a televised event to make the announcement." Annabella handed Sir William a bound report as he sat in front of his dressing table mirror preparing for his public appearance.

"Do the precincts have to agree to us changing the management of the Contagion Compound?"

"No, since the Contagions' care is included in the Department of Human Betterment, the precincts do not have a say. It's the Presidential Precedents which allow you to determine the best for the Contagions."

Sir William smiled. He was going to be a hero. "They must remain in the Compound. They will taint the purity of Society if they leave. They will always be Contagions."

"I assure you, Sir William, the Compound will continue to run smoothly outside of the Department of Human Betterment."

"Society would have been destroyed by The Path if I hadn't taken action."

Sir William tucked a white towel into his shirt collar, picked up a bottle, spritzed his face with tanning spray, and then patted his face with another towel. Orange splotches marred the fabric, and the president looked for any evidence of a tan line at his chin. He peered into the mirror and meticulously moved a few hair strands before applying a layer of industrial-strength hair spray. He applied some mustache wax before pulling the towel from his shirt collar.

"I'm ready. Let's announce this and be done. I have a table reserved at The Flodden Club."

They left the private chambers and made their way to the main corridor. A podium had been placed under the dome of the Presidential Palace, and the press were seated in rows of chairs filling the atrium.

Sir William waited for Annabella to introduce him, enjoying the fanfare preceding his time at the podium.

"I have devised a wonderful plan, a great plan, to address the needs of those contained in the Contagion Compound." He scanned the audience and waited for clapping. The press sat silently. Disappointed, he continued.

"There are some in Society who believe the Contagions are not being treated fairly. There are others questioning the expenses put out by the Department of Human Betterment to maintain the Compound. I have come up with a solution to address these concerns and more."

Several cameras flashed, pleasing Sir William. They were capturing him for all of Society to see.

"We are starting the transition to remove the Contagion Compound from the Department of Human Betterment. We are establishing a Contagion Republic. We've hired a management company to assist with the transfer. From now on, the Contagion Compound will have internal governance in addition to providing resources for Society."

A murmur could be heard around the room, and hands shot into the air.

"Sir William..."

"Yes?" The president pointed to a reporter in the second row.

"I'm with the Society Sentinel. All of the Contagions were sent to the Compound as children and have led a sheltered life. How are they equipped to take on the responsibilities of management?"

"That is why we are providing a company to assist them with this transition. Everything is outlined in this report." Sir William held up the bound brochure.

Sir William fielded a few more questions. He couldn't remember the details of the transition. "You'll see this is the best for all when you read the documentation. The Contagions will have autonomy. Self-sufficiency is the best for both the

Contagion Compound and Society. Remember, When there's a *WILL*, there's a WAY!"

He stepped away from the podium, paused for a few more photos, and then retreated toward his office.

"Excellent, Sir William." Annabella congratulated him.

"Have my car pulled around. I'm late for the Quilt Club."

"Of course."

Annabella summoned Sir William's limousine and pushed him inside. After he was safely outside of the Presidential Palace gate, she tapped a message to Jordon.

"It's done! Tonight, we celebrate."

CHAPTER 37

The Forest Seer Council was buzzing with energy. For several weeks, the loggers had been decimating the land and inching closer to their hidden community. The Source had been providing insights, but there was disagreement on what the messages meant.

The Forest is a safe haven.

Plan ahead to ease the way.

Make tomorrow better than today.

Would they be safe if they stayed? Would their livelihood be destroyed with their ecosystem damaged?

If they moved, how much further would they need to retreat into the woods? Did they have the winter to plan?

Roseleen slipped away from the meeting undetected. She usually felt so carefree and joyful in nature, but she acknowledged she was feeling the shift in the lands. It hurt her to see the remains of the once tall trees reduced to severed trunks and sawdust.

She crossed her harvest satchel over her body. The last of the fall bounty had been gathered and stored in the underground bunkers. Instead, she slipped a book taken from Society years earlier into the bag, along with a packet containing lunch for her and Triden.

The decimation of the forest highlighted how limited her interactions with Triden could become. If he went missing, he would be hunted until found. If the Forest Seers were forced to relocate, would they ever see each other again? She couldn't survive without the assistance of her community, and he couldn't leave the Compound for any length of time without facing a death sentence.

She met the young man by the fallen tree. The air was crisp and the two huddled together to stay warm. She pulled her woolen shawl closer. She'd started wearing a rabbit-fur-lined leather jacket for more warmth. The skin did not go to waste after the meat had been turned into a hearty stew.

"We may move deeper into the forest. We're going to see if the logging continues when the snow falls."

"You know I can only slip away from the Compound for a short time each day."

"I know. It makes my heart break thinking of you trapped inside."

"Really, it's not so bad. I focus on the time I have with you."

"What if I have to leave? What am I going to do without you?"

"The doctor is working on a cure. I have faith he'll find something, and then I'll be free to leave the Compound." Triden tried to sound confident, even though he had doubts.

"I wish I had your optimism, but it could take years."

"I met with him this week and he said he's making progress. We are meeting again next week. I'll try to find out more information."

Roseleen kissed Triden. "I don't know what I'll do without you."

"Don't worry yet. I'm sure it will work out. What does The Source say?"

"The bird always knows the migration path home."

"Any idea what it means?"

"Not yet. I'm feeling stressed and that usually blocks the messages."

"I don't know how, but we'll be together, I promise."

Triden looked at the position of the sun in the sky and stood up. "I have to go. I'll see you tomorrow." They embraced, and he turned and wound his way out of the woods and sprinted through the field, making sure to run through the grass on a different trajectory to minimize developing a trodden path. He hoped he wasn't lying to Roseleen by promising her what he wanted for them both without knowing how it could be their future. He was sure of one thing. He didn't want to lose her.

He looked up at the looming gray structure. The only thing keeping him sane was knowing he would see Roseleen again tomorrow. His new normal included her.

As he reentered the main workspace, the screen on the wall flashed the familiar saying.

"Lucky to Be Alive!"

Only if I have Roseleen in my life. The thought only served as a reminder a life without her was no life at all.

[⊪[

Jordon and Annabella laughed by the flickering fire in their living room. They clinked their wine glasses, the standard fare for their celebrations.

"Oh, Jordie, Sir William calls you 'Jor-dumb'!"

Jordon laughed. "It's official! I'm obviously hitting close to home to be warranted with such a nickname. Do you ever worry Sir William will let his ego put Society at risk?"

"Of course, but luckily he's not interested much in the security meetings. Those who are qualified have maintained the proper activities to preserve Society."

"Really, he doesn't pay attention at all?"

"Rarely, and even then, I don't think he fully grasps the level of information available to him. He's focused on how he looks, getting adoration at his election rallies, and planning his next meal."

"I thought it would be the Quilt table."

"That goes without saying. I wonder if he'll figure out the Precinct Ministers are throwing their hands to funnel money into his personal account?"

"How could he not see it? Does he really think he wins every time at the table legitimately?"

"Don't underestimate the size of his ego."

"His ego is going to be his downfall."

"Don't I know it!"

"Are the kids home?"

"No, they're studying at the library."

"Perfect. I want to make love to you in front of the fire."

"I think that can be arranged."

Annabella slipped out of her dress and let it fall to the floor.

"You're wearing way too much clothing, *Jor-dumb*."

Jordon laughed. "So are you, dear. Let me help you." He deftly removed her bra before unhooking his belt and stepping out of his trousers. It didn't take long for them to discard the remaining pieces of clothing. Jordon lowered her to the rug in front of the fireplace and kissed her. She was ready for him, and he entered her quickly, enjoying the look on her face as she welcomed him inside her. They moved together, power igniting their passions. They were a couple who shared the worldview that it was better to optimize one's circumstances than to be on the sidelines. They'd already managed to secure the lumber lease and now the ongoing management of the Compound. Soon they would find a way to take over the presidential role as well. Sir William wouldn't even see it coming.

∭

The doctor slid into the chair behind the protective screen separating him from Triden. The additional blood sample retrieved during his last visit confirmed it. The young man did not have antibodies for the virus.

The doctor had questions with no answers. *Without the antibodies, wouldn't Triden be at risk of death from everyone else in the Compound?* Something about him prevented exposure.

"Have you heard about the changes being made at the Contagion Compound?"

Triden shook his head, "What type of changes? Any chance

they're putting more support on housing repairs? My sink has been dripping for months."

"Really? Wow. I don't know about that, but Sir William announced the annexation of the Compound from the Department of Human Betterment.

"The department of what?"

"Human Betterment. It's where I work to find the cure to P3264."

"Annexation to where?"

"The Compound. Many citizens believe Contagions should have representation."

"Representation?"

"Yes. There are those who believe Contagions have rights and should have a place at the political table even though they live within the confines of the Compound."

"I have the freedom to live and work. I also have a moral responsibility to prevent spreading The Path."

"There are others who complain of the cost of keeping the Compound running."

"And the president... what did you say his name was?... is addressing this?"

"Sir William Newbiggers." The doctor paused. "Not exactly; he announced something he thought would make both sides happy. He's allowing the Compound to create its own agenda and moving the financial burden onto the Compound directly."

"How are we to do that?"

"They're bringing in a management firm to make the transition. You've heard nothing about it?"

"No. I would think it would have been announced on the screens."

"Me, too. I'll see else I can find out."

Triden saw an opening. "What other differences are there between us and Society?"

"There are many, and a lot of things are changing, too.

"Like what?"

"They've started harvesting wood from the forest."

"Is that unusual?"

"Very much. The land has always been protected for future generations. The current administration sees an opportunity to create income for Society instead. The president's provided access to a lumber company to cut down trees."

"All of it?"

"Not sure. I know when I drive here that I see lots of trucks heading to Society loaded with logs from the forest."

"Do you think they'll continue to cut down trees when the snow comes?"

The doctor paused. "Can you see the woods from here?"

"Not really. The perimeter wall is twenty feet high. Even on the roof of the buildings, it's impossible to see much more than the coils of wire across the top."

"Why the curiosity about the forest?"

Triden swallowed. Had he asked too many questions? He'd been surprised when the doctor had mentioned the logging and hoped to get insights to share with Roseleen.

"No reason, really. We have trees inside the Compound. I remember seeing the woods when I was little."

"Of course. I don't know how much you remember from your time before you came here."

"I remember my parents, a stuffed toy taken from me when they brought me here, and I remember the smell of the woods. Two I can never have again, but the forest is something I can still enjoy."

Triden hesitated. *How could he have said that?* "I mean, I can still smell the woods when the wind is right."

The doctor smiled under the mask. "I'm working to find a cure so you'll be able to do more than smell the woods."

"I didn't mean to make you feel bad."

"Don't worry. You're inspiring me to solve this puzzle."

"How can I help?"

"You've been helpful already. The blood samples and the interviews are helping me gain insights into P3264."

"What are you learning?"

"That it's not predictable. What is true in one case doesn't seem to be consistent with other cases."

"Really? How?"

"Well..." the doctor decided to show his hand. "For example, your blood sample doesn't show any antibodies to The Path."

"That's odd. Why wouldn't I have antibodies?"

"I'm trying to put the puzzle together. It would either indicate you've never had the virus, or it's no longer contagious, so you don't need antibodies." The doctor could see Triden processing the information. He continued, "We can rule out the first scenario. Everyone was tested for the virus before coming here."

"So, it's no longer contagious?"

"That's the puzzling part. Everyone else I've tested still has antibodies which would indicate P3264 is still dangerous."

"Then why don't I need antibodies?"

"I believe there's something about you specifically which has made it possible for you to overcome P3264. Something different from everyone else here."

Power Walker. Is this what Roseleen's message from The Source means? That he had the power to overcome P3264 and walk among the Contagions without getting sick again? Is this why she didn't catch the virus?" Triden's head was spinning.

"Do I have the virus?"

"According to your blood work, no. The rash on your body and the initial blood tests indicate you've had it."

Triden didn't ask the question pounding in his head. *If I don't have the virus, how come I am here?*

CHAPTER 38

Sir William stood at the podium and absorbed the energy around him. He loved his election rallies. He loved playing on people's insecurities and fears to make them see him as their savior.

"I have SAVED you from increased taxes. My opponent would have raised your taxes to pay for the Contagion Compound! He wants to raise taxes and funnel more money into the Compound."

The crowd booed their disapproval.

"Extravagant money to do what? Make the Contagions live a life of luxury while people in Society... good people like you... are left with NOTHING! No one has done more for the people of Society! I have protected you from increased taxes! I have protected you from the deadly virus threatening to destroy Society! Only I am able to make your world, your life, better! My opponent is going to STEAL from you the very freedoms which are your RIGHT! Do not let him make you a HOSTAGE of taxes! Do not let him STEAL your freedoms! My opponent is a SNAKE!"

The audience started to hiss loudly.

"Remember, When there's a *WILL*, there's a *WAY*"

The hissing became cheers, and Sir William smiled.

"Don't let my opponent and those who support him take from you what is yours! They will take your MONEY; they will DESTROY our economy and raise your TAXES to pay the OUTRAGEOUS BILLS! *Together we STRIVE and THRIVE!*"

Thunderous applause and stomping feet vibrated through the arena.

Sir William continued for an hour and forty-four minutes. When the audience appeared to be tiring, he prompted them to respond.

"Who is your favorite president?"

"Sir William, Sir William, Sir William," rang throughout the building.

"Who is my opponent?"

"A SNAKE... Hiss..." The audience squealed.

Sir William saw Annabella giving him the signal to wrap up. She always complained he spoke too long, but how else was he going to connect with people? The rallies were the way he was going to win reelection.

"I am your favorite president, and I will work *tirelessly* to serve you!"

He left the podium, and the cheering continued as if it were a concert and the audience was screaming for an encore.

Annabella met him as he stepped down from the stage.

"Sir William, you're meeting with the precinct minister, which should have started fifteen minutes ago."

"Oh, right. Please change it."

"You need the support of this precinct for your reelection."

"Isn't the rally enough? Everyone here loves me."

"It was a very good speech, Sir William. We want to make sure we reach everyone, and our best bet is to get an endorsement from the precinct cabinet minister.

"We play Quilt together regularly. How could he consider endorsing anyone but me?"

"I think it's important for the endorsement to be made publicly; ideally today after a successful rally."

"Excellent thinking, Annabella. The precinct cabinet minister will convey how much he believes in my message. I am the best candidate!"

"To garner his support, remind him of your history supporting the Contagions and your recent measures."

Sir William had been instrumental in creating the Contagion Compound and moving the infected children from the contaminated precincts to the repurposed space. The segregation had been deemed the last-ditch effort for mitigating the spread of The Path. It had been heralded as pivotal for stopping the spread of the virus and ending the mass terminations.

Sir William, as the Director of the Department of Human Betterment, had earmarked the children to be moved. Most of his responsibilities as director he'd delegated to appointed administrators. When the virus became prevalent, it required a more active role. Sir William had only taken on the Contagion Compound as a personal project because he saw the value to him politically.

After meeting with the precinct cabinet minister, who refused to endorse Sir William until he had provided the precinct with a detailed plan for the coming administration, Annabella managed to get Sir William inside his presidential car.

"I think it was the best rally yet! Wasn't it a great rally, Annabella?"

She stroked his ego. "Yes, Sir William, it was a shining example of who you are and what you stand for." The subtlety of her comment was lost on him.

[ ]

Annabella looked over the contract for the management of the Contagion Compound she had prepared for Sir William. It looked in order as long as he didn't ask questions. She tapped the screen and accessed his calendar.

He was scheduled for Quilt later in the afternoon before the Precinct Four dinner. She would retrieve him from the club. She knew he would be in high spirits after winning at the table, and it would be the perfect time to present the contract and minimize questions.

Republic Management would take over the Society responsibility for the Contagion Compound and receive a stipend from the Department of Human Betterment to manage the day-to-day processes. They would deflect the criticisms of having slave labor conducting everything from manufacturing to laundry by outwardly promoting Contagion inputs into policy development.

Annabella and Jordon, through Republic Management, would receive payments from Society and would cut current costs to create a significant profit margin. The goal was to promote the Compound as self-sufficient as well as minimize the expense to Society. Republic Management would reap the rewards.

Annabella reviewed the financials for running the Compound and identified a variety of places they could cut corners. Fresh undergarments and robes were delivered daily to every Contagion. There was no reason they couldn't deliver undergarments daily and switch the robes to weekly. Annabella also noticed the protein pucks were expensive. There had to be an alternative for feeding the Contagions which wouldn't cost so much.

She marked up the spreadsheet on the screen to highlight the opportunities to reduce costs. She smiled as she realized there was an even larger opportunity than she and Jordon had projected. Sir William didn't have to know how lucrative the move would be.

⬙⬙⬙

The doctor pulled the van into the Compound parking lot and maneuvered through the stream of trucks to a parking spot. Once inside, he sat behind the partition, waiting for Triden to arrive. A few minutes passed, then the young man entered the infirmary and sat across from Jayr.

"Does it bother you that you can't see my face?"

"No, not really. I can tell a lot by your voice."

"I want to make sure you can trust me. I know without seeing my face, it might be hard."

"Have you found anyone else in the study without the

antibodies?"

"Not yet. But I've only been able to collect a small number of samples when I visit. There are over 26,000 residents. I hope to find a correlation with my original sample data."

"Didn't everyone give blood samples when they arrived at the Compound?"

"That might be true. However, I've only received limited samples from Society. I'm looking for matching variables."

"Match in what way?"

"Gender, blood type, age; anything, really, to provide insights. If there's no match, I'll remove attributes one by one until I get a sample size to look for something of substance. I'm trying to determine if you hold the key to the cure."

"Because I have no antibodies? Wouldn't someone with antibodies be a better indicator for finding a cure?"

"I can get information from them, too. It's a puzzle."

"I hope you figure it out."

"Me, too, Triden. Me, too."

The doctor gathered additional samples before returning to the Society van. He stripped off the heavy leather attire and slid into the front seat.

What were his options? What if none of *the new samples matched any from the original batch?*

He had lots of unanswered questions and a nagging feeling the answer was right in front of him.

[‖]

Sir William's administrator informed Lilia she was scheduled to attend a foreign state of affairs visit with her husband the following week. It overlapped with her next treatment. She wondered if she could cancel her attendance. After all, if she was going to be in the hospital for extended "tests," she wouldn't be expected to be there.

"Tell Sir William my schedule cannot be shifted. He will have to attend to Society affairs on this matter without my presence."

"Yes, ma'am."

Lilia smiled. "Also, tell him the Be Kind Foundation is having a charity dinner in three weeks, and his attendance is expected."

"Of course, immediately."

Lilia sighed. It had never been her intention to be the Top Lady of Society. She had wanted a life of luxury with a man who could provide resources to play with to her heart's content. She was interested in the finer things in life: designer clothes, jewelry, traveling by private jet, club memberships, and the opportunity to mingle with celebrities. More recently, she saw the importance of having money to take care of her semi-annual procedures. Sir William would surely die sooner than later, and she would be left wealthy with the freedom to do what she wanted.

She had recently fired the mail delivery person. He'd started using the terms "we" and "us." Clearly, he hadn't understood his role to help her kill time as well as get back at Sir William for his dalliances over the years.

She would be on the lookout for a good replacement. The next person had to meet the same criteria: youthful and in a very junior position, so even if they talked, no one would believe them. Why would the Top Lady of Society be entertaining a mere mail boy?

Because it helps with the monotony.

She tapped the screen and looked at her schedule. She had time to fit in her favorite designer. Time for some new clothes.

CHAPTER 39

Triden and Roseleen lay together, their naked bodies intertwined between two woven blankets she'd brought with her as the days were turning colder. A few snowflakes filled the air, and they pulled the top blanket closer.

Roseleen sat up.

"Hey! You're letting the cold air in."

"Oops, sorry. I received the bird message from The Source again." Roseleen lay down and snuggled next to Triden.

"What do you think it means?"

"I don't know. I get a brief image, but it's not like any bird I've ever seen."

Tread lightly to remain unseen.

Roseleen conveyed the additional message. "I think it's our answer to you getting out of the Compound when it snows."

"You are a multi-talented, beautiful woman." Triden admired her. She was fearless and so optimistic. Even with the looming destruction of her forest home, she seemed centered and focused.

"The Source always provides," was her standard response when he questioned her about it.

"I hope you're right." After years at the Compound, he had a pragmatic outlook.

"I know I'm right." She kissed him. "You'll see. I'm going to turn you into an optimist one of these days."

"I know my fate. I shouldn't hope for a cure after all this time. It's better for me to accept that my future is the Compound with stolen moments with you as long as you'll meet me."

"I'm not going anywhere. I plan on meeting you every day until we can be together always."

"I don't want you to get your hopes up."

"Too late."

"Roseleen, you know I can't leave. They'll kill me as a threat to Society."

"I'll see if The Source has any messages."

"Can't hurt to make a query."

"It doesn't really work that way. I'll listen for a message intended for you."

"I'm curious to know what it is."

"Patience." Roseleen smiled as she realized she sounded like her mother.

"That's the story of my life." Triden pulled her close and hugged her before getting up to dress. It didn't take long to cover himself with the undergarments and brown robe. He pulled the hood over his head, leaned down, and gave Roseleen a lingering kiss. He didn't want to go, but the sun was getting closer to the horizon. He'd been gone longer than normal.

"I'll see you tomorrow."

"Be safe."

"Always."

Triden sprinted across the open field, minimizing the trampling of the grass. He reached the opening and slipped inside. After replacing the rusted bar, he picked up his tool belt, secured it around his waist, before replacing his hard hat and tracing his way back through the corridor. It took a minute to slip out from behind the barrier and push it back in place to hide the abandoned tunnel.

He made his way through the maze of pipes, smiling as he thought of his tryst with Rosey. She smelled so fresh and clean, not like the antiseptic soap available at the Compound.

As he entered the common area housing the maintenance room and office, he realized he wasn't alone. His supervisor was there, looking irritated.

"Where have you been? I've been waiting for you for thirty minutes."

Triden touched his toolbelt. "I've been in corridor 12. There's a pipe showing signs of strain. I replaced some of the anchor bolts."

"Is it as bad as we think?"

"The complex was old before they converted it for us. I can keep patching things, but if they're not addressed soon, it could become a big problem."

"How big?"

"As in a river of sewage throughout the lower level of the building." Triden took a deep breath in relief. Talking shop felt safe.

"Let's go to my office. I have something to discuss with you."

That doesn't sound good. Triden took a deep breath. "Lead the way."

He followed his supervisor up the metal stairs and down the hall of the W&W Building. They entered the small office, and the supervisor walked around his desk and sat in a black office chair. He gestured to one of the two chairs facing his desk.

"Sit, sit!"

Triden never spent time in the office and fidgeted nervously. *Had it been discovered he was venturing outside the Compound every day?*

"I've noticed a change in your behavior..."

Triden looked down and swallowed nervously. His heart was pounding, and he could feel himself breaking into a sweat under his robe.

"You've been doing a great job, Triden. Your attitude is exemplary. I want to recommend you for recognition."

Triden didn't know what to say. He wiped his sweaty hands on his robe, trying to calm his nerves.

"You've been a new person recently, a real asset to the W&W team. I know I can trust you to extend the life of these pipes as best as you can. Also, it's appreciated you're participating with the Society doctor to find a cure. You are a true asset to the Contagion Compound!"

"Thank you."

"A certificate of recognition will be great for both you and the team at W&W. It is our job to ensure the safety and happiness of everyone here. As you know, not everyone does well in the Compound. It can be difficult to know we're dangerous to others. We are pariahs on Society, and yet here, here in the Compound, we can make a difference! We're lucky to be alive!"

"Yes, thank you." Triden didn't know what else to say.

"Good! It's settled. I'll put you in for recognition, and we'll see what happens. We're competing with the other divisions within the Compound. I feel good about this year. We're going to make a difference."

"Lucky to be alive!"

"Today and tomorrow!" his supervisor responded as Triden walked to the doorway.

What if?

Jayr had been staring at the screen for so long his eyes were tired and he was unable to focus. He couldn't turn off the power; the screens were always on with the news feed. The connection to Society was not to be interrupted.

He swiveled his chair around and stared at the blank writing board behind him.

There were still no matches to the original data set, and it reinforced the folly of trying to find a match with so few blood samples retrieved each week.

"What if?" he said out loud to the wall.

He stood up, grabbed a stylus, and started writing on the information board.

Options/Known data:

Toss out Society provided data sets (for now).

Virus indicators: All test participants have rashes; some have welts as well.

Virus impact: No children have been conceived even with multiple On Book encounters; an indicator the virus causes sterility.

All new blood samples show antibodies, except Triden.

"Triden holds the key. But how?" The doctor tapped the stylus against his thigh as he looked at the board. He stepped forward and added another notation.

Virus impact: Once exposed, a host is always contagious.

The doctor had also seen the images numerous times of people dying horrific deaths when exposed to P3264.

What if?

Triden lives in the Compound and has a rash but no antibodies.

The doctor shook his head.

What if the virus is no longer contagious? What if the contagion period was longer than most viruses but still ultimately dissipated during the years the residents had been in the Compound?

This could explain why Triden no longer needed antibodies while living in the Compound. But why did everyone else still have them? How could the doctor test the infectious rate of the residents in the Compound? Was he willing to bet his life on it?

⸭

Planning without consequence is still time well spent.
There's always a fork in the road.

Boundaries are being redefined.

The highlight of Roseleen's days was time spent with Triden. She'd been happy and content before they met and yet now, the thought of him not being with her for at least part of the day made her heart ache.

Roseleen stepped to the communal kitchen and wrapped items for lunch in a piece of leather, and slid the packet inside her satchel.

She found Triden pacing. After kissing him hello, she pulled back.

"What's wrong?"

"I met with the doctor. He's exploring ways to find a cure. And I feel guilty I'm not telling him about being outside the Compound with you."

"It would put you at tremendous risk. I understand why you're not saying anything."

"I know, I keep telling myself that, too. I have a feeling I could help everyone in the Compound if I told him, though. If he finds a cure, we can be together always."

"I know, I know. There's nothing I want more."

"Can I trust the doctor to keep my secret safe? I don't want to jeopardize what I have with you. Losing you would be too painful. I don't think I can survive in the Compound without the time we have together."

Roseleen opened one of the two blankets folded over her satchel and laid it on the ground. They sat down, leaning against the back of the fallen log, and she put the second blanket over their legs. She retrieved the leather pouch and unwrapped the sandwiches, and handed one to Triden.

"You're spoiling me. I really don't want to eat Compound food anymore."

"Ick! I know why. Do you want me to bring you food to take back with you?"

"No, it's too risky, and your community needs to keep enough to make it through the winter."

"We're able to hunt some and we have a lot of things stored in our bunkers."

"I appreciate the offer. I'll be fine."

They finished their lunch and then lay down side by side on the blanket and held hands. Overhead, the leaf canopy was rustled by the wind, and the sun flickered through the branches

"I never knew the world could be so beautiful."

Roseleen smiled. "I know. There's a magical feeling in the woods."

"Any more insights about the logging?"

"Adin and I looked this morning. It doesn't appear they are going to stop anytime soon. We keep hoping the snow will be a deterrent. At least they seem to be moving toward the forest to the north. They're still expanding toward our treehouses, but it's buying us some time." She didn't mention the Council was considering options requiring them to move before spring.

"I'm glad to hear that." Triden propped himself up and looked into her eyes. "I wish I could help you."

"You can. Be safe."

"I'll do my best." He leaned down and kissed her.

Sir William looked at the recent election poll results. "Annabella! This poll is defective. How did they reach this conclusion?"

Annabella entered Sir William's office. She'd been anticipating his outburst and hovered by the entrance.

"Sir William, you know some of the precincts have different demographics. The respondents could be heavily weighted from one area. We did our own survey and found you are leading by 13 points. I wouldn't worry about one little poll."

"The other side is running such a weak person. He's boring. How can people like him?"

"There are some who are concerned about the Contagion Compound. You proactively addressed the issue and removed it from the conversation. We should prep you for the debate next week."

"Prepare? Why?! I know what the people want to hear. They want to know their borders are protected. They want to know we're not giving away our goods with weak trade agreements with the countries around us. They also want to know Society is solidly positioned for years to come, with no infiltration of secondary citizens. No one is going to take away our rights. Certainly not a small group of disgruntled, misinformed protesters."

"Sir William, I know you view the undersecretary of the Signet as an incompetent person; however, he has more years in governance than you. He's remembered as being an advocate for those who are not as privileged in Society.

"Losers! I have no interest in people who can't make their way in the world, the less privileged looking for a handout."

"I think we should focus on the role you played to ensure the Contagions were able to live in a Compound dedicated to their safety."

"Their safety? NO! The Compound was set up for SOCIETY'S protection. The virus was rampant throughout the country. By isolating the Contagions, we ensured the future success of Society. There were many good people killed by the Contagions. Good people. Upstanding citizens of Society. The Contagions are infected filth. They are lucky to be alive!"

Annabella sighed. "I understand, Sir William. However, this might not be the best message for getting reelected. There are already detractors who question your commitment to the office you hold."

"That's nonsense. No one has done more for Society than I have. I protected it when P3264 was out of control. We stopped the spread by terminating those who were infected and putting the tainted children into the Compound. Without me, how many more people would have died?"

"You were instrumental in creating the Contagion Compound, but public opinion seems to be shifting. It's been years without finding a cure or a vaccination."

"The Compound is the best place for those children."

"They're all adults now, Sir William."

"What does it matter? They are protected. They are fed. They have their lives within the Compound. Why is this such a big issue now?"

"Some are referring to the Compound as a prison."

"Nonsense. It's protection. If they leave, they could infect someone. They could kill anyone they come into contact with. Without the Compound, they would have been terminated as well."

"I think it's part of Society history many would like to re-write or ignore."

"What's done is done. There's no sense looking back. We've created a society that is the greatest in the world. The Contagions can stay in the Compound for the rest of their lives, and everyone will be safe."

Annabella smiled. With that attitude, she and Jordon would reap the reward. Republic Management would funnel money to them for years to come.

CHAPTER 41

The Barcode was abuzz with activity. The screens around the room were outlining the changes being implemented.

Triden sat with Benjam, and together they read the tabletop screen.

"Starting immediately, Republic Management will be assisting the Compound with improved processes and procedures to ensure the safety and well-being of all residents by order of Sir William Newbiggers, President, Statecraft of Society."

"What do you think this means?" Benjam looked up from the screen.

"The doctor mentioned this during our last meeting."

"You talk about this with the doctor? I try to get in and out as fast as possible. I don't want to be detained."

"I've been curious, and the doctor has been answering my questions."

"Tri, curiosity is not a good thing. You need to find a way to make your days here work."

"Don't you ever wonder what it's like outside of the Compound?"

"I used to, but it's only a hollow dream. I found it was making me crazy, so I let it go."

"I admire that you can do that."

"It's easy. I have everything I need here." Benjam picked up his drink. "I have unlimited access to Paleem and more than enough people to keep me entertained at night."

"I found a way to get outside." Triden wasn't sure why he blurted out his secret.

"Wait, what?!"

"Shh..." Triden leaned in closer. "I've been going into the forest."

"Are you serious? They can kill you if you're caught."

"I know. That's why you can't tell anyone. Swear."

"Of course. You're my best friend. I'm not going to say anything."

"The only problem is once you go outside, it makes it harder to be inside."

"I can imagine. What's it like?"

"It smells amazing. The woods have an earthy quality. The ground is soft, and there are animals you can watch for hours."

"Hours? How long do you stay outside?"

"Not long. I don't want to get caught."

"Be safe, Tri. You're one of the reasons I can tolerate it here. Don't go and get yourself killed."

"Don't worry. No one watches us because there's been no need. Haven't you wondered why there are no guards here?"

"Well, it's not a prison."

"Technically, no. But we're not allowed to leave."

"That's because we can kill people by coming into contact with them. It's our moral responsibility to protect them and ensure we live, too."

"Exactly! They've taught us to cage ourselves."

"That sounds crazy."

"I know. I never saw it this way until I went into the forest. When you see the Compound from outside, it's a prison with high walls and barbed wire."

They looked back at the screen. "What do you think about this announcement?"

"I think someone in Society doesn't like supporting us and they're passing it over to another agency."

"But they put us here."

"I know; we're lucky to be alive!"

Benjam nodded. "Take a life, and give your own."

Both men knew the mantras of the Compound.

"Time will tell what happens with Republic Management. My guess is it will be more of the same, only a different name."

"I hope that's true." Triden didn't have a good feeling about it. Maybe all of his time with Roseleen was giving him insights, too.

The two-faced woman shifts with the tides.
Ego will betray those with overconfidence.
Intentions show the motives and the means.

Roseleen pondered the messages from The Source but did not get any revelations. She knew the two-faced woman wasn't in their tight-knit community and it wasn't Triden. Whoever it was, she didn't get a good feeling about her.

Lately, there had been an underlying uneasiness and Roseleen felt it deeply. The destruction in the forest she and Adin witnessed each day when they scouted the edge of the woods also impacted her mood.

The highlights of her days were the lunches she shared with Triden. Being away from him, particularly if the Forest Seers made a quick retreat into the deeper landscape of the woods, she feared they might be separated for longer than the winter months. She'd fallen in love with Triden. No wonder her heart ached at the thought of being apart.

The two-faced woman has no opinion.

Another variation from The Source did not provide any additional knowledge.

I get it, ok?! Be leery of a two-faced woman. Roseleen answered The Source out loud.

"Everything alright, Daughter?" her mother called from the main room of the treehouse. Roseleen pushed the curtain to her area aside and smiled.

"Letting The Source know I got the cryptic message."

"Don't worry. All messages become clear when the time is right."

Roseleen smiled. "Now you're sounding like The Source."

"Patience, Daughter, patience."

"Ugh. Why do I hear the messages if they have no meaning yet?"

"So you'll be prepared when the messages become clear."

"I suppose. Sometimes I think The Source likes to make me crazy."

The two women laughed. "I know it can feel that way sometimes, Daughter. The Source can have a sense of humor. But trust the truth to be revealed with perfect timing."

"Thank you, Mother. I'm going to meet Triden."

"You enjoy this young man, do you?"

Roseleen blushed, red creeping around her freckled face.

"I'm happy for you, Daughter. However, I want to make sure you protect your heart. He's from a different world and you'll unlikely be able to have a full life together."

"I know, Mother. I'll take part of a life over no life with him."

"You say that now, Daughter. How will you feel when he's not able to be there for you?"

"I can take care of myself, Mother."

"I know you are very capable, Daughter. I'm thinking more about when you are sick or tired and need a helping hand."

"I have everyone in the community."

"Yes, dear, we are always here for you. It's something deeper. An intimacy you can share with a partner. Like the bond I have with your father."

"Thank you, Mother. I appreciate your concern. For now, I'm focused on surviving the winter. I don't know what the future holds even with the guidance from The Source."

"I love you, and I don't want to see you get hurt."

"I love you, too. I'll do my best to protect my heart, but it may be too late."

"I'm here for you, whatever happens."

Lilia dressed in a cotton medical gown to prep for her procedure. She had cleared her calendar and had her clerk post a non-committal statement to the press that she was going to the medical center for a series of "standard tests" as part of her annual physical. Her aide had been instructed to send out a second announcement the following day announcing the Top Lady of Society would be staying for some additional tests and would return to the Presidential Palace by the end of the week. She would lay low for some additional time to make sure any evidence of bruising and swelling around her face had diminished before returning to her regular schedule.

Lilia had undergone enough procedures to know her face would look dreadful at first, but her skin would settle and she'd look like a new and improved version of herself. She had been unaware after her first procedure and had threatened the doctor with a lawsuit when she first saw her new face. One of the nurses had stepped in and assured her it was swelling from the invasive procedure, and she would look amazing in a few days' time. Now she knew what to expect and would not berate the surgeon.

She had found a doctor who understood her desire to look her best without alerting those around her to the steps she'd taken to protect her youth.

"Hello, Mrs. Newbiggers, we're ready." Dr. Emery made a gesture for the anesthesiologist to start. As the face mask with the numbing agent started to flow through her infusion pump, he added, "Be prepared for the new you!"

Jayr paced the partitioned area within the infirmary. He'd already gotten additional blood samples from a variety of Compound residents, and he'd asked to see Triden again, too. He'd been informed the young man would need to be retrieved from the Water and Waste Management Building located in a different sector.

He looked at the screen overhead. It was approaching the lunch hour, and he was hoping he could convince Triden to come with him. He knew there was a stigma and tremendous fear around stepping outside the Compound walls.

As the screens overhead cycled through a variety of messages, he'd discovered a lot of information was designed to keep everyone inside the perimeter.

"Take a Life, Give Your Own!" flashed before him with gruesome pictures of those who had died of P3264, a harsh reminder the unforgiving virus spread silently and killed quickly.

The Contagion tasked with retrieving Triden reentered the infirmary.

"I couldn't find him."

"Where would he have gone?"

"There are numerous corridors bringing water and sewage from a variety of places into the sanitation tanks. It's not surprising I couldn't find him quickly. He could have been down any number of the tunnels.

"I see."

"I left him a note in the common area. We don't know when he'll see it, though. If he's doing any type of repairs, it could take a while."

"There's no way to message him other than a note?"

"No, that's not how the Compound works. Everyone has a schedule, and they know where they need to be. This is unusual to interrupt someone's workday."

The doctor was anxious to talk with Triden. So far, no one had questioned his repeated visits, but one complaint to the Department of Human Betterment could expose his unsanctioned trips to the Compound.

"Thank you for your assistance. I can wait a little longer."

〰️

Triden strolled into the main artery which fanned out to a variety of corridors, all speeding the flow of water and sewage to the respective tanks for cleaning and sterilization to then be propelled to the distribution pipelines.

He checked the pipes as he made his way down a corridor he hadn't visited for a while. Some condensation was dripping from one of the seams. He wiped it with a towel from his tool-belt and sighed with relief when it became evident the pipe was not leaking water.

About an hour later, he returned to the open maintenance area and stowed his work belt. It was almost time to meet Roseleen.

He pulled a stool from underneath the large metal table at the bottom of the stairwell. There was a piece of paper with his name on it.

How long had it been there? Triden unfolded the page.

The note was short.

"Please report to the infirmary."

The message made him sweat. He had been interested in learning from the doctor, and yet each time he was pulled back to the infirmary, he couldn't help but get nervous about the end result. Too many Contagions had gone to the infirmary, never to be seen again.

It was rumored those in the infirmary had the worst virus symptoms and therefore were on the shortlist for experimental treatments to find a cure. But his skin condition and reactions were not troublesome, so why would he keep being requested?

Previously, he'd been able to avoid the infirmary until he'd been selected as a study participant with the Society doctor. Even still, he hadn't been detained after giving samples and talking with the physician.

Messages ingrained in him for years were hard to shake. It had taken him weeks to feel comfortable with Roseleen, and he still was amazed she was immune to P3264. She was one of the lucky ones and a survivor like those in the Compound. She hadn't contracted the virus, which still perplexed him.

He packed up his things and climbed the metal stairs. It worried him the note had been left on the table. Clearly, someone had been looking for him. He may have to lay low for the next few days to avoid the discovery of his lunchtime escapes.

He tapped on the doorframe to his supervisor's office.

"I've been called to the infirmary again."

"Thank you for letting me know. Do you know how long you are supposed to be part of the study? We need you here."

"I know. I suspect not much longer. I trust the doctor is making headway on a cure."

"I stopped counting on one a long time ago."

"I still have faith. There has got to be a way to minimize the impact of the virus on other people."

"I hope you're right, Triden."

He exited the W&W Building and turned down an alley to the left. He was about a ten-minute walk to the infirmary. He replayed times with Roseleen in his head as he walked.

He loved being Off Book with her. There was no need to scan his barcode, and they could connect with a deeper sense of intimacy than he'd ever felt for anyone within the Compound. She didn't shy away from the marks on his skin. He felt as if she could see beyond everything on the surface and see him for who he was at his core.

He turned down a paved road leading to the interior administrative offices, including the infirmary. Most Contagions were dedicated to their jobs, and he was the only person on the street. He pushed open the glass door which led to the examination rooms of the infirmary. With a little luck he would be done quickly and able to slip outside to meet Rosey.

The doctor paced the interior of the infirmary. He'd presented the entrance officials with the proper paperwork to remove Triden from the Contagion Compound for his virus participation study.

Had he lost his mind?

His trips to the infirmary were still being done covertly. His manager did not know about any of the research he had conducted on the premises, and he'd forged a signature on the document to retrieve Triden.

When had he gone off the rails looking for a cure? The doctor knew the answer. The first time he'd gone against his supervisor's orders and visited the Compound.

If his research was correct, he wasn't sure who he could trust. He didn't want to think about what would happen if he was wrong about his findings. There was a reason he was continuing to operate incognito. At least Triden would be protected, and his work... well, he didn't want to think about the final outcome to his research if he was wrong.

The young man entered the room and took a seat behind the partition facing the doctor.

"Would you like a blood sample today?" one of the infirmary aides asked the doctor.

"No, thank you." There was no need to poke Triden for a blood sample that would yield the same information he'd already gathered.

"Triden, I've processed paperwork for you to leave the Compound with me."

"I don't want to go."

"I know how you feel about leaving. But I swear, you'll be protected and you will return. If you want."

"If I want? I don't really have a choice, do I? I have to be here because of P3264."

"If my research is accurate, then you will be able to choose where you want to live."

"You found a cure?"

"Not so much a cure as a workaround." The doctor was hesitant to reveal too much inside the walls of the Compound.

"But no one has ever come back after they leave here. Why will I be able to?"

"I'm asking you to trust me, Triden."

"I don't know you. I don't even know what you look like."

"That's fair." The doctor dug around in his satchel and pulled out his Society Department of Human Betterment ID. The gloves made it difficult to flip open the booklet, and it took a moment before he was able to hold up his picture to the partition between them. He watched as Triden leaned closer and scanned the card.

"I still don't know you. How can I trust you?"

"I'm a doctor sworn to provide the best care I can to anyone I treat."

"That didn't save the others who left and never came back."

"I'm not sure who those people were, Triden."

"We know people in the Compound have left for trial studies and have never been seen again."

"They weren't taken for my research. You're the first person I'm taking from the Compound."

"They showed us the images of their treatment. They showed us how they died when the supposed cure didn't work. I don't want to die."

"I swear on my oath as a doctor, you won't die with my treatment."

"How can you promise that?"

"Because I'm giving you complete control."

"Me? How?"

"I will tell you the process when we are ready to test the cure, and you can decide how you'd like to proceed."

"Why can't we do it here?"

"Because I need a controlled environment to test my hypothesis."

"I don't want to go."

"I understand. The paperwork has been submitted. I'm sorry you don't have a choice about leaving. However, I will give you a choice to return after my testing if you want."

He watched the young man fidget in his chair. He could see an array of emotions cross his face, calculating and formulating a response. The doctor could see him trying to find a loophole for going with him, but the doctor hadn't provided one.

"I need you to promise me something."

"What?" He watched as Triden searched for words.

"I want to be able to walk in the woods when we first leave here."

"The woods?"

"Yes. I want to be free to go into the woods."

"Can I come with you?"

Triden hesitated and then nodded affirmatively.

"Sure, we can go for a walk in the woods."

"OK, then I'll come." Triden stood up. "Where do I go to meet you?"

"The infirmary aides will show you the exit."

⊏◍⊐

Triden looked at the photo of the doctor pressed against the clear partition. He was stalling for time, trying to figure out a way not to go with the doctor. He shifted uncomfortably in his chair.

He had to see Roseleen. He had to let her know what was happening. He thought of the messages she had shared with him and looked at the doctor again. He didn't have to see the photo on his identification to know who he was; he had to see the doctor as he was, dressed in heavy leather clothing with an odd mask, a mask with a bird beak-shaped filtration system.

The bird always knows the migration path home.

The doctor is the bird. With the realization, he knew he would be alright, but he still needed to see Rosey.

"I need you to promise me something."

With the doctor's assurance he could enter the woods, Triden stood and looked at the infirmary aide.

"Come this way."

Triden followed the aide to an area of the Compound he'd never been to before. The large partition slid aside, and he was led to the opening where the doctor stood. There was no resistance or delay in leaving. The Compound attendees were obviously aware the doctor was taking his patient with him.

Triden could see a large parking lot behind the doctor. Lots of large commercial trucks rumbled past the entrance. The stream of traffic halted their progression into the parking area; it was the first time Triden had stood within six feet of the doctor without a partition.

"How can I come with you without exposing you?"

"I have a medical van. You can ride in the back if you'd like."

There was a pause in the flow of trucks, and Triden followed the doctor to a white vehicle parked on the far side of the lot. An emblem for the Department of Human Betterment was on the side. The doctor opened the back hatch door, and Triden saw a large, empty black case.

"That's for the clothing I have on," the doctor answered the unasked question. "You can take a seat there." The doctor pointed to a bench folded along the right side of the interior. He placed his medical bag next to the open case.

Triden climbed up into the van interior and pulled the bench down. He found a belt integrated into the seat and strapped himself in place. The doctor closed the back door and walked to the driver's side. He unlocked the door and was a bit clumsy trying to climb into the seat. There was an opening between the front seats and the back of the van, and the doctor turned toward Triden.

"I've never driven with all this stuff on. It's harder to fit behind the steering wheel than I thought."

"I'd offer to drive, but I don't know how."

"Give me a minute. We're not going to go far. I promised you a walk in the woods."

"Thank you."

The doctor struggled to move the folds of heavy leather and squeeze behind the steering wheel. He released the seat lever and moved the chair to its furthest position but still felt uncomfortable as he started the van and moved the gears into reverse. After waiting for a truck to pass, the doctor exited the parking lot.

[][

Jayr didn't drive far, only until the Compound slipped from view. He pulled off the road behind some brush so they would be barely visible from the road. It was time to find out if he was correct or not.

"Before we take our walk, I have something I have to tell you."

"Can it wait until after we walk?" Triden was looking at the sun in the sky; he knew Roseleen would already be at their meeting spot.

"Let me come around to the back. It will make it easier to tell you." He moved to the interior of the van and closed the black case to sit on top.

"I've been researching for a cure for P3264 for years. Whenever I thought I was getting close, a mutation or variable would occur, and I'd find myself back at square one. I've been using data samples provided by the Department of Human Betterment. Recently, I asked for new samples and was denied."

"But you've been getting samples."

"Yes, but not to the knowledge of anyone in my department."

"Why are you telling me this?"

"Because I want you to know why and how I've come to my discovery about the contagion. I also want you to know that no matter what happens, you will not pay the price."

"Pay the price?"

"Yes... Take a life, give your own."

"You're making me nervous."

"That's not my intention, but I do want you to know you are protected and can return to the Compound without any issue."

The doctor reached into his medical bag and pulled out several envelopes. "This is the paperwork for you to return to the Compound at any time." He extended his hand, and Triden took the paper.

"This one is to leave in the van if something goes awry."

"What are you talking about?"

"I'm going to touch you, and if I die, this letter says I took my own life because of the stress of not finding a cure."

"Wait! Why are you going to expose yourself? That's suicide."

"Not if my findings are correct."

Triden shook his head. "No, I can't let you do that.

"We have to trust each other."

Triden struggled. He would have to tell the doctor about Roseleen. He didn't know how he was going to be able to see her without letting the doctor know. "I've been leaving the Compound most days during my lunch break."

"How?"

"I found an abandoned tunnel at my work."

"You've been going outside?"

"Yes. And I met someone, a woman. She says we can be together because I'm the Power Walker."

"The Power what?"

"She says I have the power to walk between the worlds."

"And she's the reason you want to walk in the woods?"

"Yes. I have to tell her I'm leaving."

The doctor reached up and pulled off the bird beak and lowered the cap of the cotton undergarment. His tousled dirty-blond hair was matted on his head by the straps of the mask.

"Wait! What are you doing?"

"Triden, you confirmed what I've already suspected." The doctor smiled and held out his gloved hand and then pulled it back and removed the glove.

"It's nice to meet you, Triden."

Triden tried to pull himself away from the doctor's hand. "I can't touch you."

"Yes, you can. Do you remember I told you that you don't have antibodies to The Path?"

"Yes, but you've seen the rashes. You know I have the virus."

"What I suspected and what we're confirming is you are a healthy young man."

"I feel fine, but I'm still infected."

The doctor shook his head. "No, you're not. You don't have the virus. The doctor laughed. "It never occurred to you that you weren't carrying the virus by being around her?"

"No. She said we could be near each other because I'm the Power Walker."

"Let's go find her."

The two stepped out from the van interior.

"We need to hurry, or we may miss her."

"Lead the way."

Triden set a quick pace, and the doctor followed behind.

Lilia looked in the mirror the nurse handed her. There was still a little swelling but nothing of significance. Her face looked fresh and it would be radiant by the end of the week when she was scheduled to leave the hospital. The surgeon was masterful and had done exactly what she had asked for, nothing more, even though he'd made a variety of suggestions.

"Avoid any topical agents for a few more days. Certainly, no exfoliants or microdermabrasion." The nurse tucked a pillow behind Lilia to prop her up. "You'll want to keep your head above your heart to minimize swelling."

"I know the drill. Thank you."

"Here's a cold compress. Use it as much as possible."

Lilia applied the ice pack to her face along her hairline. A little cold was insignificant. She knew these short-term procedures would ensure healing without lasting discolored pigmentation.

"Can you get me some water? I need to hydrate."

"Of course, I'll have the hospital cafeteria send up some water along with your lunch."

Lilia leaned back into the pillows and closed her eyes. All she had to do was relax and enjoy. Her husband wouldn't be able to talk to her for five glorious days.

⫙

Annabella met with the Society administrator supply agent responsible for Compound logistics.

"So, we're agreed the clothing distribution will be altered to every other day for undergarments and weekly for clean robes." By her calculations, the changes would yield a significant profit for Republic Management.

She looked at the next item on her spreadsheet.

"I'd like to discuss the food shipments."

"The Contagion diet is sanctioned by the Lab of Human Betterment."

"Yes, but they no longer handle the affairs of the Compound."

"Regardless, the diet cannot be changed."

"What do you mean? The protein pucks are expensive."

The administrator looked bored. "Look, all I know is the diet has been customized for the Contagions to mitigate the effects of P3264. It's detrimental to anyone in the Compound not to consume the food provided."

"Really? Food makes a difference?"

"The meals have been validated by a medical nutritional team to ease the symptoms of the virus."

Don't kill the messenger, Annabella told herself as she looked at the supply agent.

"Who is this nutritional team? I want to discuss menu changes with them. There has got to be a way to lower the costs of feeding everyone in the Compound." Annabella had identified food costs as a big opportunity to line their pockets with more profits. She wasn't going to give in so easily.

"I'll have to do some research. It's been a long time since the protocol was put into place."

"Fine. I want the information by tomorrow morning." Annabella turned to exit the office. She was determined to make a change, and it would happen with or without the supply agent's assistance.

CHAPTER 43

Triden cut into the woods, and the doctor followed. They didn't talk; Triden focused on finding his way. The doctor was panting to keep up with the younger man.

Looking at the sun through the treetops; Triden could tell they were cutting it close. The doctor slowed him down, and the young man set a pace to ensure his companion didn't fall too far behind.

"Our meeting place should be near here." He was regretting cutting into the woods before reaching the Compound. The landscape was different than the path he normally took. Instinctively, he was traversing forward to intersect with his normal route, and yet he couldn't be sure from the new angle.

Time was ticking as he pushed on. He knew Roseleen lived deeper in the forest and he would not be able to find her if he missed her. He wanted to call out her name, but breaking the stillness of the air made him uneasy. He didn't want to run the risk of being overheard with the recent logging activity in the woods.

He glanced to his left and right repeatedly, looking for a landmark to show him where he was. He pushed on, trying not to feel panic.

The forest floor was soft and lush as the two men made their way through a myriad of roots and leaves. Moss covered the north side of the tree trunks, and the air was brisk. Triden stopped and looked for anything to indicate where he was in the woods. He was debating retracing his steps, losing valuable time, to find the trail he usually used when he saw a cluster of familiar trees. Sighing with relief, he pushed on.

"It's up here to the left."

The doctor fell slightly behind the younger man as they continued the last stretch.

Rosey!" Triden called out as he saw her familiar charcoal-colored woven shawl. He had barely arrived in time as he observed her collecting her things, getting ready to depart.

She turned, her copper hair catching flecks of sun as she faced him, relief flooding her features.

"I was getting worried." She stopped short when she saw the doctor emerge from behind Triden.

"Roseleen, this is the doctor I told you about."

She looked puzzled.

"He checked me out of the Compound. I had no choice but to let him know about us."

She eyed the older man carefully.

The bird always knows the migration path home, echoed in her ears. It didn't make sense. As she looked at him, she saw a middle-aged man with hints of gray in his hair and creases around his brown eyes. He was still catching his breath after the trek following Triden into the woods.

"Triden," she nodded toward the doctor. "The bird always knows the migration path home."

"Yes! I thought the same thing."

The doctor looked confused. "What do you mean."

Roseleen looked at the older man. "I got a message about a bird migrating. I didn't understand until now it's not a bird with feathers; it's a bird made of leather."

The doctor looked perplexed. Triden stepped forward.

"Rosey gets messages. She knew you would be coming. That's how I knew it was safe to come with you."

Jayr wanted to ask more questions, but they'd already lost a lot of time. "I'm sorry to rush you, but I have to get Triden to a safe place and return the van."

Triden turned to Roseleen. "I love you."

"I love you, too."

"I'll be back as soon as I can."

"I'm coming with you. I don't want to lose you now."

The doctor stepped forward. "I didn't plan for two people."

"I'm going to come with you. I'm sure we can work out something."

The doctor assessed the situation. If Roseleen was with Triden, there was a better chance of the young man staying to help find the antidote for P3264.

"Alright, but we've got to go now."

Roseleen slung her satchel crosswise over her body. "I'm ready."

The three started to traverse toward the van.

⬛

Triden and Roseleen sat on the folding bench in the back of the van, holding hands. The doctor had stripped off the outer layer of heavy leather clothing and packed it in the large black container before sliding behind the wheel of the van.

The traffic back into Society was dense, and the doctor stopped and started as he navigated toward the parking garage of the Department of Human Betterment. His mind was active as he ticked through the next steps for assessing options for a vaccine. He would document every variable he could think of related to Triden and then cross-reference to the data sets he'd gathered. He was looking for anything unique to Triden and not found within the data sets of the other participants. By isolating variables, he could try to mimic the criteria to develop a vaccine. This was the closest to finding a cure he'd been in years.

He glanced over his shoulder. He hadn't planned on the girl being with them. She was dressed in unique attire that would highlight she was not part of Society. She had a woven wrap across her lap. She was wearing a leather tunic and pants, along with leather slippers. Cords tied the items against her body; there was no ornamentation, only purely functional clothing. She was tall and slender and had moved through the forest with familiarity and ease. She was unwrapping a leather packet and extracting sandwich-like items the two shared while he drove. They were engrossed with each other; his presence had been forgotten. His curiosity would have to wait until they were safely settled in his home to learn more about the two.

CHAPTER 44

"Newbiggers Receiving Emoluments"

Jor-dumb was at it again. Sir William screamed at the screen. "Annabella!"

The advisor stepped inside Sir William's office.

"Your fool of a husband is spreading lies. He has got to be stopped."

"What is he saying now?"

"Look!" Sir William pointed to the screen on his office wall. "He has no proof of this."

"Sir William, is there anything, anything at all, which could be considered an abuse of your power? Are you getting any type of support from any of the precincts?"

"Of course not! That's absurd."

"I don't know Jordon's source, but I suspect he found something that is strong enough to make the statement whether or not it's true."

Annabella watched Sir William pace around his office. A vein at his temple was throbbing, and his face was red as he raged. The advisor knew there was truth to Jordon's accusations. She intentionally had not discussed his media schedule with him, but she knew him well enough to know he wouldn't make a blanket statement without something to back it up.

"Sir William, have a seat. I'm sure this will all blow over."

Annabella pulled out a chair and sat facing Sir William. "Tell me, is there any business venture you have which may be construed as a conflict of interest?" She already knew the answer. She'd done a thorough investigation of Sir William before taking the position as his advisor. The Statecraft valued loyalty and believed political success was hinged on the players you partnered with. It was imperative one knew who they selected to enhance their personal advancement. Annabella had seen an opportunity when she learned more about Sir William. A narcissist who demanded loyalty in exchange for power offered a unique opportunity. Placate his ego, boost his personal opinion of himself, and identify the opportunities within the topics which bored him. That's how Annabella and Jordon had manipulated their way into two lucrative contracts, with a third underway.

"My businesses are being managed by my son. You know I made him the Executive in Charge when I was sworn into office. I am not involved."

Annabella nodded agreement even though she knew Sir William's child from his first marriage was the CEO on paper only. Sir William still dictated the business objectives.

"What about The Flodden Club?"

"What about it?"

"Some could consider it a conflict of interest since you entertain at a club you own."

"That's nonsense. I play Quilt with my personal funds."

"Yes, but you do make money from the food and beverage side of the house."

"How is that an emolument? It is food eaten by those in Society."

"Yes, but you have entertained visiting dignitaries as well. It might be time to host those events at a Statecraft venue until this news blows over."

"Tell your husband to cease his inaccurate and false accusations."

"We barely talk, Sir William. We live in different parts of the house." The lie was easy to sell.

"I don't like it, Annabella."

"I know, Sir William. But I'm a mother with her children to consider."

The doctor, Roseleen, and Triden transferred to the doctor's car after returning the van. It was late afternoon, much later than the previous excursions, and the doctor felt anxious at the possibility of drawing attention to the two passengers. Neither Roseleen nor Triden were dressed as others in Society. It would be important to change their attire as quickly as possible once they were safely secured at his home.

Jayr was surprised they both adapted to the movement of the vehicles so easily. Triden would have been previously transported to the Compound. However, based on the young girl's attire, he doubted she'd ever been inside a moving vehicle. But the two were intent on each other; the movement was not their focus.

He lived in the northwest section of Precinct One, close to the Presidential Palace. The sun was beginning to set as he pulled his car into the parking structure of his housing compound. The tall structure had twenty-eight floors, and the doctor lived in the penthouse at the top. His reserved parking space was located near the main elevator bank; he was thankful they wouldn't have to walk far and could minimize their visibility.

He parked the car and turned to his two passengers.

"I'm going to step out first and make sure no one is around. I will signal you to join me when I feel confident we won't be seen."

Roseleen and Triden nodded with understanding, and the doctor opened his car door. He tried to look relaxed as he stepped toward the elevator and casually looked around the stalls. A light flickered overhead; otherwise, there was no movement.

He turned toward the car and signaled for the two to join him as he pressed the call button. Roseleen and Triden joined him as the doors slid open and the doctor stepped inside. Triden stepped forward, but Roseleen hesitated.

"What is this?"

"It's an elevator."

"A what?"

Triden reached out, offering her his hand.

"It's OK. We have them at the Compound. It will move us between the floors of the building."

Roseleen stepped forward hesitantly, and the doors slid closed behind her. The three of them stood inside, and the doctor flashed his ID to trigger the button for his residence. Triden noticed he did not have a personal barcode on his left wrist like all the Contagions. He understood why Roseleen didn't have one, living in the woods, but wouldn't the doctor have had the same type of identification?

The elevator jerked slightly as it started its quick assent to the top floor. Roseleen, sure-footed in the forest, was surprised by the movement and clutched at Triden's arm.

"It's OK. That's the worst of it."

"Really? Can you tell my stomach? It feels like it's in my throat."

The two of them laughed, trying to defuse the tension.

The doors opened to an alcove with two residence doors. The doctor turned to the one on the left and scanned his card again to open the door.

"The other side belongs to a cabinet member. Fortunately, they travel a lot for their work."

As the three stepped inside, Triden marveled at the space. It was nothing like his own quarters. No cement blocks with a bed and simple mattress. It was open and airy. The space could easily house his studio ten times over.

There was an upholstered sectional and chair with a low table in one area with a large screen nearby. A high glass-topped table with chairs was in another section. And a third section contained things he'd never seen. The doctor was walking them through a tour.

"This is the kitchen area. Let me know if you'd like anything to eat or drink."

"Down this hall are the bedrooms, my office, and a home gym."

"A what?" The doctor was reminded again of how the two people in his home did not fit into Society.

"I'll show you."

The doctor led the two down the hallway, pointing out the bedrooms and his office. Then they walked into a room filled with a variety of equipment Triden and Roseleen had never seen before: an odd plank wrapped with rubber, benches, and metal bars with black plates on either end.

"I'm going to test your physical endurance here."

"What for?"

"I'm looking for anything that sets you apart from the others in the Compound. But it can wait until morning. Let's get some dinner."

The three walked back to the main living area. The doctor opened a cold cupboard and pulled out vegetables and meat, and started to prep the meal.

"Can I help?" Roseleen offered. Triden was watching, unclear what he was looking at as the doctor started to scrape the surface from several orange rods.

"Sure, can you peel these?"

"What are they?"

"Carrots. You've never seen a carrot?"

"No." Triden looked at the other items on the kitchen counter. "What are those?"

"Onions."

"And this?"

"Pork chops."

Triden knew that the flavors of the protein pucks correlated to non-processed food, but he'd never seen what the food looked like. Nothing on the kitchen counter looked like the protein pucks he'd consumed since entering the Compound.

He looked at Roseleen. She seemed familiar with the food; he suspected she'd seen similar items in the forest and surrounding fields.

Soon, the kitchen was filled with interesting aromas, and Triden felt hunger gripping his stomach. The sandwich he'd shared with Roseleen earlier had served its purpose. His priority had been finding Roseleen before venturing to Society with the doctor and he'd missed his normal meal.

He couldn't believe she was here. She'd left without concern for her family. Wouldn't they be worried about her when she didn't return? He was looking forward to time with her alone. There was so much he wanted to share with her, and he wanted to savor the extended time together.

"Triden, there are plates in the cabinet." The doctor gestured toward a door over the countertop. "Can you set the table?"

He found a variety of dishware in the interior, pulled out three large plates, and moved to the table. He wasn't sure how to set a table. He'd been eating protein pucks without a plate for years. He was only familiar with the glasses at the Compound containing either tea or one of the fermented beverages at The Barcode. He placed a plate in front of three of the chairs.

The meal was luxurious to Triden. He savored each bite and asked questions about the food and how it was prepared. Roseleen was also curious about some of the ingredients. As Triden watched her, he realized they both were navigating their way in a strange new world.

"Tomorrow, I'll get you clothes so you'll blend into Society easier. Triden, your family was from Precinct Nine, correct?"

"Yes."

"Precinct Nine no longer exists. It was turned into a mass graveyard for those who were terminated and the buildings were abandoned. If anyone meets you, tell them you are visiting from Precinct Three."

"Is that where my parents are buried?"

"It's impossible to know, but it's highly likely they are buried at Memorial Park in what used to be P9."

Triden had vague memories of his parents. He wondered if they had suffered or had died quickly. He had been separated from them when he was little, and his memories had faded.

Roseleen reached for his hand under the table and rubbed her thumb over his palm as comfort. He turned toward her and their eyes locked in understanding.

The Forest Seers had lost loved ones, too. Many had refused to heed the messages from The Source and had stayed behind in Society. Only those who had ventured into the woods had survived.

"Roseleen, based on your clothing, I take it you live in the woods?"

"Yes. We moved into the forest when it was evident there was a shift happening in Society. We left several years before the terminations."

"And no one in your community contracted P3264?"

"No. We have stayed to ourselves for the past thirty years. I was born in the woods."

"That's interesting. The pathogen moved quickly in certain precincts; others were less impacted. Society acted hastily to isolate and stop the spread, but it still had devastating effects on parts of the Statecraft."

"Will your family be worried about you? We didn't give you an opportunity to notify anyone you were coming with us."

Roseleen smiled. The doctor didn't know she was able to communicate with her family mentally by leveraging The Source. "It's alright. They know I'm with Triden and I'm safe. I am safe, aren't I?"

"There's no one here who wishes you harm. We've been looking for a cure for P3264. The only reason I'm asking for secrecy is because I've operated outside of normal protocols to continue my research. Once I can present my findings to the Statecraft, it will be possible to introduce you, and you can move freely."

"Triden said you told him he could return to the Compound anytime."

"That's true, but I'm hoping he'll stay long enough for me to find the missing component to my research."

Triden looked from Roseleen to the doctor.

"I'll stay as long as I feel we're making progress. It is vital to find a cure, and I hope one day everyone in the Compound will be able to move freely again."

"That's my hope, too, Triden."

⁂

Hello, Mother. I'm with Triden, and I'm fine. Roseleen closed her eyes and willed the message to her mother. It was the easiest conduit to her family when her mind was clear, without distractions from the world around her.

Dearest Daughter, I suspected as much when you didn't return. Still, I worry about you. The loggers have been making deeper advances into the woods.

I am in Society with Triden and the doctor.

You're not in the woods? Daughter, that distresses me.

We are safe. The doctor is the bird.

The migrating bird?

Yes, Mother. I am on my path.

Roseleen's head started to hurt. It took effort and focus to communicate. *I'm tired, Mother. I will connect with you tomorrow.*

Thank you, Daughter. I love you.

I love you, too.

Roseleen cleared her mind and turned to settle next to Triden. His breathing was slow and rhythmic as he slept. She had fantasized about spending more time with him since they'd first met. She wrapped her arm around his waist.

The day had been exhausting and filled with many new sights and experiences. Roseleen had heard about Society as it had existed decades earlier, yet nothing matched the technology and framework she'd observed today.

She could tell Triden had been operating on adrenaline, and she hadn't been surprised he'd fallen asleep quickly once his head touched the pillow. The doctor only had one guest room, and the two had opted to share the large bed instead of relegating one of them to the couch in the common area. The doctor had accepted their decision and had given them night clothes, toothbrushes, and other toiletries.

Both Triden and Roseleen had been intrigued by the sweet paste used to scrub their teeth with a soft-bristled brush. While Triden had a similar toothbrush at the Compound, Roseleen used the fibers of tree branches to brush hers.

The clothing, a cotton top with drawstring pants, felt cozy, and the room was almost too warm with the clothing, blanket, and Triden sleeping beside her. She was used to the cool night air in the treehouse, and her skin felt dry. She pushed the blanket aside and was grateful for the cooler air around her.

Ego will betray those with overconfidence.

Roseleen couldn't sleep. What did the message mean? Who's ego? The doctor? Hers or Triden's? She tried to shake the sense of dread she felt about the message. She finally drifted into a fitful sleep haunted by images of the doctor and Triden being escorted by men in military attire.

[ll[

Benjam waited at his usual table at The Barcode and scanned the room for Triden. It wasn't like his close friend to be so late. It was the social time for everyone in the Compound to connect after a day at their various posts. No one missed the time to interact with others since the majority of their days were conducted in silence. Without the outlet at The Barcode and On Book sessions, the monotony of living in the Compound could make anyone go stir crazy.

He finally tapped the screen at the table and searched the log for Triden's name. Whenever anyone was off their regular schedule, it was posted on the screens to minimize concern when protocol and expectations did not align.

It didn't take long to scan the list since so many in the Compound avoided the infirmary. Triden was listed as a vaccine trial participant who had been taken off-site. Fear gripped Benjam, and he tried to push down a wave of anxiety.

This wasn't good. No one had ever come back from research trials. Benjam feared he'd never see his friend again, and he hadn't even been able to say goodbye.

⫸

Triden ran in place on a rotating conveyor belt. Sweat glistened on his bare chest, accentuating his crimson rashes. A variety of electrodes were taped to his body, all gathering data related to his heartbeat, body temperature, and oxygen levels. The doctor was developing a wide array of data points to help him hone in on the variables Triden presented to his research.

It had only taken Triden a few minutes to get comfortable running on the device, and he'd quickly found his stride.

The doctor tapped the screen on the wall by the treadmill and watched several moving bars displaying Triden's vital signs. He was in excellent shape. The diet at the Compound was controlled, and while everyone was allowed to take as much as they wanted, obesity was not common. It appeared the protein pucks were viewed as mandatory sustenance and nothing more. Overindulging was not an issue.

Gleekma, a sweet delicacy, was eaten by many in Society

but had not been offered at the Compound. The doctor marveled when he watched both Roseleen and Triden nibble at it tentatively. Roseleen had made a face and commented on how sweet it was. Triden had eaten the whole pastry as if he'd discovered food for the first time.

Triden had devoured everything on his dinner plate the evening before and asked for seconds at the breakfast table. The doctor enjoyed watching him try the different dishes placed before him. Roseleen was also curious about items found outside of the forest. They both savored each bite, and the doctor was looking at the food he took for granted with fresh eyes.

"Thank you, Triden. You can stop running. I have enough data for today."

The doctor pressed the buttons on the treadmill and the conveyor belt slowed. Triden stepped off and picked up a towel to wipe his face.

"It feels strange to run and not go anywhere."

The doctor smiled. "I'm grateful on days when the weather is bad to have a way to exercise indoors."

"Did you find anything?"

"I'm going to input this information into my system and analyze it. I'm looking for anything outside of normal ranges which could be a differential in the data set."

Roseleen had been quietly watching Triden on the treadmill when she got a message from The Source.

Intentions will show the motive and the means.

She hadn't shared her abilities with the doctor beyond the moment in the woods. She knew from the stories of the Forest Seers that those with her skills had often been persecuted. People who did not understand often reacted with fear and distrust.

The doctor tapped the screen and requested his car be pulled to the front of the building.

"I won't be long. I'm also going to pick up clothes for you

both so you can go outside. Until you can assimilate into Society, please don't leave my flat. I should return in several hours."

Jayr made his way to the door and turned to face his two visitors. "Help yourself to any food in the kitchen. Also, I told the building security guard my cousins are visiting from Precinct Three in case anyone asks. My advice: don't answer the door if anybody comes up."

"I'm going to shower." Triden stepped into the bedroom they shared. Roseleen continued to the large living space. She explored the cabinets in the kitchen area and found several interesting pastries. She pulled a packet of dried tea leaves from her satchel and boiled some water to steep the familiar beverage. She wanted to feel a sense of normalcy in this strange place.

Soon Triden joined her, his hair still damp. He wore the familiar brown Compound robe, tied at his waist. He'd left the hood in their bedroom.

"I made us some tea, and I found these." Roseleen held out a plate with the cream-filled pastries.

They moved to the dining table and marveled at the taste of the confection. It was light and delicate with a hint of fruit essence neither could place.

"I'm not sure how I can go back to the Compound after this. The protein pucks leave a lot to be desired after tasting all this food."

"Don't remind me. The piece I had was enough." Roseleen laughed at the memory.

"I hope the doctor can find a vaccine. I've never thought anyone would be able to leave the Compound, and I'm beginning to have hope."

"Me, too." Roseleen paused. "I'm also hoping he can find out more information about the loggers cutting down all the trees."

"We both have a lot to gain from the doctor."

"He's a good man."

"Yes... and he won't be back for a while. Care to join me in the bedroom?" Triden stood and extended his hand. He loved connecting with her.

Roseleen stood and took his hand.

"Lead the way!"

The loggers stopped cutting. Snowflakes were starting to fall, and a storm was brewing on the horizon. Their work would have to wait. The foreman looked at his personal screen. They had cleared ten acres before the weather had turned. It would be a sufficient contribution for the day. The goals were aggressive, and they would be able to return in the morning after the storm had blown through.

Adin and his father stood within the tree line and observed as the members of Society climbed into their trucks and pulled away from the clearing.

"Unfortunately, they'll be back."

"Yes. I think it's time to make plans to move. It will take time for us to set up a new camp, and we don't want to be left without shelter as winter turns harsher."

"Do we really have to dismantle the treehouses?"

"Yes. If we leave a trace of our homes, we could be targeted by those who don't want people living outside of Society. We learned the hard way, before we left Society, that those with a different viewpoint are ostracized and ridiculed."

The two could still smell the slight burn of wood from the electric saws which mowed through the thick tree trunks with ease. The numerous tree stumps and sawdust powder dotted the landscape and reminded the two of how much had been lost in the few weeks of the logger's presence.

⫷

Sir William handed his tableau board to his game steward and assessed the pile of betting tiles. He had amassed a small fortune, and the game had only been in play for little more than an hour.

His mind wandered from the table. There was no need to

reintroduce the Contagions back into Society. An excessive amount of money had already gone into funding research that could be utilized elsewhere. Sir William had other plans for the funds budgeted for research. Canceling the program would allow him to divert the monies without having to engage with the Budgetary Committee of the Signet. He pushed his chair away from the table.

"Players, you will have to forgive me. I am unable to stay longer."

He stood and waited while his steward gathered the betting tiles and counted them with the dealer. Once the amount had been confirmed, he was given a voucher indicating the amount of funds being transferred to his club account. As usual, he begrudgingly tipped the dealer and his game steward the minimally acceptable amount.

Mallor entered the Quilt room and motioned to Sir William. The president was thankful for the added reinforcement to leave the room. Generally, it was frowned upon to clear the table of betting tiles unless game play had been underway for at least two hours.

Sir William said his goodbyes and moved to the hallway.

"Who is responsible for these protests?"

"You're not going to like it, Sir William."

"Tell me."

"Jordon Connor has been orchestrating a variety of media promotions encouraging people of Society to take to the streets."

"He has got to be stopped."

"Would you like me to bring him in for questioning?"

"No, no, not yet. Let me discuss it with Annabella. If she can't control her husband, then it will be a matter for your expertise."

"Very well, Sir William. I will wait for your direction." Mallor knew the president counted on him for his skills; however, the jowly man did not want to know the details of his work other than he was effective at what he did. Mallor appreciated Sir William's apathy. It allowed him to navigate more efficiently without the need to be concerned about human rights. It was easier and more enjoyable to use pain and fear to get to his end result.

[III]

"I guessed on the sizing." Jayr unwrapped several packages containing a variety of clothes. The doctor had purchased multiple outfits for each. Triden slipped into a button-down shirt with long sleeves and a collar extended upwards to frame his neck. Light blue stripes were etched through the fabric. Sleeves extended below his fingertips, and the doctor showed him how to fold the cuffs and clip them into position. Each arm had ribbon-like strands to tie to form an elaborate finish. The shirt was comfortable, with the exception of feeling bound at the wrists.

The doctor handed him a pair of dress pants that he slipped on over his cotton Compound undergarments. They were made with a ribbed fabric and had suspenders to pull over his shoulders. It felt very different than the brown robe he was accustomed to wearing.

"Good, the fit is correct. I made sure to get you long sleeves to cover your barcode."

Triden was still getting used to moving around the doctor's residence without scanning his wrist at every doorway. It was second nature to wave his left hand at the Compound, and only now, when it wasn't a requirement to move, was it triggering feelings of ambivalence about the human-made mark on his skin. He had only begun to understand the differences between the Compound and Society, and he wasn't sure he liked them. The waste and indulgence seemed to infiltrate every detail, and after the sparseness and minimalism at the

Compound, it was hard to understand. *Why did his shirt need ribbon ties? Why all the extra effort to present oneself?*

The food was their highlight. Both Triden and Roseleen were giddy trying the different morsels they found in the kitchen. They both favored the forest tea Roseleen had in her satchel over the syrupy and sweet nectars they discovered in Jayr's pantry, but the savory and sweet items they'd consumed were unlike anything either had tried before.

The doctor handed Roseleen several bags. "I'm not familiar with women's clothing, so I relied on the shop assistant to guide me."

She carried the bags to the bedroom and extracted several dresses folded between thin sheets of paper. She quickly swapped her own clothing for the smooth, crisp, cream-colored fabric of one of the gowns. It was light compared to the leather pieces which comprised her outer wear, and it felt strange as she buttoned the double-breasted panel. The dress was designed to accent her figure and was tailored at the waist. Long sleeves with a floral pattern accented the solid fabric of the skirt and placard of fabric with a notched collar high at her neck.

Not all is how it appears. The message from The Source rang in her ears.

She found a pair of leather boots with a slight heel, which curved inward in an ornate fashion, and thin stockings to cover her feet. The boots felt tight and confining compared to her hand-sewn leather slippers.

She looked in the full-length mirror on the back of the bedroom door, and she didn't recognize herself. The girl of the woods had turned into a woman of Society. She felt uncomfortable as she exited the bedroom to rejoin Triden and the doctor in the main living area. She walked unsteadily on the angled boots, and the folds of the fabric rustled softly as she walked.

"Wow." Triden's expression showed her he liked what he

saw. The doctor smiled as well.

"The clerk was about your size, and this is what she said would work. She was right."

"Are we going out?" Triden looked to the doctor.

"I want to make sure we don't create any suspicions, and this way, if we need to go out, you'll have a better chance of blending in. Remember, if you cross paths with anyone, Triden, you're my cousin and Roseleen is your girlfriend, and you are both from Precinct Three."

"What if they start asking us questions?"

"I should be with you, and I'll take the lead. If you're alone, shut down the conversation. Tell anyone you don't have time to chat."

Roseleen stepped out of the boots. "Is it alright if I don't wear these in the house?"

The doctor nodded. "I do ask you to wear Society clothing while you're here, but it's fine not to wear the shoes indoors."

Roseleen sighed with relief. Accustomed to being barefoot, the leather shoes did not feel comfortable even though they fit her feet properly. She would adapt with time.

⁜

"Annabella, you have got to control your husband. He's agitating Society and undermining our efforts."

"I'll see what I can do, but I can't promise anything. Jordon has a mind of his own."

"There's no reason we need to keep funding research that hasn't yielded a vaccine when those in the Compound are safe. There's no risk of spreading P3264 with them contained. There hasn't been a recorded case in Society in over twenty years. Your husband shouldn't be agitating the situation."

Annabella nodded. As long as the Contagions were living in the Compound, Republic Management would be profitable. A vaccine would undermine their plans. It was time for Jordon to dial back his rhetoric. The goal had been to create a diversion in order to establish the privatization of the Compound with minimal scrutiny. Since they'd been awarded the contract, Jordon could maneuver attention to another topic.

Mallor entered Sir William's office as Annabella stood to leave. The advisor was not a fan of the middle-aged man. She couldn't put her finger on the feeling she had, but her gut advised her to stay out of Mallor's way. She knew very little about his role in Sir William's inner circle, but she'd heard enough rumors to know side stepping was her best option.

"I'll leave the two of you and see what I can do about Jordon."

"Just put a muzzle on him. That should do the trick." Mallor smirked, and Annabella couldn't leave the room fast enough.

There's always a fork in the road.

Roseleen knew she'd been diverted off her normal course and she was trying to adjust to being indoors, sequestered in Society. She and Triden observed the world below from the windows of the doctor's penthouse suite. Strange vehicles propelled people around Society on tracks. Cars and vans like the one the doctor had used to transport them to his home filled the streets below. Horns and other sounds echoed upwards; there was an energy and hum around her making it difficult to communicate with her mother and others in the Forest Seer Communion.

The two were dressed in Society outfits but remained barefoot. They curled next to each other and held hands on the couch. The doctor left early in the morning for the Lab of Human Betterment, and they were left on their own.

The screen to their right flashed news articles and commentary. They had learned the bottom banner was a direct feed from the President of Society. Images of Sir William Newbiggers showed him to be a rotund older man. With a dark mustache, splotchy skin, and hair twirled atop his head, he struck them both as self-absorbed and overly indulgent. It was perplexing that this was the person chosen by Society to lead government functions.

"When there's a WILL, there's a WAY!"

"Wow, he even uses his name."

The image on the screen showed Sir William with his wife leaving the Presidential Palace. She was a tall, willowy blond who appeared to be decades younger than the president. Their two daughters each held one of their mother's hands. Sir William waved to reporters and appeared oblivious of his family's presence.

"It is so strange here."

"I know. I'm not used to all the noise, and the images and voices are non-stop."

They had already lowered the volume on the screen to the lowest setting, but it was impossible to fully silence the device.

"I had no idea this is what Society is like. The memories with my parents are so different."

"Tell me."

"I don't recall very much. I remember my mother always seemed to be smiling, and my father, he was kind. They were always so loving toward me."

"Why didn't they go with you?"

"They were transferred to a holding facility for adults who tested positive for P3264. Children were separated from their families when it was evident younger people were more resistant to the virus. Most of the adults died from the virus. Others were terminated to stop the spread."

"The Seers tell the story of how The Source informed them of shifts in Society. We didn't know at the time the virus was the cause of the changes. We knew we needed to leave. Not everyone listened to the messages, but my family, along with others, invested in developing our community deep in the forest."

"What happened to the ones who stayed?"

"I'm not sure. I hope they survived, but it's impossible to know."

"What does The Source say?"

"Nothing particular about this. The messages are to inform action. Since there's nothing to be done to reunite with the ones left behind, no messages come forth."

"I love you have this ability."

"You don't think I'm a freak?"

"Hardly. If anything, I'm the freak. I'm marked by the virus."

"It's interesting. I noticed the rashes at first, but now I don't see them. I see you."

They leaned in and kissed each other. It didn't take long for them to remove their Society clothes. Their naked bodies intertwined, and they kissed again. They moved together in a rhythm of their own which drowned out the noises of Society around them.

███

The doctor stared at his data. "There has got to be a variable I'm missing," he mused aloud. Tapping the screen, he selected a different grouping of data and looked at the generated graph. Nothing appeared as an outlier. Everyone in the Compound matched with others in a statistically significant way. But Triden was different. Besides not having antibodies and naturally fending off P3264, there had to be another trait Jayr could isolate.

He rubbed his eyes. Staring at the screen was taking its toll, and he stood to stretch. He exited the lab and made his way down the hall to the break room, and poured himself a cup of coffee.

The screen on the wall blared out the news. Sir William stood in front of a podium and addressed a crowd outside the Presidential Palace.

"Over the years, Society has dedicated itself to finding a cure for P3264 using both financial and intellectual resources, and to date, there has been no vaccination found to halt the spread of this deadly disease."

The doctor watched the screen.

"We have shown isolation can control the spread of P3264. Ever since the Compound has been in operation, no new cases of P3264 have been reported. Those in the Compound are contributing members of Society who have full lives within the Compound. It is time to accept this as the new normal."

The doctor pulled out a chair at a table and sat down. *This doesn't sound good.*

"That's why we're halting all research on finding a cure for P3264. It is time for us to focus our resources and time on efforts which support all in Society."

The doctor lurched forward, sloshing coffee out of his cup. He absentmindedly grabbed a towel and wiped the hot liquid from the tabletop.

Did his supervisor know about this change?

He tossed the remainder of his drink into the sink, rinsed his mug, and quickly returned to his lab. Tapping on the screen, he sent a message to his manager.

"I saw the news report. Sir William is halting all P3264 research. Please advise."

He started pacing the room. Waiting for a reply was untenable. It was time to see his supervisor in person. He grabbed his medical bag and personal screen and made his way down the hallway to the office located at the north corner of the building.

The doctor knocked on the open door leading to the interior of his manager's office. Masha, about ten years his junior, looked up from her desk.

"Jayr, I know why you're here, but I don't have any answers. I've been trying to get information. Sir William only made the announcement today without letting anyone in the department know his intentions beforehand."

"Can he do this? I'm making strides in my research. I know I'll have something soon."

"You've had these feelings before, and yet something always changes."

"True, but..." *Did he dare tell Masha he'd gone against her wishes and been visiting the Compound and this time was different?*

"Can you give me two weeks?"

"I don't know. You might be done as of today. I'm still trying to learn the implications of the announcement."

"This is inhumane. Of course, the Contagions have a life,

but it's not like ours. They are confined to the Compound. How can the administration decide their fate so randomly without consideration?"

"There's a growing shift in Society. Many believe the resources assigned to finding a vaccine should be used differently since the threat to Society has been eliminated as long as the Contagions are kept segregated in the Compound."

"I thought the protests highlighted the public interest in the work we're doing. The goal has always been to reintroduce those infected back into Society."

"Sir William apparently believes sentiments have changed and only a few still desire funding the research. Regardless, it's out of my hands."

Jayr made his way back to his lab. He knew he was getting close. Finding Triden and adding more samples to his data was the most significant advancement he'd made in years. He had to find the key before his work was shut down.

⫼

Lilia smiled as she saw the aide assigned to her task force. He was young and fit, unlike her bloated husband. He had easily replaced the mail clerk dismissed weeks earlier.

"Please come in. I have some items for you which aren't quite ready. I only need a few minutes."

The young man entered her office, and she shut the door, unconcerned about how it looked to those with desks outside. They had signed privacy documents that forbade them from discussing anything occurring at the Presidential Palace. Besides, she was a married woman and the aide was young enough to be her son. No one would believe it.

It didn't take long to undo his belt and pull his pants down, and with a few hand strokes, he was ready. She liked the feel of his youthful body inside her, their toned skin intertwined.

The last time she'd welcomed Sir William into her bed, she'd been assaulted by the rolls and sags of his stomach as he tried to thrust into her. Since then, she hadn't entertained having relations with her husband. He'd only gotten more bloated with time, and she'd already achieved what she wanted by having a union with him. Sir William provided her with the lifestyle she craved. She had procreated with him to ensure her foothold within the upper echelon, and now she was Top Lady of Society.

The president had more to lose than she did. He needed her to play her part entertaining dignitaries. She knew he had interludes with a variety of people, breaking their wedding vows. She felt no remorse; he had destroyed any feelings she'd had for him as she learned about the string of conquests. Her payback was to engage sexually with many youthful men who came across her path. One day, when Sir William was out of office, she would divorce him. Retaining Top Lady as a title, she would have no trouble attracting one of the most eligible men in Society, someone who actually was successful versus paper rich and monetarily poor. Lilia had been tricked by Sir William's façade, and only after they'd gotten married did she learn about his financial house of cards. With his Quilt addiction, hush money paid to avoid sexual scandal, and businesses funneling money to support a lavish lifestyle beyond their means, Lilia learned she needed to protect her assets. She was not going to divorce Sir William without ensuring every penny she'd earned being his wife would be hers.

The aide had an orgasm quickly, faster than she would have liked, but the act wasn't about sexual pleasure. It was sexual payback. She would find a time to reveal her indiscretions to Sir William, and she would make sure he squirmed, hearing every little detail.

Jayr, Triden, and Roseleen sat at the dining table, finishing a breakfast of fruit encased in a light, feathery pastry. Triden could tell he was already putting on weight in the few days at the doctor's home. The sweets, along with meat and eggs, filled their plates, and Roseleen and Triden enjoyed every bite. The doctor smiled. Seeing the food through their eyes renewed his appreciation for the items he took for granted each day.

The doctor's personal screen pinged, and he glanced at the device and shook his head.

"P3264 research has ended as of midnight. You have been reassigned to another project. Details below…"

The doctor didn't read further. He already backed up most of the research data to his personal screen when he first heard the news. The data could be archived at any moment now the news was official, and he'd no longer be able to access information. He'd siphoned as much of it as he could.

"It's official. I've been reassigned to the hospital for general practice rotations."

"You're not looking for a vaccine anymore?"

"Not officially, but I'm not giving up."

"Don't you need access to a lab to develop a vaccine?"

"I'll still be able to use my lab. I just won't be able to be open on the nature of my research."

"Are you taking a big risk?"

"I don't think so. No one will be paying attention to my research, and I can always work on it at night."

Jayr realized, now that the announcement had been made, it would be impossible to visit the Compound. He was thankful Triden had come with him to Society.

The answer was buried somewhere in the data he was transferring to his device. He was bound to find it given enough time. He couldn't bear the thought of his work being for naught.

Jayr confirmed access to the download. He knew there would be a record of his data access, but he doubted anyone would pay attention to a scrapped project.

He activated his personal screen and typed a memo to his supervisor. "Permission requested to provide a final recap of vaccine study findings to Lab of Human Betterment Board of Physicians. Please advise time and place for meeting." It was customary protocol to present findings whenever a study ended. The doctor wasn't sure exactly what he was going to convey at the meeting, but he had until then to find the missing link.

Triden sighed. "Maybe we're destined to be at the Compound. I know I feel safer there."

"My life work has been devoted to finding a cure to reunite those infected back into Society. We're so close, I have to try."

The picture shows the wrong story. The words boomed in Roseleen's head. It was the strongest message she'd received since she'd entered Society.

"Is there a different way to look at your data?"

"I'm sure there's another way."

"I think we often believe we have the picture in front of us, and yet there's always a different viewpoint." Roseleen didn't want to share The Source message verbatim with the doctor to avoid him questioning her insights.

"It's a good reminder of the basic decrees of research. I'll try to put a fresh lens on my work."

Roseleen had hope. "I'm optimistic you can find it. We wouldn't be here otherwise."

Sir William was bored. He looked at the time in the lower corner of the screen on the wall next to his desk and was relieved he could leave for the Quilt Club in less than an hour. He'd been on a winning streak, and he was eager to play. The precinct head was droning on about some nonsense related to resources. Where was Annabella? She should be here to manage the information flow within the room. There was no need for him to be bothered by this tedium.

He picked up his personal screen and typed out a message to his followers. *"We are going BIG! When there's a WILL, there's a WAY."*

The ribbon of text rotated across the bottom of the large screen. He didn't elaborate, liking the hint of information to keep people attached to their screens, wanting more.

"Presidential Rally next week! Come and hear about the progress we are making!"

Sir William enjoyed the control of the information banner. Annabella apparently had some success with *Jor-dumb*. His face had been absent from the media feeds for the past few days.

The conversation stopped, and Sir William realized the group was looking to him for a response. The Precinct Two Head looked at him expectantly.

"Sir William?"

"Yes. You must forgive me. Urgent Statecraft business calls." He stood, inferring he'd received a message on his personal screen. "We can convene again tomorrow."

"But Sir William, what about the trade agreement?"

"Impossible to respond right now. I will give my reply to Annabella, and she can distribute."

The precinct head stifled his feelings of frustration. This meeting had been similar to many before. Sir William's apathy prevented any actions. His lack of involvement had almost halted the passing of the Statecraft budget, cutting vital resources to many in Society.

"I guess next time, I need more pictures." The Precinct Two Head addressed the Head of Precinct Three as they filed from the room.

"Or use his name more. That's my trick to keep his attention." Both heads of state looked at the screen.

"The Quilt game is scheduled to start soon. Are you playing today?"

"Fortunately, no. I was able to get the approvals I needed for infrastructure last week. My budget can't support another Quilt game until next month after appropriations."

"I know how you feel. Last year, it cost double what it needed to for implementation of our policies."

"Do you know Jordon Connor?"

"Yes, I met him at a Statecraft dinner last year."

"Maybe it's time to give him a call. An anonymous tip about Statecraft business practices might help us."

"I've thought of it. However, The Flodden Club is outside of the Justice Halls of Parliament. Any money lost at the table is considered a matter of private affairs and does not pertain to State business."

"Even though the table is funded by precinct money?"

"With Sir William appointed to audit oversight, I doubt it will get a lot of traction."

"That seems criminal."

"It is. Let's give it time. I suspect Sir William's ego will be his downfall."

"One can only hope. As far as I'm concerned, elections can't happen soon enough."

※

Annabella and Jordon lay in bed, bodies intertwined.

"You're going to be late, Bella." Jordon kissed the top of his wife's head.

"I blocked off my calendar. This morning is the standard precinct briefing, and then Sir William will be heading to the Quilt table."

"How many hours does he actually work?"

"Let's not go down that path. Let's just say he works enough for us to get what we want."

"Brilliant!"

"Thanks for laying low for a few days. It's really annoying Sir William you're getting so much screen time."

"Well, we got the contract and the research is being halted, so the Compound will be around to generate income for us for years to come."

"It is a genius plan."

"You laid the foundation, Bella, and queued it up perfectly."

"Once you get to know him, he's pretty easy to manipulate."

"It's a good thing our foreign counterparts haven't figured it out yet."

"Don't be so sure. Sir William doesn't treat anyone appropriately. In or outside of Society, he demands loyalty and servility."

"That's a scary thought."

"I try not to think about it." Annabella slid out of bed. "Time to babysit our President. See you tonight."

⚊⚋⚊

Jayr collapsed onto the couch. Triden and Roseleen were in the kitchen, concocting a meal using the items in the pantry. The doctor had shown them how to access recipes on the screen, and they filled their days learning new techniques.

"Really, you don't have to cook. I can help."

"It's fun."

"Yes, but you aren't responsible for making every meal." The doctor looked tired. "I've been scheduled to present my research."

"So, it's done?" Triden looked worried. "No cure and no chance of leaving the Compound now?"

"I copied as much data as I could. Don't give up hope yet."

"I've loved being outside the Compound. Before I found a way to the woods, I was content. Now the thought of being confined is agonizing."

"I can only imagine."

"Does he have to go back to the Compound? Or could he come to the forest?"

"As far as I'm concerned, you can both stay here or go back to the woods. That said, I hope you'll stay a few more days."

"With the research being halted, does that put us at risk?"

"I don't think so. I've observed that the Compound and Society don't share information often. The screens are on different feeds. The two communities operate independently with the only interaction related to the shipping of items both in and out of the Compound."

Roseleen and Triden looked at each other and nodded.

"We can stay longer. It's for the benefit of all in the Compound to find a cure while there's still a window of time."

"I'm glad you see it that way. It's never been my intention to detain you against your will."

Triden laughed. "Isn't the saying in Society: When there's a will, there's a way?"

"Don't get me started!" Jayr laughed in return.

Sunlight filtered through the blinds in the guest bedroom. Triden slept next to Roseleen, his arm draped across her body in a protective manner. The sounds of Society drifted up from the streets below as the city was coming to life. Roseleen stirred and stretched. She was surprised at how quickly she'd adapted to sleeping in the luxurious bed.

Triden awoke and kissed her shoulder.

"Good morning."

Roseleen turned onto her back and looked at the sunlight streaming across the ceiling from the window.

"I love sleeping next to you."

"I know. I love it, too."

Neither was quick to get up and instead snuggled closer while they gradually awoke.

"I hope Jayr finds a variable which will lead to a vaccine."

"Me, too. I have a lot of friends confined in the Compound. It would be wonderful if they could leave someday and live full lives. I didn't realize how much I was missing until I met you."

Roseleen kissed his cheek.

"I wonder if we can explore today? I'm not used to being so inactive."

"I know how you feel." It was the third day in the penthouse, and while part of the time had been devoted to research, the times when the doctor was at the Lab of Human Betterment had felt confining for the couple.

"I do enjoy being in bed with you, but it might be time to venture outside."

Triden sat up and slid out of bed, unconcerned about his naked body.

"Oh my, God. Triden!" Roseleen's voice sounded urgent.

He turned, concerned. "What's wrong?"

"Look at your skin!"

He looked down and couldn't believe his eyes. He quickly moved to their private bathroom and flipped on the light switch, illuminating the room and the mirror. He stared at the image reflected back to him.

Roseleen followed him.

"The rash is almost completely gone."

"How can that be?"

Roseleen slipped into a robe and handed Triden the second one hanging in the bathroom.

"Come with me."

The two ventured into the hallway and turned to the open space.

"Doctor! Jayr! Come quick!"

The older man was brewing his morning coffee and turned to find Roseleen and Triden in front of him.

"Show him!"

Triden pulled up the sleeve of his robe and extended his arm. A few faint pink patches were visible but nothing like the deep color splotching his skin for as long as he could remember.

"What am I looking at?"

"The rash is almost gone, and it's not anywhere near as inflamed as it's been since I've known him." Roseleen's voice was rapid with excitement.

The doctor looked at Triden. "What does the rest of your body look like?"

"It's the same. The rash is almost entirely gone. Why is that? I've had it for as long as I can remember."

"I don't know. What's changed recently?"

"We came here."

"True, but you haven't gone outside. This is effectively a controlled environment." The doctor started pacing. "Triden, tell me about a day in the Compound. Anything that's different than being here."

"I get up, go to the dining commons, then to work. I've

been spending an hour or two outside with Roseleen for the last several months. Then, I go back inside to spend time at The Barcode before going to my apartment."

"Did you notice any change to your rash since you've been in the woods?"

"Not really. It might have been a little better, but not really. Rosey, did you notice anything?"

"No. The rash has looked the same here as it did in the forest. At least, until today."

"Something has changed from your time here and at the Compound."

"Well, the food is a lot better."

"Of course! But why would it make a difference? The rash is a reaction to the virus." The doctor paused.

"What is it?"

"I have an idea. Triden, is there anyone at the Compound you trust completely?"

"Yes. My friend, Benjam. I think you met him in the infirmary."

"I remember. And you trust him to be discreet?"

"Yes, absolutely."

"Great. He's going to help us test my hypothesis."

"Which is what?"

"I think I found the key I've been missing. We don't have much time. I've been scheduled to give my final report next week. I should be able to visit the Compound without detection if I go before the presentation."

The doctor moved to the pantry and started tossing a variety of food items onto the kitchen counter. He also selected bottles of water.

"How many meals have you had here?"

"This morning will be my eighth."

The doctor counted out the packages before him.

"This should be enough for five days." He pushed the items

into several canvas bags and headed toward the entrance to the apartment.

"I'll be back soon. Sit tight."

[ ]

Annabella sat at her kitchen table and reviewed the poll numbers for Sir William before leaving for the Presidential Palace. The numbers had been holding constant for the last few months with minimal fluctuations in his trajectory. Regardless, more than half of those in Society disapproved of his performance. Questions related to his policies, his business investments, and his treatment of those in the Contagion Compound enraged some or were casually dismissed as non-issues by others. The prior year, when news broke of the payment of hush money to a young woman in Precinct Three related to a sexual escapade, many precinct administrators foresaw the end of Sir William's presidency, and yet it had not swayed public opinion dramatically. The polls had only dipped two points, and the affair blew over without repercussions... except possibly from Lilia. Sir William's wife had distanced herself from the story and refused to comment. Publicly she had been photographed supporting her husband, but behind closed doors, Annabella had quietly observed a much different response.

Rumors circulated that Lilia was pursuing extra-curricular activities of her own. Annabella admired the strength of the Top Lady. Her own ambitions had gotten her to where she was today, and she was not letting Sir William define her. Annabella was thankful Lilia never questioned her involvement in Sir William's Signet. It would have made her role as his advisor nearly impossible.

"Good morning, Bella." Jordon, done with his morning shower, smelled fresh as he leaned down to kiss his wife. His light brown hair was slightly damp, and his face was smooth.

"I'm heading to the Presidential Palace soon. I have to meet with Sir William before his afternoon commitments." Both of them knew Annabella referred to his near-daily trip to the Quilt Club.

"Did you know Sir William was the head of the Oversight Committee for Development of the Contagion Compound?" Jordon queried his wife.

"I knew he was involved. But considering how apathetic he is as president I suspect his contribution years ago was minimal at best."

"He had to have been productive on some level to make it to the presidency."

"True. It's hard to believe he does any work which doesn't directly line his pockets." Annabella sat before her personal screen. "Jordie, I know how you feel about him. Do me a favor, though, and don't make any public statements for another day or two. I'm laying the foundation for our next internal coup."

"Yes, dear!" Jordon waved a mock salute towards his wife. "The first lumber exports have gone through, and it's proving very lucrative. We should be able to yield enough profit to roll over to our other ventures. By this time next year, we should be fully functioning with money flowing in, not out."

"With the announcement of P3264 research being halted for more worthy studies, the main doctor, a Society member named Jayr Lenus, will present his findings. Once that's done, we'll be free to implement our Compound changes."

"When is the briefing?"

"It's been scheduled for next week. Considering there have been no conclusive findings to date, it's only a formality. It should have no bearing on our management of the Compound."

"I love you, Bella." Jordon kissed her again before heading to the door. "Be brilliant!"

Annabella smiled. All the pieces were coming together. She reviewed the documents on her personal screen for their next venture; everything was in order. She would slip it in between several other State initiatives just before Sir William was scheduled for The Flodden Club. With his mind on the Quilt game about to commence, she doubted he'd ask any questions.

CHAPTER 49

Power to Quad Four had flickered and gone dark. Benjam stood in front of the offending electrical panel looking for the cause. It didn't take long to identify the faulty fuse and replace it. Flipping the switch on the breaker box, the power was restored. He locked the panel and returned to the Electrical Station. His manager handed him a note as he entered: "Please report to the infirmary immediately."

Benjam tried to quell the rising panic in reading the words. He knew he'd been released from the infirmary after the Society doctor had taken blood samples and asked him questions about his family and health. Still, he feared being called to the Compound hospital.

His manager looked serious. "Remember, Citizen, you are doing your part to help all Contagions."

Benjam nodded. "I'll be back as soon as possible." At least he hoped he'd be returning. Triden had been taken away three days ago, and he wasn't sure he'd ever see his best friend again. Benjam put away his toolbelt and scanned his wrist to exit the control room. Maybe he could get information on his friend.

As he entered the medical room, the heavy-leather-clad physician stood on the other side of a plexiglass barrier. Two infirmary attendees were also in the room on Benjam's side.

"Thank you for coming on such short notice."

Benjam slid into the chair facing the doctor.

The doctor addressed the two attendants, "Thank you for your assistance. You are free to go. I would like some time for a confidential conversation with my patient."

The two men paused and watched as the two orderlies left the examination area. Benjam was the first to speak when they were alone.

"Did you take Triden?"

"Yes. He's doing well and sends his regards."

Regards? That didn't sound like Triden.

The doctor continued, "We've had some initial success with my research. Triden said you can be trusted."

"He's my best friend. I trust him with my life."

The doctor paused. "I understand you don't know me, but I need you to be discrete with what I am going to share with you. I don't want to spread false hope if the results are not as I suspect."

"Do I have to come with you?"

"No. There is a risk of spreading P3264, so it's better to keep you here."

"But you took Triden. Why?"

"I needed to gather additional information, and it was easier to do it within Society."

"I see."

"Can I ask for your discretion? It's imperative what I share with you does not go any further."

Benjam leaned closer. "Does Triden trust you?"

"Yes, I believe so."

"OK. What do you need?"

The doctor had transferred the food items into a medical bag before entering the Compound. He inserted the leather satchel into the special vacuum compartment to pass the bag through to Benjam.

"This contains food from Society. I'm asking you only to consume things from the bag for the next five days."

"How is that going to help?"

"We may have isolated something which counteracts the virus."

"In food?"

"Possibly. I'll have more clarification after five days."

"All I have to do is eat this?"

"Yes. And Benjam, you do need to be discreet. Please don't let anyone in the Compound know you aren't eating or drinking Compound food. I'm trying to establish a baseline for the research."

"Ok." The young man wasn't sure why others couldn't know of his special diet, but he would keep quiet. He would agree to most anything that could lead to Triden returning to the Compound. He missed his friend.

"Oh, and Benjam, please avoid going to The Barcode during this time. It will be helpful if you can abstain from physical contact with others in the Compound."

"Only for five days, right?"

"Yes. After five days, you can do whatever you want."

"Sounds manageable."

"Thank you. I can't tell you enough how important this is for you and the others here. I will check in with you halfway through the experiment."

"Sounds interesting. Let's see what happens." Benjam stood up and waved to the doctor on the other side of the plexiglass barrier. "See you in three days."

Jayr stood and started to the exit behind him. He connected with the Contagion who had escorted him to the infirmary meeting room.

"Hello. I missed lunch today. Would it be possible to get something to eat?"

"Of course," the young steward answered. "Give me a few minutes."

It didn't take long for him to return with the customary bagged lunch consumed by all in the Compound.

"Thank you. I appreciate it. Have a good day. I'll be back in several days."

Jayr was relieved the news feeds were different between Society and the Compound, and his visits could be performed covertly without alerting his supervisor.

The doctor returned to his vehicle and, once inside, looked into the bag. Several protein pucks and a sealed glass with tea were enclosed. It was a good starting point for performing a food analysis. He was determined to find the variance between the food available in Society and what the Contagions were eating in the Compound.

◊

Boundaries are being redefined.

Roseleen's mother worried about the latest message from The Source. Was the perimeter of their home about to be breached? She closed her eyes and inhaled deeply several times, trying to quiet her mind. She hoped The Source would provide more guidance. No additional messages appeared, and she was left to interpret the message on her own. Communications with her daughter had been limited because the distance between them distorted their telepathy. She was not worried about Roseleen; she was strong and capable and was with the Power Walker. Shira hadn't yet met Triden, but she knew of his presence through her daughter. Since he had arrived in her life, Roseleen had blossomed and found ease. There was no more uncertainty. They shared a destiny.

Not all want to do good in the world.

Shira pushed away the thoughts of the second man who was on the horizon. Roseleen would cross paths with this dark power soon. She willed her daughter a sense of strength and resolve. She would need it.

◊

The doctor tipped the brown bag and spread the few items on the lab tray. It was sterilized, and he wore surgical gloves to avoid any contamination. The objective was to keep the items intact, just as they were provided within the Compound.

Several large protein pucks, dried nutritional elements shaped into round disks, comprised the main course. There was also one smaller puck. The doctor smelled each one and discovered the larger disks were meat and grain-based while the smaller one smelled like a concoction of fruit.

He inserted the first food sample into the gas chromatography chamber used to analyze everything from the presence of pesticides to the percentages of every ingredient contained within food items. It would take a while to separate the ingredients and perform the analysis.

Jayr's research presentation on P3264 was scheduled for the beginning of the coming week, and he had received permission from his supervisor to summarize his work. He was thankful he still had access to the lab even though his data sets had been archived. His manager was not aware of the backup he'd made nor of his continued efforts. He would be able to remain below the radar for a few more days. If his hypothesis was correct, that was all he needed.

⚊⚊

You will continue to be tested.

Roseleen was used to this type of message from The Source. Along with the other Forest Seers, she received the messages as a "life manual," helping guide them to lead fuller, richer lives. Learning how to hear and interpret the messages was a core value of their community.

Not all want to do good in the world.

She had received this message for months, but after spending a few days in Society, the message felt more urgent. At first, she had questioned the doctor's intentions with his research. It didn't take long for her to see he was a man of science and compassion. He definitely fit in the "do good" column.

She was feeling restless. The Society clothes felt confining, as did her time in the doctor's penthouse. The novelty of their new setting was beginning to feel normal, but she wanted more exercise than the time she spent running on the treadmill in the home gym. She would ask the doctor if they could venture outside when he returned from his lab.

Triden moved to the private bathroom in the guest bedroom. After breakfast, he'd returned to their room and slipped out of the robe. He looked at his skin. It was smooth. The rash had retreated, leaving behind a bare whisper of inflamed skin. He couldn't remember a time he hadn't had the rash covering the bulk of his body.

Was there really something in the food from Society that could offer a cure? He didn't know much about nutrition other than the protein pucks had been developed to offer optimum ingredients to live a hunger-free life with the proper balance of vitamins, minerals, protein, and fats. If all his nutritional needs were being met with the protein pucks, was it an overlooked, nonessential food item that could provide a cure?

He hung his robe on a hook on the back of the bathroom door and quickly dressed in one of the Society outfits provided by the doctor. He felt cautiously optimistic that the days of being confined in the Compound might actually come to an end for all the Contagions.

Mallor didn't trust Annabella. As far as he could tell, she was highly motivated by her own self-interests. Sir William trusted her implicitly, but Mallor knew people well enough to know when someone with her background of political canvassing moved to an advisory role, she likely had an ulterior motive.

He tapped the screen in his office and logged into the Statecraft Signet files. He'd been granted the highest security clearance by Sir William to aid him with his work for the president. Recently, two contracts had been pushed through using irregular channels. Most initiatives followed specific protocols presenting the pros and cons at a Signet hearing with heads and other representatives from each precinct in attendance. While one precinct might benefit from certain initiatives, the goal had always been to ensure any proposals were presented to provide equal consideration across the precincts.

It didn't take long for Mallor to find the proposal for logging the nearby forest land. It took longer for him to dig through court filings and corporate registrations to find the information he was looking for related to the company ownership.

Alpine Resources Management.

Cross-referencing the corporate name with the board listings, his suspicions were confirmed. Jordon and Annabella Connor were the CEO and COO.

The second initiative moved the management and the day-to-day maintenance of the Contagion Compound out of Society budgets to a private entity. He retraced the same steps to find its incorporation history. It didn't take long to find information about the second corporation, Republic Holdings.

Jordon and Annabella Connor were also listed as the owners. The findings didn't surprise Mallor. Was it in his best interest to push Annabella out or wait to see if there was a way to use the information to benefit himself?

Mallor had been watching Sir William's poll numbers and it amazed him the president still had the loyalty of so many constituents in Society. But Compound protests were becoming more vocal and prevalent. Sir William ignored them, seeing no reason to worry about the Contagions who were contained in their own community. As long as they did not leave the Compound and risk exposure to those in Society, they could survive. Their work provided significant support for the various precincts. Without the contributing labor by the Contagions, goods and services would come with a much higher cost.

Mallor knew Sir William's message at the next presidential rally the following week would reiterate the slogan that Contagions were "Lucky to Be Alive!" Even the recent announcement about the cancellation of the vaccine research had barely created a blip on the poll numbers. The protests appeared to be isolated in several pockets within the precincts.

Mallor would keep his eye on Annabella and her nefarious husband. Apparently, their marriage was much stronger than either let on.

⸭

Sodium hydrochlorizide

Sulfite benzicynide

Synthetic polyestesgen

The doctor read the list of ingredients with disbelief. The protein pucks included meat and grains common in Society food; however, the additives were unconscionable. Three particularly harmful inflammatory ingredients were included that were not normal in any nutritional guidelines published by the Lab of Human Betterment.

Clearly, someone or a department within Society had reasons for including the ingredients, and the doctor was beginning to formulate a hypothesis. Fear twisted inside of him. He would have to be careful with his next steps.

[ll[

"Contagions are people, too! Find a cure, find a cure!"

The shouts of the protesters were irritating Sir William. He watched the media feed on the screen; the chants played with a stereo echo on the screen and outside his office window.

"I thought we released an ad campaign showing how productive and satisfied Contagions are in the Compound."

"We did. The reel played for several weeks before we announced the cancellation of the vaccine study."

"Then why are there so many protests?"

"This is only a small number of people in Society. It will die down soon." Annabella and Jordon had a vested interest in keeping the Compound functioning with the new privatized management. The vocal response by protesters spanning each precinct had surprised her. Nothing in the poll data had indicated that halting the research would cause such an outcry.

"Find a cure, find a cure!"

"Call out the Signet Guard. Can't they clear the streets?"

"That's one option. However, it might be better to let this die out of its own accord. Remember what happened with the photo op?"

"It's better to fight than be walked all over. I am not a loser! It's not a time to show weakness!" Sir William paced behind his desk.

"I agree. However, if you call out the Guard, it could cause a reaction bigger than if we let them grow tired and go home. Giving them no response will be more demoralizing. Let's not fan the flames."

Sir William growled at the screen. "Don't they see it doesn't matter? It's not necessary to reintroduce them to Society. The Compound is fully functional. They are lucky to be alive!"

"Give it a day or two, and I promise the protests will stop, particularly after the research report shows no evidence of progress. The monies will be better spent elsewhere. Those in Society will come around. All in good time."

"I will not be bullied!"

"Of course not." Annabella spoke in a soothing voice and tried to distract the portly man. "I have a few items needing your attention." She reached for her dossier and extracted papers for the president to sign.

"What's this?"

"A formality. Nothing to worry about. Sign here and here."

Sir William absently scrawled his name and returned his gaze to the screen.

"If they are back tomorrow, I'm having everyone arrested."

She would address the protesters in the morning. For now, she had everything she needed. She tucked the signed papers back into her folder.

CHAPTER 51

The doctor paced the vestibule in the infirmary, waiting for Benjam to arrive. He'd spent the last two days performing research and was fairly certain he'd identified the key he'd been looking for, and Benjam provided the lock to be opened.

The young man entered the room, and the doctor could feel his heart rate elevate. This was the closest he'd come to solving the riddle of the virus. He knew he was emotionally invested, and he had to be careful he wasn't fabricating a solution.

Benjam looked nervous as he sat down in front of the clear barrier separating him from the doctor. He looked around the room to see if anyone from the Compound was nearby.

"What was in the food you gave me?"

"Nothing special. It was food from my pantry."

"It had to have something special about it."

The doctor leaned closer to the divider. "You noticed a change?"

"Yes. My rashes are almost completely gone. How is that possible?"

"I have a theory." The doctor paused. "You haven't told anyone, have you?"

"No, I wanted to talk with you first. Besides, Triden's the only person I would talk with, and he's not here."

"It's imperative you don't tell anyone and don't let anyone see that your rashes are going away."

"Why can't I tell anyone?"

"Because I don't know who can be trusted and who can't."

The young man cursed. "Am I in danger?"

"You should be fine as long as no one knows. It's also a lot safer here than in Society."

"What's next?"

"I want you to start eating the protein pucks again. Go back to your regular Compound diet."

"Ugh. They're going to taste awful after the food you brought."

"I know. It's only for a few days. I'll be back to check with you."

"Can you bring more Society food with you?"

"Of course. Anything in particular?"

"Yes. That pastry thing."

"Gleekma. I'll be sure to bring it when I come back."

"See you soon, Doc."

"I am so grateful for your help. You are critical to solving the mystery."

"Anything to get out of here."

The doctor turned to leave the infirmary. The screen overhead flashed the customary message.

"Lucky to Be Alive!"

The doctor just needed his luck to last a few days longer.

[◦◦◦]

Triden and Roseleen stepped out of the elevator. The activity of Society churned outside the entrance, and they slipped their hands together to face the unknown awaiting them. The doctor knew they were going stir crazy inside his home and had said it would be alright if they went for a walk.

"Try not to engage with anyone outside. Fortunately, since you are together, it is unlikely you'll be approached."

Roseleen was getting used to the elevated heel of her boots. The stiff linen and cotton clothing felt scratchy against her skin, and she missed the smooth texture of the leathers she normally wore.

Triden was faring better in his new clothing. The materials were similar to his Compound robe and undergarments, and he enjoyed the expanded view without the encumbering hood. His Compound boots were similar to the dress shoes provided by the doctor, and he was able to walk with ease.

As they pushed open the doorway, the cacophony of the world around them assaulted their senses. Vehicles flashed before them, and they paused a moment before merging into the pedestrian traffic on the sidewalk.

Triden squeezed Rosey's hand as they walked, both hesitant to talk for fear they might be overheard and draw attention to themselves.

Roseleen looked at the women of Society. Her clothing mirrored their style. She wondered what their reaction would have been if she was in her customary Forest Seer attire. She had never been compared to anyone in her home, and now she was hyperaware of the need to blend into the world around her.

The smells around her were also a distraction. There was nothing familiar to the scents. The aroma of the forest had a fresh, natural quality. The tang of Society included exhaust and steam rising from sidewalk grates intermingled with the fragrance of cooked foods.

They turned to the right, making a mental note of their surroundings so they could retrace their steps. Tall buildings loomed overhead, and the frenetic energy around them was palpable. After the calm of the forest and Compound, it was overwhelming and exciting at the same time.

Large screens broadcast media feeds and advertisements. It was easy to get distracted by the images. Triden leaned in closely.

"Are you alright?"

Roseleen nodded.

"There's a lot to take in," Triden whispered to her.

The messages from The Source were scrambled with all the distortion around her. The familiar messages were oddly absent, which made her feel uneasy. For as long as she could remember, The Source had provided wisdom and comfort.

She looked up at the screen overhead and saw an image of the president. He was in a room with several others, and when she saw them on the screen, she stopped short.

Not all want to do good.

She didn't need The Source to remind her. She'd been seeing images of the man not to be trusted for months. Now she knew he was part of Society.

"Triden, look!" Roseleen gestured to the screen.

"The president? I'm tired of seeing him."

"I know... but look at the man behind him."

"Who is it?"

"Not all want to do good in the world."

"That's him?"

"Yes, we need to tell Jayr."

"What can he do?"

"Maybe he knows who it is."

Returning quickly to the doctor's penthouse, they shared the oracle with the doctor. The news feed on the screen had changed.

"Without an image, I'm not sure who the man is. How long have you been getting this message?" Like Triden, the doctor was beginning to understand the intuitive powers of the young woman.

"For months."

"Let me know if you see him on the screen again."

"Our paths are going to cross."

"I can assure you, you're safe here." Triden embraced Roseleen. "I'll protect you."

Roseleen didn't share her internal knowledge that the encounter would be inevitable and no one could shield her.

The doctor was stuck in traffic. He resisted the urge to lean on the horn. While it might feel good to hear the noise, it wasn't going to get him out of Precinct One any faster. He'd hardly slept the night before, and anticipation made him a nervous bundle of energy.

A bag of pastries was on the passenger seat next to him. He hoped he would have a reason to celebrate with Benjam. He was grateful for Triden's recommendation and Benjam's understanding of the need to be discrete.

Finally, traffic started moving, and he turned onto the thoroughfare to take him to the Compound. His nerves were stretched; he willed himself to pay attention to the vehicles around him. If his suspicions were correct, he was going to present a shocking final report on his research.

The medical van felt small and overpowered by the big container trucks rumbling alongside him, all with the Compound as their destination. Fortunately, the vehicles progressed in unison, and it wouldn't be much longer until he arrived.

After parking in the far corner of the parking lot and slipping into his protective gear, the doctor made his way to the entrance. He was buzzed inside and greeted by one of the residents who he'd seen multiple times before.

"Welcome, doctor. We received word today research has been concluded. There is no longer a need for you to risk infection."

How could his luck have run out today of all days?

"Yes, it is ending; however, I have one final interview with a study participant."

The Compound resident shifted his weight back and forth, unclear how to proceed.

"I've received notification. The research has ended."

The doctor looked at the pastry bag in his hand. He hoped Benjam would forgive him.

"I have some treats from Society I was going to give to my study participant. Would you like them?" The doctor opened the bag so the resident could look inside. The sweet smell of pastry, sugar, and custard rose from the interior.

The resident paused, eyeing the unusual food. It smelled nothing like the protein pucks.

"Alright. You may enter today, but no more visits after this. Agreed?"

"Agreed." The doctor sighed with relief. Today should be all he needed.

The heavy metal gate slid back, and the doctor stepped into the familiar vestibule. As soon as the partition closed behind him, the barrier before him slid aside. He quickly arrived at the infirmary.

Benjam entered the room a few minutes later and sat on the other side of the barrier. Looking at him through the glass, Jayr saw a hopeful sign. Benjam was smiling.

"You ate only the protein pucks, correct?"

"Yes."

"What happened?"

Benjam looked around; there were no other residents within earshot. He leaned closer to whisper to the doctor.

"The rash is back."

"That's what I suspected."

"Now what?"

"I'm going to present my research early next week. It's my hope this information will allow you to return to Society."

"And if it's not?"

"I'll still fight for you. I made a pledge to find a cure. I'm a man of my word."

"Did you remember the pastries?"

"I did, but they became a donation at the entrance. I'm sorry." So much for being a man of his word. He hoped the young man would understand.

Benjam looked disappointed.

"That's the way of the Compound."

"What do you mean?"

"There are the written rules, and then there's a set of

unwritten codes of behavior." The doctor suspected that was true everywhere. Benjam didn't mention he orchestrated a lot of the Off Book encounters by leveraging his electrical skills to override the screens.

"Hang in there. I hope to have more news for you soon."

"If there's one constant in my life, it's my routine here."

The doctor nodded. It was time for that to change.

CHAPTER 52

Annabella referred to her notes and looked up at Sir William. He was distracted and angrily tapping out a message for the rotating banner along the bottom of the screen.

"When there's a WILL, there's a WAY."

The message was losing its appeal. Those in Society had loved the play on words at first, but as time progressed, and Sir William had done little or nothing to address their concerns, the phrase was sounding more and more like a hollow promise.

"Sir, the final research findings for the P3264 vaccine are being presented in two days. I think it would be helpful if you attend. I will set up a post-presentation interview so we can control the narrative."

"Is it important?" Sir William barely shifted his focus from the screen as he replied.

"It's a way to minimize the message of the protesters."

"If you think it will make a difference, I guess I can go. Can you see if Lilia will attend with me?"

Annabella made a note. "I'll see what I can do. Generally, she requires at least a week's notice for changes to her schedule."

"People in Society love her, and if they see she's in support of stopping the research, it should shut those foul protesters up once and for all."

Annabella didn't know how the Top Lady felt about halting the research. She suspected the other woman hadn't given it much thought.

"I'll make the arrangements." Annabella wasn't sure what the Top Lady would want, but she knew she'd ask for something in exchange for her presence at the function.

Jayr sat with his manager, reviewing his findings before the presentation would be made public. She looked up from the report.

"Is this accurate?"

"Yes."

"Where did you find this information?"

"In the Lab of Betterment files on the Compound."

"Haven't all the files been archived?"

"I had some backed up on my personal screen." The doctor decided not to share he'd downloaded every file he could when he heard of the cancellation of his work.

"Really? This was part of the lab's files?" She continued to flip through the pages of the presentation, flicking her finger across her personal screen.

"Yes."

"I would have thought this would have been part of Housing and Comfort."

"I don't have access to those files, only the ones pertaining to The Path."

"Of course, that makes sense. You know what this means?"

The doctor had been feeling a sense of dread ever since he'd discovered the document.

"Yes. That's why I think it's important to discuss it at the research review."

"I can't guarantee you'll be heard."

"I know. But I have to try."

⫍❖⫎

The logging machines spewed sawdust and exhaust as the forest trees were toppled in an unrelenting cascade of leaves and bark. Branches were stripped from the massive trunks, and the skeletal remains were loaded onto large flatbeds to be cut into planks to sell at auction.

This too shall pass.

The Source message defined the visual in front of Roseleen's father. The logging had been non-stop, and acres and acres of land had been reduced to a sea of exposed, ringed tree bases. Traditional forestry practices of thinning the wooded area were being ignored, and the entire forest ecosystem was at risk.

Animals fled deeper into the woods, fear palpable in their movements. The normal vibration of the woods had taken on a feverish pitch, and even the ground under Skylar's feet pulsed from the throbbing diesel machines rumbling from the tree line to the main road.

While The Source message seemed comforting and reassuring, it was likely that moving away from the Forest Seer treehouse community would be a necessity. At first, he'd hoped the logging would come to a stop with a quota fulfilled by the fallen vegetation. Unfortunately, no such indication was evident, and the longer they waited, the more difficult it would be to relocate undetected.

It was time to dismantle the treehouses and remove any evidence of their existence. They would join the melee of animals moving deeper into the recesses of the woods. They would rebuild. They would survive, as long as the cutting stopped before the entire forest was depleted.

Skylar pushed the thought from his mind. The forest was already being hobbled. The thought of it being completely decimated defied all reason and left a foreboding sadness he couldn't shake.

It was the morning of the research presentation. The doctor reviewed his notes. He was about to go out on a limb, and it could have dire consequences.

Triden and Roseleen were both dressed in Society clothing, ready to join the doctor. All three had nervous energy feeding upon one another.

It didn't take long to make it to the Lab of Human Betterment presentation hall, where the three joined a middle-aged woman by the lecture podium.

"Jayr, good to see you. We will stream your report to the screen overhead and throughout Society."

The doctor introduced his supervisor, Masha, to Triden and Roseleen. She did not ask questions about their presence.

It was customary for those within the Lab of Human Betterment to attend in person, and the doctor watched as many of his colleagues began filling the room.

Masha looked up from her personal screen with a look of surprise. "Sir William and Lilia Newbiggers are attending."

Triden and Roseleen exchanged looks. The President of Society? Why would he be coming? They had seen the portly man on the screen in the doctor's home. Roseleen knew the dark souled man was in the president's inner circle. She would be extra careful.

The security detail for the president arrived and scoped out the auditorium. They reserved the front two rows for the presidential staff and precinct heads. Roseleen was allowed to sit in the row as well after it was explained she was with Jayr.

Triden and the doctor were seated at a table on the stage, watching the audience filing into the space. A buzz of conversation started as a hum and grew as more and more seats filled with Society patrons.

The start time came and went, and still, the two front rows

remained empty. Protocol required they wait for the president to arrive. Time ticked slowly and the conversation tapered off as the audience anticipated the start of the report.

A set of double doors, one of three in the back of the room, burst open, and a self-important group of people strode inside. A blond woman in a navy dress appeared. Roseleen recognized her from the screen as an advisor to the President.

The two-faced woman shifts with the tides. So that's her, Roseleen thought.

A variety of officials filed in with her and flowed into the seats in front. No messages came forth for the majority of officials.

After another pause, as if waiting for full attention, Sir William and the Top Lady entered the room. Everyone stood and applauded as the couple made their way to the center seats.

Ego will betray those with overconfidence.

Lastly, a middle-aged man in a gray suit entered, and Roseleen caught her breath.

Not all want to do good in the world. It was the man who had been haunting her. She instinctively knew he was linked to the president. He sat down a few seats from her, and she fought the urge to run. She was protected in the crowd, and she caught Triden's gaze on the stage. She subtly nodded in the older man's direction, and Triden followed her nod. Looking back to Rosey, he tilted his head in acknowledgment. He would watch her.

Sir William cleared his throat and advanced to the stage. He stood at the podium without looking at the panel seated behind him.

"Members of Society...Today marks a historic day in the story of our Statecraft. We have successfully contained P3264 and created a livelihood for the survivors. The Contagion Compound is a testament to the efforts of Society to provide a safe haven for those inflicted with this deadly disease. While they have tainted blood and as carriers cannot be included in

Society, they are lucky to be alive, and they bear the fruit of their existence within the walls of the Contagion Compound."

Triden felt a wave of anger wash over him. The message from the president was filled with platitudes.

"I have done the most to support the Contagions. They have food and shelter. They live within their own community. Isolated, they are not harming Society. Their disease is contained and is not spreading." Sir William paused for effect. "The Time of Mass Terminations is behind us. We have prevailed regardless of whether or not there is a vaccine. It is time in our illustrious history to look forward. It is time to look to the future of Society and invest in making us the greatest nation."

Applause filled the auditorium, and Sir William basked in the noise. "Join me later today! We are holding a rally to celebrate our achievements and to pave the way for a solid future for Society!"

The president smiled and waved to the audience.

"And now it's time to wrap up the research and move forward in our quest to make Society strong and whole as a nation!"

The doctor stood and approached the podium. Jayr waited for the president to take his seat and for the noise to quiet in the auditorium. His heart was pounding, and he took a deep breath. He had to get his message out to a large audience and throughout Society on the screens. It was the only way to ensure his safety and to protect Triden and Roseleen. His supervisor nodded, and he started to speak.

"I started my research of Pathogen 3264 nineteen years ago. We found what looked like a promising cure early into our research, and yet the disease mutated quickly and often." Jayr clicked through his presentation. He was grateful it was being live-streamed throughout all the precincts. There would be no going back after he had completed his report.

"I have been relying on data samples provided by Society. I have analyzed it by parsing and looking for any unique or repeating variables. More recently, I ventured to the Contagion Compound, using established protocols, to gather additional blood samples to compare to the samples provided by Society."

Murmurs hummed around the room with this news, and the doctor continued. "At first, I did not find any alternative findings to my research. That is, until I met 36MA46RA23. This Compound resident did not have any antibodies to P3264 in his blood work."

Several members gasped. Others looked expectantly at the doctor, and he pushed on.

"There are several reasons a person would not have antibodies. I explored which hypothesis would be accurate, and I have found the key to The Path."

Roseleen could feel the energy shifting in the room. The president looked agitated, while the Top Lady looked bored. The others around them looked on with interest. Roseleen was surprised to make eye contact with the man from her Source messages. *Why was he looking at her?* She looked away quickly, hopeful it was only a coincidence.

"It is possible to reintroduce residents in the Compound back to Society!"

Sir William stood up from his seat, his face splotchy and red. "NO! They are filth! They are not fit to be part of Society."

The doctor tried to speak over the voices. "We have been told they are Contagions. We have been told they will always be infected and kill anyone who comes into contact with them."

Sir William sputtered. "That's true! They are CONTA-GIONS!"

The doctor gestured for Triden to join him at the podium. "This is Triden. Also known as 36MA46RA23. He was given this number when he entered the Compound. It was tattooed onto his wrist. Show them."

Triden lifted his left arm and showed the mark.

Screams filled the air, and people rushed for the exits. Fear of exposure after years of brainwashing drowned out the voice of reason from the doctor. Roseleen stood, trying to make her way to the stage to join Triden.

"Wait! Wait! It's completely safe. Please listen!" The doctor's voice was drowned out.

Roseleen was being pushed toward a side exit by the frenzied crowd. A hand gripped her arm, and she turned to find herself facing the ominous man in the gray suit. His eyes were cold, and his face expressionless.

"Come with me."

"No!"

"I don't think you understand. It isn't a question."

"Triden!" Roseleen tried to get his attention to no avail. The man in the gray suit was propelled her forward, and the crowd swallowed her from Triden's view. The presidential security detail blocked the perimeter and quickly escorted the president, Top Lady, and aides away from the melee. Triden and the doctor were blocked from exiting the stage. Pandemonium prevailed.

❙❙❙

"We have to find her." Triden was anxious. He'd seen her point out the man in the gray suit. Neither knew who he was, but Triden had no doubts he was dangerous. He trusted Rosey's messages from The Source after all the time they'd spent together. He didn't understand how it worked, but he didn't need to. It was part of her, and he loved her.

"The man we told you about was here."

"The one who doesn't want to do good?"

"I'm sure he took her."

"Come with me." The presidential security detail was finally dispersing after Sir William and the Top Lady had been ushered from the room. He moved toward his supervisor.

"Masha, we need to find Roseleen. She doesn't know Society, and we have reason to believe she was taken."

"Taken? Why?"

"We're not sure, but there was someone here who might have kidnapped her. He was in the front row. Is there a way to find out who was with the president?"

"I'm sure we can review the footage. Let's go to my office."

CHAPTER 54

Make tomorrow even better than today.

The message was loud and clear. She didn't need much insight to decipher that she didn't need to fight the man next to her.

You have the power to heal.

The man pushed her into the passenger seat of his car. "Don't try to run or you'll only make your situation worse." Roseleen felt a wave of calm as she sat in the seat. She took a deep breath. She could sacrifice herself for a better tomorrow. The Source would guide her.

It didn't take long for him to navigate the streets of Precinct One. She saw replays overhead on the screens capturing the images from the research presentation. None of them had expected the crowd to erupt with fear when presenting Triden. They had thought revealing the barcode would show the risk had been mitigated. None of them understood how strong the programming had been to tell a narrative of the Contagions infecting Society.

Roseleen closed her eyes and tried to connect with her Mother.

HE is here. Send me protection.

You are loved and protected, Daughter.

If only she could reach Triden telepathically. She could feel his worry and panic.

Triden, I love you. I am strong. Don't worry.

She hoped he received some sense of calm through her message, even if he couldn't hear the words. As the car moved forward in traffic, she had to push all outside friction aside and center her feelings. It would take all of her strength to deal with the man by her side.

Mallor drove the car toward his private offices. He had seen the doctor and the Contagion talking with the young woman. If his instincts were correct, she had information that would be helpful. At the very least, she would provide an afternoon of entertainment. It had been a while since he'd interrogated anyone, and he missed the power and control of having a target squirm and crack under pressure.

He glanced at her as they were driving. She seemed surprisingly calm for someone who had just been forcibly put into a stranger's car. She must be feeble-minded if she didn't understand the situation she was in. He smiled. As soon as she saw his interrogation room, he would see realization dawn on her face. He loved watching someone's last shred of hope vanish into fear. He would be in control. It looked like the afternoon was going to be better than he anticipated. He pressed the accelerator down and looked forward to what was to come.

He pulled his car into the garage space and pressed a button to close the door behind him. The redhead next to him could attempt to run, but there would be nowhere to go.

He got out of the car and walked to the passenger door, and pulled it open. "Come with me."

Roseleen opened her eyes and looked up at her captor. His dark eyes were calculating and cold. She wondered why he was the way he was. The Source provided her with the answer she'd known instinctively.

A mother's love is not always given.

He gripped her arm and guided her down a hallway, past several offices, to the end room. He used his free hand to open the door and swing it open. Facing them was a thick wooden chair with leather straps at the base of the legs and armrests. It was not designed for comfort. Along the wall hung an array of devices. Roseleen had never seen anything like them, and yet she could guess what they were used for. This was where the man before her gathered information. This was a room for torture.

She walked into the room and went straight to the wooden chair.

"I'm assuming this is where you want me?" She looked expectantly at the man in the gray suit, and she saw surprise cross his face before he stripped away the hint of emotion.

"I want to know your connection with the doctor and the Contagion."

"Who says I have one?"

"I saw you interacting at the auditorium."

"I see." Roseleen smiled. "You know nothing."

"I know more than you think."

"But you still want to question me, and you have no idea who I am."

Mallor didn't like being caught off guard. *Why wasn't she scared? Didn't she know the tactics he would use to extract information?*

"If you don't cooperate, this could get messy." Mallor sat down on a bench by the door and slowly removed his dress shoes. He placed them methodically under the bench and slid into his knee-high rubber boots. He also removed his suit jacket and replaced it with the long, rubberized coat. He pulled on latex gloves and covered his face with a clear shield to protect him from any bodily fluids or projectiles.

Embrace the one in front of you to know their truth.

Mallor stood and walked slowly toward Roseleen. "We can do this the easy way or the hard way. It's up to you."

"That's an interesting concept." Again, she saw a hint of surprise cross the man's face.

"How so?"

"If I understand this correctly, you want information. But you're not going to trust anything I say when I first tell you because you don't know me, and you won't know if I'm lying to you. Your only option is to take steps to validate my words."

"Give me a reason to trust you."

"That's the problem. I can tell you anything, and you won't know if it's true or not."

"Trust me, I'll know if you're telling the truth."

"Really? So, if I tell you I live in a treehouse, you'd believe me?"

"Of course not. That's ridiculous."

"Is it?" Roseleen smiled. "I know the truth, and I also know whatever I tell you won't be believable until you've tried to torture out an alternative story from me. The irony is I can make up a completely fabricated story to begin and then tell you the truth or start with the truth and make up something to get you to stop hurting me. Either way, you'll never know what to believe. You will always have doubts."

She wasn't as feeble-minded as she'd appeared in the car.

Triden was beside himself. He'd raced around the perimeter of the Lab of Human Betterment. The streets were empty,
and he couldn't locate Roseleen. He feared the man in the gray
suit. She'd seen premonitions of him, and now she was missing.

He returned to the office of the doctor's supervisor. Masha
and Jayr were huddled in front of a personal screen, looking at
a replay of the live broadcast captured while the doctor was
on stage. Behind them, on the larger screen, played a media
feed with a frenzy of activity.

"Contagion escaped from Compound!"

"Is there a cure?"

"Mayhem at Lab of Human Betterment."

Triden saw how quickly misinformation was spreading
throughout Society.

"How can we find Roseleen?" He tried to keep desperation
out of his voice.

"We're trying to identify who was with Sir William." They
zoomed in on the front row of attendees in the replay.

"Next to Sir William is the man in the gray suit. We don't
know who he is. On the president's other side is Lilia, the Top
Lady, and beside her is Annabella Connor, a presidential advisor. There are also other precinct heads, but they don't seem
connected to the man in gray."

"I think our best bet is to reach out to Annabella Connor."

Annabella rode with the president and Top Lady back to the
Presidential Palace. What were the implications of the Contagions being reintroduced to Society? She and Jordon would
have a contract to maintain an empty facility.

The media stream on the screen in the executive car was broadcasting a loop of the meeting at the Lab of Human Betterment.

Sir William sat next to her and glared at the images.

"Contagions are filth and cannot and will not be reintroduced into Society. The spread of misinformation must be stopped."

"I understand. However, the feed is playing throughout all the precincts. Members of Society are going to be asking questions."

The president reached for his personal screen and typed out a message for his private banner. Annabella watched it scroll along the bottom of the screen moments later.

"There has been a mistake with the final report from the Lab of Human Betterment. Dr. Jayr Lenus has falsified information in an attempt to provide credibility to his work on P3264. Do not listen to his lies."

Annabella struggled to find the words to counsel the man beside her. When he was in a rage, it was almost impossible to divert his attention.

"The replays are showing the Contagion's arm with his barcode."

"Lies! His presence has been fabricated to spread false information. I bet it's someone from within Society and the barcode is fake. I want them arrested immediately."

"On what charge?"

"Crimes against the Statecraft! Endangerment of the members of Society. It is imperative that all in Society know these lies will not be tolerated."

Sir William tapped out another missive for the presidential banner on the bottom of the screen. *"Those involved in this deception inflicted upon Society will be arrested. This behavior will not be tolerated."*

Mallor scanned the tools at his disposal, looking for the perfect item to create fear in the young woman strapped to the chair behind him. She hadn't struggled when he'd tightened the leather straps, and she'd looked up at him with calm and what almost looked like serenity. He was unnerved by her reaction. Usually, at this stage, his subjects would be displaying a heightened heart rate, shallow breathing, and fear at the unknown facing them. His most recent victim released his bowels before he'd even made a move.

He selected an item he enjoyed; two metal balls encased in a soft silicone cover, connected by a strap. The heavy balls would inflict pain, and the soft covering would minimize bruising. He could extract the information he needed using force.

He turned toward his victim and let the balls swing together as he approached her.

"Let's start with your name."

"Roseleen."

"What is your last name?"

"I don't have one."

"That's absurd. Everyone has a last name."

"Really? Are you sure?"

"Stop wasting time. Tell me your last name!"

"I can't tell you something I don't have. Would you like me to make something up instead?"

Mallor watched her closely. *Still no fear or physical reactions. How was that possible?*

"What precinct are you from?"

"Most recently? One."

"What were you doing at the Lab of Human Betterment today?"

Roseleen didn't know how to lie, and she had nothing to hide. The truth would prevail. "I was there for moral support. Why were you there?"

"This isn't about me."

"I would disagree." Roseleen smiled at her captor. "You enjoy this. It gives you a sense of power."

"This isn't about me," Mallor repeated. He heard his voice shift, and it disturbed him she wasn't fearful. He swung the balls forward, connecting with Roseleen's right shoulder. Pain flashed across her face, yet there still wasn't fear. He swung again and again, each time the balls connecting with a different part of her body. He could hear her ribs crack.

"Just because your mother didn't show you she loved you doesn't mean you have to do this."

"What did you say?!" She'd made it personal. She had no right to mention his mother. He swung again, connecting with her leg. He enjoyed the sound of contact from the balls. He would get the information he wanted.

Roseleen closed her eyes. She could see the man as a little boy. *Mallor. His name is Mallor.* The Source was flooding her with messages.

No one is exempt from learning in this lifetime.

Only future actions can undo the past.

"She did love you, Mallor. She didn't know how to show it."

"Stop!" Mallor swung again; blind fury enraged him, and he pummeled her body.

"You can take a different path; love has no boundaries."

"You will tell me what I want to know!"

"The world changes whether we are ready or not."

Mallor struck, again and again, trying to evoke fear on her face and wipe out her words.

How did she know his name?

"Tell me, what is your connection to the doctor?"

Roseleen's head drooped. The messages from The Source stopped, and her world went dark.

CHAPTER 56

Jordon watched the screen as the auditorium broke out into chaos. The Contagion had shown his barcoded wrist, and the orderly meeting had descended into a stampede of fear. He could understand the reaction after years of propaganda. Even separated by a screen, his initial reaction had been to pull away.

He was intrigued as well. The man with the barcode had been in the room for the length of the meeting, and yet there had been no adverse effects. The doctor also mentioned a breakthrough in his research, and those two pieces of information meant there was a bigger story, a story he was going to break across all media channels.

Jordon tapped the screen and accessed the Society Assignments Directory to find Dr. Jayr Lenus and his supervisor, Masha Stevenson. Their offices were located at the Lab of Human Betterment.

There was no time to waste. He pushed his personal screen into a messenger bag and left his home. He checked the timetable as he entered the public transportation portal. Seven minutes before the next car arrived for the center of Precinct One. He tried not to pace on the platform. The news of the Contagion in Society was being discussed by everyone around him. Anxiety and fear blended with curiosity. He knew how they felt. The Contagions had been confined to the Compound and there had been no known breach of Society for years until today.

The train arrived, and Jordon stepped inside, scanning the car for a place to sit. It was more crowded than usual, and he realized the information replaying on the screens had sparked a flood of movement in the precinct.

"I don't feel safe on the streets." Jordon overheard a conversation between two people beside him.

"I'm heading home and locking the door."

This was the biggest story since The Path had taken hold. Jordon willed the train to go faster. He looked at the route map overhead. Seven more stops before he reached his destination.

Sir William paced his office. "This is treason! There is no cure for the virus. That doctor and his fake contagion will be arrested for falsifying information and stirring up Society."

The large screen still replayed the images from the reporting two hours ago. Commentators were trying to fill in the gaps for news which was still unclear.

Annabella looked down at her screen. A private message arrived from her husband. "I'm on my way to find the doctor. This story is big, and I'm going to be sure to be the one to tell it."

She subtly typed a reply. "Sir William is going to have them arrested. Be safe."

"On what grounds?"

"Falsifying information and causing social unrest."

"Stall him. I need to get the story first."

"I'll do my best."

She looked up from her screen. "Let's discuss our options. What is the motivation for the doctor to lie?"

Sir William stopped and glared at her. "He's obviously lashing out because his research was halted. Now he's trying to fabricate a story to validate his work. It's unacceptable. I want the Society Security Patrol to arrest him and the impostor immediately, along with his supervisor, for condoning this behavior. The fake Contagion is clearly a hired actor playing a role and should be arrested too. I will expose them as the frauds they are."

Annabella got up from the couch and started for the door.

"Don't worry, Sir William. I'll take care of it. I'll contact the patrolling officer and make sure the doctor and the others are taken in for questioning."

"Questioning?! NO! They need to be charged with fraud."

"It will be hard to charge them until we have more information."

"Where is Mallor? He can take care of it."

"I think it will be better to go through the proper channels. If what you say is true, having the Society Security Patrol involved is important."

"Of course, it's true! There's no other explanation," the president sputtered. "This doctor is a quack and needs to be stopped." He pounded his desk. "Tell me when they're in custody and find Mallor!"

"Yes, Sir. I'm on it."

Annabella left the room and leaned against the closed door behind her. She could stall for a few moments more.

⫟⫠

Mallor looked at the unconscious woman. She was in her mid to late twenties, although freckles made her appear younger. Her copper hair hung around her face. She was dressed like many of the women in Society, and yet something was different about her.

He looked closely at her hands. Her nails were short and unpolished, another oddity for someone from Society. Her hands were clean, but he observed they were callused. This was a woman who used her hands for work. She wasn't an office worker or socialite with soft skin. He pushed up the left sleeve of her blouse. There was no barcode on the underside of her wrist, which ruled out her being from the Compound.

She had been unfazed by him. She showed no fear, even while he beat her. His afternoon had promised to be enjoyable and full of sport. He loved the weakness of others; it made him feel strong. Instead, he felt weak.

What had she meant about his mother? How could she know anything about a woman who had died before this girl had been born? And how did she know his name? While he was·often around Sir William, he made a point not to be featured in media reporting. He was one of many suits in Sir William's orbit. He did not drive policy or hold a top Society position. He operated below the radar.

Returning to the wall of items at his disposal, he picked up a capsule filled with ammoniaethonal. He broke it open under Roseleen's nose, and the pungent aroma jerked her awake.

"We're going to try again."

Roseleen's body felt sore. She suspected her skin was purple and blue with bruises inflicted by the contraption Mallor had used. He'd hung the strapped balls on the arm of the chair he moved in front of her, and he sat facing her.

The world is changing. Society will not be the same.

The messages from The Source resumed, and she shared the missives flooding through.

"It is time to embrace love. Love for everyone. More importantly, Mallor, it is time for you to love yourself."

"How do you know my name?" Fear flashed on the face of the man.

"I've seen you for a long time. I know you did not feel loved by your mother. That's why you hurt people, so they feel the hurt you felt by being ignored by her."

"Stop it! There's no way you can know that!"

"I only know what The Source chooses to share."

"The Source? What nonsense is this?"

"It's the power of the universe. We are energy. All of us. I feel the energy of those around me."

"You're crazy!" *When had he lost control of the interrogation?*

"It's time for change. There has been corruption and hate

for too long. The Power Walker is here to traverse between the two worlds."

"The Power who?"

"Triden is here to bridge the worlds. He will restore order and peace."

"We are not at war."

"There is a hidden war. It is a war of class and society. Too long have those entitled to a place in Society been denied their rights. You have played a role in encouraging inequities."

"I have a job I do very well."

"You are fueled by pain and suffering. It is time for you to do good in the world."

"Who are you? How do you know this?"

"I'm the Oracle. I see the future."

"No one can do that."

"I can see your past, and now I see your future. You have a chance for greatness, but you must shed your armor. You must be vulnerable and stand for truth. You have documented all the secrets. With this information comes power. You can choose your power for good, or you can continue down a path of corruption."

How did she know about his insurance—all the notations made so he would have ultimate protection?

"If you choose to protect yourself, you will not survive. If you use the information to restore balance, you'll live a full life."

"You listen to me. I'm in control."

"Not everyone wants to do good in the world. You get to choose your path."

Mallor froze in his tracks. This girl had him rattled. A girl! How was it she showed no fear? How could she speak of the things she knew nothing about? He picked up the torture tool and struck her again.

Jordon exited the train car and dodged between the throng of people in the terminal station. He'd passed the Lab of Human Betterment numerous times but never had a reason to enter the large, official building. Columns flanked the entrance, and the emblem of the institution hung overhead. He took the stairs two at a time. The large interior atrium was impressive, and he walked the marble floor looking for any information to guide him to Masha Stevenson's office. Knowing Society Security Patrol was likely on their way caused his heart to pound.

The building was surprisingly quiet, considering the turmoil from the meeting held earlier in the day. He pushed down a long hallway. Lab rooms on his right were visible through glass panes embedded in the closed doors. On his left was a series of offices. He was looking for C-136. The offices were part of block A. At the end of the hall, he saw a staircase and signage indicating B and C offices were on the higher floors. He sprinted up the curving marble staircase and, at the top of the first flight, determined he needed to go up one more.

He turned left and made his way down the hall: C-150, 148, 146... His heart pounded, and he realized he'd been holding his breath and let out a sigh when he saw C-136. He looked inside: empty. Had the Society Security Patrol been there already?

He pulled out his personal screen and tapped a few boxes. The doctor's office and lab were also on the C level. He sprinted down the hall and found the doctor's office, C-128. Also empty.

He turned toward the lab doors. C-127 was assigned to Jayr Lenus. He pushed open the door and found himself facing the doctor and the Contagion. He'd made it in time.

He extended his hand. "Hello, I'm Jordon Connor. My wife is an advisor to Sir William Newbiggers. I'd like to talk with you about the meeting this morning."

The doctor did not respond to the offered gesture. "Are you here for the Statecraft?"

"No. I'm here as a representative of Society Media. I want to tell your story."

"Tell it or bury it?"

"Why would I want to bury it? This is the biggest story since the Compound was created years ago."

"What is your affiliation with Sir William?"

"As I said, my wife is an advisor to him."

"And you?"

"Well, I think he's pompous and arrogant. We don't get along."

"Why should I trust you?"

"Because I know Society Security Patrol is on their way here to arrest you and..." Jordon looked at the young man. "Triden?" The young man nodded affirmation.

"Look, I know why you may not want to trust me, but can we go somewhere else to discuss this? No strings attached. You can tell me as much or as little as you want, whatever makes you comfortable, but for now, let's get you away from the Society Security."

"Sir William ordered the Patrol to arrest us?"

"Yes, according to my wife."

"Let's go." Jayr and Triden collected a few items, and the three moved to the door.

"Do you mind taking off your lab coat? I don't want to draw attention to us as we're leaving." Jayr slid out of the long white garment and hung it on the back of the lab door.

"Is there a back way out of here?"

Jayr pointed down the opposite hall. This will take us down to the parking garage. There are several exits we can access from there.

"Follow me."

The three men made their way to the stairwell at the back of the building. Jordon descended the steps quickly, pausing briefly to allow the older man time to catch up. Triden moved with ease, certainly not as Jordon would have expected from a virus-infected Contagion.

He probably isn't a Contagion. How could the doctor be next to him without worry? Jordon felt his pulse race with excitement for being the one to convey the story.

He slowed as he made it to the bottom of the stairs. Society Security Patrol could be seen at the opposite end of the hallway, pushing through the rotating doors into the large rotunda.

They watched as the patrol made its way up the first internal staircase and then continued. Once in the parking garage, the doctor motioned to his car, and they climbed inside.

He pressed the ignition, and the car came to life. Jayr tried to look calm as they drove past the Society Security Patrol cars and pulled into traffic.

They rode in silence for a few minutes.

"Are we in trouble?" Triden looked anxious.

The doctor assured the young man. "We've done nothing wrong. We have to be careful. There are those who are going to want to bury your story."

Jordon smiled, "I can put it on all media screens in Society before the day is done."

"How can we trust you?"

"I saved you from being arrested, didn't I?"

"What do you get out of it?"

"I get an exclusive story. Something tells me this is big."

The doctor nodded. "I won't tell it unless we're live on the media screens. We need protection."

"I'll make the arrangements." Jordon knew he was taking a chance. His instincts told him to trust the doctor and his curiosity about the man with the barcode outweighed any fears of potentially promoting a fraudulent story. Either way, he could expose the story as either truthful or an elaborate lie. He didn't have anything to lose.

✺

Mallor felt exhausted, broken. As he looked at the young girl's limp body, he couldn't shake her words from his mind.

Not everyone wants to do good in the world. You get to choose your path.

Usually, he didn't waste his time thinking about being good or evil. He had a job to do, and he had been given a wide berth to accomplish the goals of the Statecraft. And yet, he wasn't here because of a directive from Sir William. He was here, torturing this girl, because of what he'd seen in the auditorium.

He had seen a loving connection between this woman and the Contagion on the stage with the doctor. He wanted to cause her pain. He realized he enjoyed the sport of wielding power over someone else, and she had looked petite and fragile, someone easily manipulated.

What had started as an intention for empowerment had quickly turned to feelings of weakness and vulnerability. His mother had taunted him as a child. She would beat him with a belt and chastise him when he cried. "You're not strong. I didn't suffer through birthing you to have a weakling for a son. You are pathetic! You are not a man!"

He had spent years proving her wrong. He was strong. He had power. Until now. Mallor lowered his head and started to sob.

✺

"We can't risk going to your home. Let's go directly to the Society Media office. We'll set you up in a studio to broadcast your message freely."

Jordon pulled his personal screen from his bag and started to type a message. Jayr looked concerned. "No messages. We must arrive unannounced. If what you say is true and we're to be arrested, I do not want to give anyone an upper hand."

"Good thinking." Jordon put his screen away.

"We have to find Roseleen." Triden had been quiet and agitated as the doctor drove.

"I know. We can send a message to her through the broadcast. We'll find her."

"Who's Roseleen?" Jordon looked confused. Jayr was quick to respond.

"She's part of my research team. She got separated from us during the presentation. We were hoping she'd find us at my lab."

Jordon gave Jayr directions, and soon they pulled into the underground parking structure of the building where Society Media content was broadcast to all the screens in the Statecraft.

"Can we broadcast to the Compound as well?"

"No, the Compound is on a different system. Everything displayed at the Compound is regulated. Nothing is broadcast without Statecraft approval from the Office of Contagion Services."

"It's important both communities hear what I have to say."

"I'm sure we can get approval once your story has gone live throughout Society."

The doctor nodded. "I don't want to risk another situation like the one earlier today."

The three men exited the car and made their way to the elevator. As they entered the media offices, Jordon introduced the doctor and Triden to the production team. It took thirty minutes to set up a studio, perform volume checks, and position the doctor along with Jordon on set. The two men sat in armchairs. The doctor pulled up his presentation on his personal screen and tapped into the bigger screen overhead, and linked the data.

"Can you tell me anything before we get started? I want to make sure I conduct the interview as smoothly as possible."

"Can you have the Society Media security close the building to visitors?"

"Is it necessary?"

"If the Society Security Patrol is looking for me, they'll be here within minutes of the start of our broadcast. We need to buy time to get the message out to Society."

Jordon nodded. He left the room and came back a few minutes later.

"Done. It'll give us about ten extra minutes. They have been instructed not to let anyone inside without proper permits. Since Sir William issued the arrest order, it will only be a temporary hurdle."

"Thank you." The doctor took a deep breath to steady his nerves. "It's important I'm not censored."

"Censored? Why would you get censored?" Jordon felt the hairs on the back of his neck. It was a bigger story than he expected.

"Promise me, if we get arrested, you'll do everything you can to tell the truth about the Compound."

"Done. Ready?"

The doctor nodded. Jordon turned to the production manager and gave a signal to go live. Jayr watched the countdown and saw the studio light turn red.

"Good afternoon, citizens of Society! I'm Jordon Connor, and joining me today is Dr. Jayr Lenus, the key researcher looking for a cure for P3264. Earlier today, his research report was cut short by panic at the Lab of Human Betterment. This broadcast will address all of your questions. Welcome, doctor."

"Thank you. Recently I've been conducting research on-site at the Compound to compare to data samples provided to me by the Lab of Human Betterment. For years, I have relied on samples provided by the Statecraft. Several years into my research, we found a lead for curbing the virus; however, a mutation was discovered, and we were not able to roll out a new vaccine. Since we've all seen how the virus has mutated, I felt it was important to retrieve current and relevant data directly from the Compound."

"I trust you found something new with the additional data?" Jordon leaned closer.

"Yes, I met Triden. He is a resident at the Contagion Compound. I found he did not have any antibodies to P3264."

"No antibodies? How is that possible?"

"There are several explanations. There could be herd immunity which means everyone builds up a resistance to the virus over time. Most likely, though, we would still see antibodies in blood samples."

"What is another way?"

"I believe Triden may never have had the virus to begin with."

Jordon looked surprised. "How is that possible?"

"Great question! I discovered the answer when I brought Triden to my home in Society. He started eating a diet from Society, not Compound food. His rashes, attributed to the virus, started to clear up, so I returned to the Compound and got food samples, and did an analysis. I found high levels of sodium hydrochlorizide, sulfite benzicynide, and synthetic polyestesgen."

"I don't understand. What does that have to do with P3264?"

"It is my hypothesis that the residents in the Compound have been detained illegally. They have been told they are highly contagious, and the rashes indicate they have P3264. Triden was told he was contagious, yet he shows no antibodies, and his rash cleared up when he went off Compound food."

"That's quite an allegation. Can you prove this?"

"Yes. I returned to the Compound and did a controlled study with a resident who has P3264 antibodies."

"What happened?"

"His rashes also went away when he stopped eating Compound food. Someone has been deliberately poisoning residents of the Compound to visually make it appear they are dangerous and a threat to Society."

"That's hard to believe."

"I know. And then I did further research."

"What did you find?"

"The residents at the Compound are predominantly from three of the prior precincts. Two of the precincts were eradicated during the mass terminations until there was a public outcry about the treatment of children."

"We all know the mass terminations were done to stop the spread of P3264."

"Yes, initially. And yet, it also provided a convenient cover for 'cleansing' Society."

"Cleansing? What do you mean?"

"It is my belief the precincts which were the most vocal about their dissatisfaction with Society policies were targeted. And precincts with members of a certain heritage were also isolated."

"That doesn't make any sense."

"That's what I thought at first, but my data confirms that the residents of the Compound fall outside of what some people believe makes a desirable Society."

"What do you mean?"

"One portion of Society saw themselves as superior to another group and found a way to isolate the 'undesirables' at the Compound."

"That's preposterous!"

"I agree, and yet..." The doctor motioned for Triden to step into view. "This is Triden. He's been living at the Compound since he was six. He's been living with others who have anti-bodies for P3264, and yet he has none. As you can see, we can be near him without any adverse reactions."

"Viewers, I can confirm I have been with Triden for a few hours this afternoon, and I feel fine." Jordon faced the camera. "There is no need to be alarmed. But, doctor, I have to ask you because I know this is a question going through Society minds right now... How do we know Triden is from the Compound?"

"He has a barcode on his wrist. All residents at the Compound were assigned a number when they arrived. Society members know this is a mark of a Contagion. It's the reason the previous meeting ended so abruptly."

"He isn't dressed like someone from the Compound. Do you have any other evidence to support where he's from?"

"Yes. Here's a copy of his bloodwork and the release papers filed to remove him from the Compound. The documents show both the date and time." The doctor projected the documents onto a screen devoted to their interview. Jordon paused for effect.

"I'm still not sure who would be motivated to restrict the Compound residents."

"This is a big unknown and gives me concern for myself, Triden, and my research assistant, who has been missing since the meeting earlier today."

"Tell me about your assistant."

"Roseleen is in her twenties. She is tall with copper-colored hair. If anyone knows of her whereabouts, please contact the Lab of Human Betterment."

Commotion outside of the studio indicated officers from the Society Security Patrol had arrived. A team of guards filled the exterior room, weapons drawn.

"Society members, we are being invaded by the Society Guard." Jordon stood and opened the studio door; the on-air signal remained lit overhead.

"Who is in charge? State your business!"

An officer dressed in tactical gear stepped forward.

"We have warrants to arrest Dr. Jayr Lenus and the person known as Contagion 36MA46RA23."

"On what grounds?"

"Falsifying information and causing social unrest." The officer showed the documents with the presidential seal.

Jordon turned to face the transmission lens.

"Society members, I pledge to find the answers. There is more to this story. Stay tuned for updates as soon as we have them."

The officer stepped forward with handcuffs.

"We aren't lying!" Triden looked for a way to escape, but the entrance was blocked. Being arrested as a Contagion outside of the Compound would be punishable by death, even if he hadn't taken a life. He knew he was protected by the paperwork filed by the doctor, and yet if it was deemed counterfeit, his life was in jeopardy.

"We'll be alright, Triden." The doctor stepped in between the officer and the young man.

"As a member of Society, I invoke my rights for fair representation and a communal trial. I also take responsibility for Triden, Barcode 36MA46RA23, and will bear all his consequences."

"Are you aware of the magnitude of your statement?" the commanding officer addressed the doctor. "By being culpable for his actions, you will serve any punishment deemed appropriate during sentencing."

"I understand."

Triden stepped forward. "I can't have you do that."

"You've done nothing wrong. You shouldn't be punished for my actions."

"You haven't done anything wrong, either."

"Hopefully we'll have the chance to show that to Society."

The doctor held out his wrists and allowed the officer to

handcuff him. Triden felt a chill reverberate through his body. *How would they find Roseleen from a jail cell?*

Not all want to do good in the world. You get to choose who you are. Roseleen's words echoed in his ears. Mallor knew it was time to leave. He fingered the files documenting Sir William's history of graft and deception. The papers were his protection, and he'd intentionally kept them off his personal screen where Society monitoring could expose them at any time.

He slid the folders outlining his work for Sir William for the last two decades into a metal case and placed it at Roseleen's feet. She was still unconscious. He'd checked her vital signs and determined she would wake shortly. Shame at beating her washed over him as he looked at her. She'd stood up to him with no fear, only wisdom belying her age.

Along with the paperwork, he had a variety of aliases documented on travel documents. It was time to retire Mallor and become someone else. It was time to start anew. He'd amassed enough funds that he did not have to work. It would be easy to slip away undetected.

Once he was safely out of Precinct One and well outside of Society, he would alert authorities to Roseleen's whereabouts.

He checked her pulse again and saw bruises on her arms. She would be in pain for a few days. The last bit of his resistance had been taken out against her by flogging her unconscious.

"I'm sorry." He knew she couldn't hear him, and yet it gave him a small amount of comfort to say it. Where had he gone astray? Why had he been willing to assume the role he'd played for so many years? Sometimes the truth is so simple it's hard to see. He had no excuses for his past, but he could make amends with his future.

It was time to be a better person. He gently tucked a tendril of Roseleen's hair behind her ear and made his way to the door.

‖

Annabella entered Sir William's office and saw him tapping out a succession of banner messages on the screen. The stream of words sounded unhinged and deranged. She had to get him away from his posts.

"I'm sure you saw on the broadcast the doctor and Contagion have been arrested per your orders."

"Yes. Your husband was interviewing them. Your husband! He's spreading lies about the Statecraft. I should have him arrested as well."

"He's a reporter, Sir William. He was only interviewing them."

"He's helping to spread lies, lies about the Contagion Compound and lies about Society."

"I'm sure all will be explained at their trial."

"It can't happen fast enough. Already there are protests on the streets by those who saw the arrest. We have to stop this flow of misinformation."

"I'll see what I can do."

"Where's Mallor? I haven't seen him since the assembly today."

"He's been unreachable."

"I want him to interview the two men arrested. And I want to find the third person. Who is this woman they mentioned during the broadcast?"

"I'm not sure. We can't find any record of a 'Roseleen' at the Lab of Human Betterment, and records show the doctor has been working alone."

"Find her or don't even bother coming back."

Annabella left his office. Leaning against the closed door for the second time, she felt tired. Babysitting the petulant president was taking its toll.

Jordon watched as the police took Jayr and Triden into custody. He motioned to the camera operator to capture the arrest as they were escorted from the sound booth.

"Citizens of Society, there is more to this story, and I'm making a personal pledge to find the truth. Whether this is part of an elaborate lie to cause panic within Society or a breakthrough in P3264, I will find the facts. I'm Jordon Connor, your feet on the street!"

After passing the media feed over to the sound booth, Jordon left the studio and met his supervisor on the other side of the door. "The messages are overwhelming our systems. And Sir William is asking for your resignation for promoting falsehoods."

"He's going to have to arrest me if he wants me to be quiet."

"Do you have any proof what the doctor is saying is true?"

"I've seen some initial documents, and I believe him. But I need more."

"Dammit, Jordon! With this story, Sir William could break our media presence in Society. He's been after domination of our airwaves since he entered office."

"Either way, this is the biggest story since the start of the pandemic."

"If it is determined the doctor lied and fabricated the residency of the Contagion, we could be shut down permanently. For all of our sakes, you better hope the doctor is telling the truth. The alternative will destroy us."

"Any messages related to the research assistant? If we find her, we can corroborate the story."

"Lots of people are claiming to have seen her. We didn't get much of a description. A red-haired woman in her twenties doesn't narrow down our options very much, so I suspect every Society redhead is being reported.

"Keep me posted if any solid leads come in to find Roseleen. I'm going to the Guard Patrol to see if I can find out more about the charges against the doctor and Triden."

Outside the Propaganda Office of Society, he pulled out his personal screen and tapped a message to Annabella.

"Thank you for stalling. I'm assuming you saw the feed?"

"Yes. I'm trying to find one of Sir William's loyalists. He's been missing since the reporting session."

"That's strange. The doctor's assistant has been missing since the meeting as well."

"That's probably a coincidence."

"I don't know what to think today. I'll keep you posted."

"Be safe, Jordon."

"Don't worry about me. More soon."

He tucked the screen back into his bag and made his way to the security building.

⟦ꞮⱁꞮⱦ

Roseleen opened her eyes and tried to focus. Her head hurt, and every muscle ached. She moved slightly and winced. The room was empty, and a metal file box was at her feet. She was still strapped to the chair. It didn't matter. She didn't have the strength to stand.

You have the power to heal. Even with a pounding headache, she received the message from The Source.

Mallor was nowhere to be seen. She wondered if he would return and beat her again. She had centered her mind and turned inward when he started pummeling her. She was able to separate her mind from her body to diminish the pain. Bringing her consciousness back to the room brought with it a wave of discomfort. She started doing a mental assessment of her condition. Slowly moving one leg as much as she could with the restraints, her thighs ached, but her bones felt intact. Fortunately, he had not swung at her knees, and most of the blows had been to her upper body. The restraints had protected her hands and wrists, but she suspected she had several fractured ribs. He'd also spared hitting her in the head, most likely to keep her coherent during questioning.

It could have been worse. She understood his soul from the messages from The Source. He had strayed off of his purpose in life. His path had taken him to a dark place where he wanted to punish those around him the same way he'd been punished by his mother.

Roseleen shuddered. The energy of his mother had a strong vibration that reverberated throughout her body. She closed her eyes and pushed the energy away. Mallor's mother would no longer have control over her son.

Take time and be truthful with yourself to be led down the right path. Instinctively, she knew the message was for Mallor, and he was on his way to correct his course.

She drifted back to sleep, knowing he wouldn't return.

Annabella looked at the alert on her screen. It was unusual for Mallor to contact her directly.

"A person of interest can be found here." The address of a building in Precinct Three followed the message.

She typed a reply to Mallor requesting more information, but he did not respond. She forwarded the address to Jordon. She had to deal with Sir William, and she trusted her husband to take care of whatever mess Mallor had created in Precinct Three. At least she didn't have to deal with the unpleasant man or spend more time trying to track him down.

After a moment, she added a message. "Be careful, Jordie. Do not engage with Mallor any more than necessary."

She put her screen down and pushed open the office door. As she suspected, Sir William was glued to the large screen and sending out banner feeds to Society.

"Society will not tolerate misinformation regarding the Contagion Compound. The hack doctor and actor portraying the Contagion will be dealt with appropriately. No one has escaped or left the Compound. All is safe in Society!"

The media feed replayed the arrest as well as interviews of members of Society on the street.

"I'm afraid of the Contagions. They could kill us all!"

"I believe the doctor. I don't know why he would lie."

"I heard it's really an actor hired to pretend to be from the Compound."

Annabella could see Sir William had successfully created doubt within Society. She wasn't sure why it was so important to him. She was curious about the doctor's story. Was it an elaborate hoax in order to make a statement about his work at the end of his research assignment? What was the purpose? The lie would ultimately be revealed and destroy his credibility.

"Sir William, do you want me to cancel your Quilt game this afternoon?"

The pudgy man looked up from his newsfeed. "Yes, cancel the game." He paused. "On second thought, now that the doctor has been arrested, we can put a stop to this fabricated story. Going to the club is exactly what I need this afternoon."

"Also, I heard from Mallor. I'm going to Precinct Three on his request."

"Tell him to meet me at The Flodden Club."

"I will. Enjoy your game."

Thankful for her cleared schedule, she decided to join her husband. She wanted to get Jordon's insights and didn't trust the communications over her personal screen when it came to the matters of the morning. There was no reason to threaten her position of loyalty within Sir William's Cabinet by having a intercepted message cast doubt on her commitment to the president.

Jayr and Triden sat in a jail cell. Upon arrival at the Guard Security office, they were informed they would be detained while the Society Federal Court reviewed the charges recorded against them. Several others shared the cell with them. However, when they saw Triden's barcode, they moved to the opposite corner of the cell.

"I didn't realize how scared everyone would be of me."

"This is short-term. As soon as we can share the rest of your story and the condition of those in the Compound, we can address their fears," the doctor reassured him.

"I'm worried about Roseleen."

"Me, too. I'm sure Jordon will find her."

"She wouldn't have left on her own."

"I'm hopeful she got swept up in the outflow of people from the auditorium, nothing more. When I can access my screen, I'll see if she's made it back to my apartment."

"I hope you're right."

"Me, too." He didn't want Triden to be alarmed, so he kept his concerns to himself.

Jordon scanned the sea of pedestrians around him, looking for Annabella. He was thrilled when he got her follow-up message saying she would join him. The excitement of being in the middle of the biggest news story—whether it was true or fabricated—was better shared with her.

It didn't take long for his wife to emerge from the transit station. Together they walked the few blocks to the nondescript building at the address Mallor had sent.

Jordon rang the bell. The sound could be heard echoing inside. No answer. He knocked on the door, creating a muffled sound through the thick wood, and still no answer.

"I thought Mallor would be here."

"Me, too. Is it locked?"

Jordon tried to turn the handle, but it didn't give way.

"Let's walk to the back."

Together they rounded the perimeter of the building. Windows were closed with blinds pulled down—no sign of life, only an eerie feeling emanating from the dark, cement structure.

"I've got a bad feeling about this."

"Me, too. Can you message Mallor?"

"I keep trying, but he's not answering." Annabella pulled out her device and tapped another message to the missing man. "He's not reading his messages."

"Why would he send you this address and not be here? There's no evidence of anyone of special interest either."

"There's the back door. Let's try it."

Jordon stepped forward and pounded on the door, and paused. Silence. He pounded again.

"I guess we're too late."

"It would seem so. It's still fun to see you during the day." Jordon grabbed his wife's behind and gave it a playful squeeze. "Not all is lost."

Annabella giggled and leaned toward her husband. "It is a nice change to our daily routines." She kissed him. "Any chance I can see more of you this afternoon?"

"I'm sure that can be arranged." He slid his hand under her skirt and pushed her panties aside, and felt the warmth between her legs. Annabella looked around to see how much privacy they had behind the building. She arched her body toward him, encouraging him to continue.

"What did you say?"

"Hmmm, I didn't say anything."

"I thought I heard something."

"Don't stop."

"There it is again. Did you hear that?"

"No." Annabella paused and listened. She heard a subtle sound like a moan of a child. "What is it?"

"I don't know, but it sounds like it's coming from inside." Jordon pulled away from his wife and stepped toward the door again. He tried the handle and it turned in his hand. He tentatively pushed the door inward and stepped inside.

"Hello?" he called into the interior. "Hello? It's Jordon and Annabella Connor. We're looking for Mallor." He looked back to Annabella and stepped inside after motioning her to stay outside. "I'm coming with you!" she whispered behind him.

They stepped into a long hallway. There was a stairwell to the right leading down to the basement below and the floors above. Offices flanked the hallway, but the building looked like it had been abandoned for some time. Some of the rooms were boarded shut, and most of the offices looked like storage spaces.

They moved tentatively down the length of the floor and didn't see anything.

"Let's look on another floor, closer to the back of the building. We wouldn't have been able to hear anything from this far away."

"Good thinking." There was another set of stairs located at the front of the building, and they started to descend to the lower level.

"Hello?" Jordon called out again, listening for any response as they moved toward the back of the building. Looking into the various spaces, abandoned and unused, was unnerving. A fluorescent bulb flickered overhead, and Annabella moved closer to Jordon and took his hand.

"I don't feel good about this."

They reached the end of the hallway, facing a closed wooden door. Others on the floor had glass window insets. This door was solid. Jordon knocked before turning the knob.

He carefully pushed the door open. A large wooden chair that looked like those used by an executioner was placed in the center of the room. Strapped to the chair was a redheaded woman. He suspected he'd found Roseleen. Her head hung down.

"Help." Her voice was almost indistinguishable. He hoped they'd found her in time.

※

Roseleen started to awaken, but she didn't want to open her eyes. Her body was stiff and sore, and she didn't want to see the wall of torture tools again. Maybe if she kept her eyes shut, she could delay another beating. As her mind began to focus, she realized she was no longer constrained and was lying down on a soft surface, covered with a blanket. She slowly opened her eyes to see a white, sterile room. A screen displayed the customary Society media feed and to her right was a series of cables linking her vitals to a medical device. She didn't know what the symbols meant, and she turned toward the interior of the room again.

There was an upholstered chair at the end of her bed and on it was a silver metallic case. She remembered Mallor had left it by her feet, but she had no idea what it contained. Had he brought her and the case here? It didn't seem likely. She had a vague recollection of him leaving the interrogation room.

Her ribs were taped, and upon closer examination, she realized her arms were badly bruised. Mallor had pelted her repeatedly, and while restricted she'd been unable to fight off the blows.

A medical person pushed open the door to her room.

"Good, you're awake. We were worried you might be suffering from a coma."

"Where am I?"

"You're at the Precinct One Medical and Rehabilitation Facility."

"Where's Triden and Jayr?"

"Oh, sweetie, those two have been arrested for fraud against Society. Their trial is starting tomorrow."

"Fraud? I don't understand."

"They fabricated a story, and they're going to pay the price."

"They're telling the truth!"

"Don't worry. The trial will reveal what is true and what isn't."

"I have to see them."

"That's not possible. They're being contained at the Society Security facility."

"How long have I been here?"

"Three days."

"What?"

"You came in pretty beat up. Someone really did a number on you."

"I have to let Triden know I'm alright."

"Sweetie, the doctor is going to talk with you. We couldn't find any prior medical records for you. We don't even know your name. You're an enigma!"

"Please help me. There has to be a way to get a message to Triden."

"I'll see what I can do. Here, take this." The aide handed her two small tablets and some water.

"What is this?"

"It will help you with the pain."

"I don't want this."

"You've been on it since you got here."

No wonder she didn't feel like herself. Her eyelids kept wanting to droop, and her mind felt full of shadows. She pushed the medication back.

"I'll add it to your IV." The nurse retrieved a syringe and pressed a liquid into one of the tubes attached to Roseleen's arm. She drifted back to the shadows before she could pull the line free from her arm.

Triden and Jayr met with their Society assigned barrister, a young man who was only a few years older than Triden.

"I've been unable to find any records supporting your story. Your supervisor said you requested permission to go to the Compound, but it was denied."

"Yes, that's true. I went without her knowledge."

"I see."

"I don't think you do. I've found the Contagions are being detained for no reason. In fact, their containment is being manipulated by poisoning their food to look like they are infected with P3264."

"Doctor, the Society barrister is going to present you as a disgruntled fraud who is manufacturing a story to make relevance out of your failed work. He is going to show you did this when your research was canceled."

"Look at Triden. He's proof what I'm saying is true."

"He's being touted as an actor solicited by you to support your lies. We've been unable to find his Society records."

"That's because he's from the Contagion Compound."

"This is a Society trial, and I can only present documents from Society."

"You mean you can't pull Triden's records from the Compound?"

"There's no precedence for this. The law states Society records are to be used. There is no method for accessing the Compound files."

"Can't you request an exception?"

"I did and received a lecture on law practices from the judge. It is in your best interests to make a retraction statement and apologize for the stress and pain you have caused Society. You'll be lucky to keep your license to practice."

"I'll do no such thing. I'm telling the truth, and it's important everyone in Society knows the residents in the Compound can be released and reintroduced into Society without fear or worry."

"If you don't enter a plea, you're signing away your career, your reputation."

"If I agree to a plea, I won't be honoring my oath as a doctor."

"Have it your way, but I guarantee you'll be facing more prison time. You'll be stripped of your doctorate, and you will be a pariah for the rest of your life."

"What will happen with Triden?"

"He will be deemed a Contagion since he's chosen to impersonate one. He will be sent to the Compound as his punishment and will most likely die when he is exposed to P3264." The lawyer started stowing his files in a case, preparing to leave the meeting room.

"I will see you in the courtroom tomorrow morning. Please be prepared to apologize for your misconception, and I will do my best to minimize your sentence."

Neither man spoke until the barrister had left the room.

The doctor faced Triden. "At least you'll be able to return to the Compound. That's what I promised you."

"You can't take the plea."

"I have no intention of bargaining with them. It appears someone in a high position within Society is behind the food alterations, which would explain why no one is willing to test my hypothesis."

"You didn't do anything wrong."

"I did by going outside of Society protocol, and the prosecutor is going to use it against me. If I was willing to break the rules, it's conceivable I am exactly what they say, a frustrated researcher looking for a thread of recognition for my efforts."

"There has got to be a way to prove your findings."

"Unfortunately, I'm using my own notes and research. There's nothing generated within the formal study of P3264."

"But you've been researching this for years."

"Yes, however, by ignoring my manager's denial request to go to the Compound, I undermined my own alibi."

"I wish there was something I could do." Triden hung his head in defeat. "I'm also worried about Roseleen. There's been no word about her since we've been here. Jordon hasn't been in contact either."

The doctor reached over and placed his hand on Triden's arm. "This is where the Society screens will work to our advantage. I'll make a public announcement during our hearing tomorrow. I hope someone watching will have information about her."

"I hope so. I never should have brought her here. She would be safe in the woods."

"Don't worry, Triden. She's going to be fine." The doctor didn't mention the feeling of dread he'd had since their arrest. No good would come from articulating his fears and would only drag Triden into the same pool of despair. Better to remain silent.

CHAPTER 60

Jordon sat in the armchair at the foot of Roseleen's bed and watched the young girl sleeping. He and Bella had gotten her an ambulance and treatment as quickly as they could. He'd made a promise to Triden and the doctor to keep an eye out for her; he'd never expected to find her in a torture room.

The doctor had clearly triggered an alarm by coming forward. Why else would someone need to detain Roseleen? Bella was convinced Mallor had inflicted the wounds and, for some reason, disappeared, leaving them to clean up his mess.

The medical staff assured Jordon that Roseleen would survive. She needed time to heal, and they were keeping her medicated to ease her pain. It could be hours before she woke.

He looked down and saw her case, a sealed metallic box. Jayr said she was his assistant. Did it contain the information supporting the doctor's research? The security patrol had interrupted his interview, and there was still a story to tell.

He reached down, released the clasp, and flipped open the case. A variety of folders were inside. He pulled out the first one expecting to find data related to the Contagions. It didn't take long to realize the information was unrelated to the doctor's work. Instead, it contained file after file of information outlining the transgressions of a self-indulgent president, his graft, and corruption.

Jordon scanned the documents and stopped short when he discovered information about the Compound. As he read, he realized he had a dilemma. Did he expose the information that could free every Contagion, or should he bury it and keep Republic Management in business?

He extracted several files from the case and slipped them into his bag undetected. He closed the container and looked at the unconscious girl.

Roseleen drifted in and out of consciousness. She was aware of medical personnel coming into her room, checking her status and murmuring words of treatment and questions about her background.

As the power of the pain medication began to wear off, she was able to drag her eyelids open and sit up. While the drugs allowed her to move with minimal pain, her body was stiff.

"I wondered when you would be awake." A middle-aged man with dark brown hair and blue eyes sat in the chair at the foot of her bed.

Make tomorrow even better than today.

She had wondered when the messages from The Source would start again.

"Who are you?"

"I'm Jordon Connor. My wife and I found you in Precinct Three and brought you here."

His name sounded familiar.

"You're the reporter."

"Yes. Are you Roseleen?"

"How do you know my name?"

"I interviewed the doctor and Triden. You fit the description of their assistant who was separated from them at the Findings Report meeting."

Assistant. She made a mental note.

"Do you know why you would have been taken to an interrogation room?"

"Someone thought I had information I didn't have."

"We've been searching for him."

"He's gone."

"We've been looking for him for several days. He's vanished without a trace."

"He won't be back."

"How do you know?"

She had no interest in sharing her insights with this man.

The two-faced woman has no opinion.

She was too tired to try to make sense of the messages.

"I need to see Triden."

"The two have been arrested. Their formal hearing to charge them officially is tomorrow."

"I have to go."

Jordon looked at the young woman. She looked better than when they'd found her unconscious, battered, and bruised, but she didn't look like she had the stamina to leave her bed.

"I think you should stay here. I'll be at the courtroom tomorrow broadcasting for the media office. I'll make sure they know you've been found and are safe."

He stood up to leave and reached down to return the metal case to the chair.

"We brought your documents. They were by the chair when we found you."

Roseleen eyed the case. It was Mallor's, not hers.

"Thank you. I appreciate it."

"I'll come by tomorrow after the court hearing."

"Can you give Triden a message for me?"

"Of course."

"Tell him to remember who he is."

"That's it?"

"He'll know what it means." She watched as Jordon left the room. She slowly pushed the blanket aside and sat up. Pain shot through her ribs, the tape not enough to stop the strain against the fractured bone. Ignoring the sensation, she willed her legs to the edge of the mattress. She rested a few minutes before attempting to stand. The plastic tubing connected to her arm was restricting; she hoped it would be long enough to get to her destination.

More pain as her feet connected with the floor. She didn't have to go far. She steadied herself using the bed and reached the end of the mattress after a few deliberate steps. She mentally removed herself from her body to minimize the pain. She had done it when Mallor was beating her; she willed the pain away.

She reached the metal case. Why would Mallor have left it by her side? She opened it and found a variety of folders and envelopes. She pulled them from the case and put them on the bed before retracing her steps. It wasn't graceful, but she managed to climb back onto the bed, ignoring the searing pain jolting through her side.

Pulling the blanket toward her, she manipulated the pile of files within easy reach. She opened the first one and started reading.

The fall morning was bright and crisp. Triden and Jayr had been led from their detention cell to the courthouse several buildings away. A bird overhead cawed, and Triden marveled that nature had found a way into the bustling precinct of Society.

"You should make the plea."

"I already told you. It goes against the oath I took as a doctor. Do no harm."

"You're not harming me. I'll be fine in the Compound."

"It will be harmful for all residents in the Compound. You deserve a better life, and Society needs to know the wrongs implemented by an elite few."

"I'm lucky to be alive. Remember?"

"I want you to be lucky to be alive...and free."

They entered the courtroom and were led to the defendant's table. The security patrol officer removed their handcuffs but left their ankle chains in place. They didn't pose a flight risk. There would be nowhere to hide in a world filled with media screens anyone could tap and use to report them.

An older, balding man dressed in a black robe with a Signet crest entered the room and settled at the desk. Media cameras were set up on the left side of the room, transmitting the court proceedings to all in Society. Triden felt nervous, unsure of what would happen in the room.

He saw Jordon; the sandy-haired man waved and made his way to the railing dividing the proceedings from the media.

"I found Roseleen. She's safe."

"You found her?" Relief flooded his body, and Triden relaxed for the first time since they'd been taken into custody. "Where is she?"

"She's extremely tired after her ordeal. She wanted me to tell you to remember who you are."

Before they could continue the conversation, the court clerk called the hearing to order. Jordon retreated to his camera and started the video stream to Society.

"Hear ye, hear ye. We are gathered today to review the matter of crimes committed against Society. These are grave charges, and it is this court's responsibility to uphold the Law of the Signet of the Statecraft. Counsel, have your clients been informed of their rights in this matter?"

"Yes, sir."

"Signet Solicitor, are there any modifications to the charges brought forth as outlined in the court documents?"

"No, sir."

"Let us proceed."

The charges were read aloud and mirrored the information provided by their barrister the day before.

"Is there anyone who has additional information pertinent to this case?"

The doctor whispered to the young attorney, "Did you present my research?"

"I did, but it's unlikely to be considered because it's based on your data, not supporting information provided by a third-party source."

The judge continued. "In light of no additional information..."

"WAIT!" Triden jumped to his feet. "I have information which has not been considered."

"Young man, you have counsel who represents you. Do you not feel he has done his job?"

"He has done a lot to explain the process here, but I am from the Contagion Compound. Our protocols are different."

"From everything I've read on this case, you are jeopardizing your future by continuing to assume a role of a Contagion. There is no cure for P3264, and yet you walk among us. The only plausible explanation is you are lying. The doctor has convinced you to play this part to your own detriment."

"I am Barcode 36MA46RA23. It's even etched onto my wrist." He pulled up his sleeve to show the tattoo. "I am a Water and Waste Engineer in the Compound. I have lived there since my parents were killed in the mass terminations. It is the only home I remember before the doctor brought me here."

"Please sit down. This proceeding is to accept information and make formal charges. You will have a chance to speak your position when we move to the trial. During this hearing, we accept evidence for the trial. Do you have any documents showing you are a Contagion?"

Triden had never had to prove who he was. The barcode and rash visually showed his fate. The rash had disappeared, and the barcode was his only identification.

"Only my barcode and the paperwork submitted by the doctor."

"Those will be taken into consideration."

Triden sat down. He did not understand the nature of the proceedings. He knew the doctor had taken on his plea, but he couldn't let him bear the burden.

The doctor leaned closer and whispered in his ear. "Someone has been misleading Society for years about the state of the Compound. It's obvious the court is closed to consideration of other information. We'll see how this unfolds."

"It's not fair."

"Sadly, life isn't always fair."

"Quiet, please. Prepare for the reading of your formal charges."

⌷⌷⌷

Sir William watched the trial proceedings with glee. How dare that doctor come forward with accusations about the Compound. The president had done everything he could to protect the citizens of Society from the inferior specimens kept in isolated confinement.

He tapped out a message for his banner. "Forced assimilation of Contagions into Society is detrimental to our future. We must secure the existence of our people and a future for the children of Society, or else we all perish! Do not forget the Time of Mass Terminations!"

He looked up as Annabella entered his office. "It's a good day! This nonsense will soon be behind us."

"Sir, you have a game scheduled this afternoon at the Quilt Club." The blond woman looked tired.

"Perfect. Any word from Mallor?"

"No. He hasn't been seen since the formal meeting to report the research findings." Annabella did not tell the president about the interrogation room and the young girl they found.

Sir William sighed. Occasionally, Mallor would be gone for several days as he tracked down opposition to the president's actions. He was bound to return soon.

"Who is playing today?"

"The usual cabinet members from Precincts 2, 3, and 5."

"Good. It will be a nice distraction from this nonsense." Sir William gestured toward the screen. "As far as I'm concerned, they should lock those two up and throw away the key."

Roseleen read for as long as she could before the pain medication interfered again. She drifted in and out of sleep with fitful dreams and mixed messages from The Source. She struggled to awaken and sit up as her nurse entered her room.

"Would you like to try the tablet this time?"

Roseleen nodded and accepted the pill and water. She popped the capsule into her mouth and drank several gulps of water while the attendant watched.

"You made progress today. As soon as you can take your own medication regularly, you'll be considered for discharge."

Roseleen nodded and closed her eyes again. She listened while the medical aide presumably checked the equipment readings and made notes. A few minutes later, she heard the door open and shut, and as soon as she was sure she was alone, she opened her eyes. She reached for the glass of water on the bedside table and spit out the pain pill she'd tucked under her tongue. The coating was beginning to dissolve, and she swished water around and spit the liquid out. She could handle some pain. It was imperative she make it to the courthouse.

The Forest Seer looked at the needle in her arm and carefully removed the tape holding it in place. She pulled it out quickly, wincing slightly as the metal needle scratched her skin. Several drops of blood appeared, and she applied pressure to stop the flow.

She got up and looked for her clothes. They were neatly folded inside a dresser, and she struggled to pull on the unfamiliar garments. If only she had her leathers from the forest, although she knew they would be impractical for navigating the streets of Society and would make her stand out in a crowd. It took a while to dress as her body groaned in response to moving her arms and legs to manipulate the clothing onto her figure.

Roseleen pushed the files into the metal case and peered out the door. No one was in the hallway, and she stepped out of her room. She walked as straight and quickly as she could and ducked into the stairwell.

[◫]

Don't forget who you are. Roseleen's words echoed in his mind. She called him the Power Walker, but Triden didn't feel very powerful at the moment. He sat next to the doctor and their lawyer and listened to the proceedings. The protocols were unfamiliar to him and nothing like the Town Hall meetings conducted at the Compound on rare occasions.

He looked at the large screen and saw his image, along with others in the courtroom, being transmitted to everyone in Society. He felt uncomfortable knowing many throughout the precincts would see his image and make assumptions about who he was without hearing the truth first.

He had been born in Society, and yet the life he knew and understood was at the Compound. He was used to his insular world, and the stimulation of all the activity around him in Society added to his uneasiness.

He brought his attention back to the charges being read. "We will determine in this courtroom the extent to which Dr. Jayr Lenus and his accomplice have acted to defraud Society."

Behind him, he heard a commotion as the doors to the courtroom were pushed open. Turning in his chair, he saw Roseleen enter, carrying a silver case. Her head was bandaged, and she was walking with a limp. He could see pain etched across her face, and he wanted to rush to her side and ease her burden.

"Silence! Silence!" The judge pounded a gavel on his desktop to quiet the room. "This is a closed session only open to those being charged and media. Please leave at once."

"If you are charging the doctor and Triden, then you'll have to charge me, too." She continued to advance to the front of the room.

"Who are you?"

"I'm Roseleen of the Forest Seer Communion, and I request a closed-door session with the honorable judge presiding over these proceedings."

"That's ridiculous. We are in the middle of registering the charges in this case. You have already missed the protocol request for submitting additional information."

Roseleen had read the papers in the case carefully. "Even

though the request for documentation has officially con-cluded, any information unknown at the time of the query can be admitted at any time. Neither the doctor nor Triden know of this content, and therefore their barrister could not intro-duce it following hearing protocols. I request a closed-door session due to the sensitive nature of the documents I'm bring-ing forth as evidence."

The judge hesitated and yet was bound by law to abide by the request. A growing murmur could be heard around the room.

"Order, order! I will not tolerate insubordination during this hearing."

"Roseleen, is that your name? Come with me."

All eyes watched as she exited the room and followed the judge to his chambers.

CHAPTER 62

The dealer called out the cards on the game tableaux. "Blue primary, yellow high, green low. Red dual. Seat one, winner!"

Sir William watched as the dealer pushed the tiles from the Bank toward him. His game steward stepped forward and started stacking the betting tiles in groups of five.

It was turning into a wonderful day. His Quilt account was at its highest balance, even after Lilia had siphoned funds before the Signet Dinner. He'd taken a break on his way to the club to enjoy the pleasures of a young girl, and he was about to enjoy a decadent feast at the club.

It wouldn't be long before the doctor and impostor were destroyed. The doctor would be stripped of his credentials. He didn't care about the Contagion. Sir William had quickly bored of the trial proceedings and stopped watching the screen. All he cared about was they were about to be crushed.

He had no time to waste on those who were not loyal. He looked at the cabinet heads at the table with him. They had proven their loyalty week after week at The Flodden Club. He was well on his way to being reelected. Ironically, the doctor had helped him. The protests about the containment of the Contagions had dissipated and been replaced with Society members fearful of P3264 spreading through their communities.

He dipped his spoon into the luscious dessert of chocolate and meringue and savored every bite. He motioned to the waiter to bring him a second serving.

The door to their private dining room opened, and instead of the second dessert, two Society Security personnel entered the room dressed in black protective gear.

"What is the meaning of this?"

"Sir William Newbiggers, President of Society, Overseer of Precincts of the Statecraft, we have an authorization of arrest."

"That's absurd. You can't arrest me. I'm the president."

"In cases of subversion and duplicity, charges can be made against a sitting president."

"What do you mean? Subversion and duplicity? I have dignified this office."

"By articles of the Signet, you are hereby alerted you are entitled to representation."

"You're going to lose your jobs for this!"

"We're following orders."

Sir William turned to the men around him. "Do something!"

"We have warrants for the cabinet members of Precincts 2, 3, and 5, as well."

Sir William watched as the men around him were handcuffed.

"I refuse to go with you. I want to talk to my attorney. Where is Mallor? He can help with this."

"I have my orders, Sir. Please come with me, or I'll be forced to sedate you."

"Sedate me! You're crazy!"

"This is your last notice. If you don't come with us now, this is your alert, you will be medicated."

"I'm not going."

"As you wish."

An officer stepped forward, and before Sir William could protest, he made contact with an electrical weapon rendering the rotund man helpless. Next, he injected a sedative making it impossible for him to fight.

"Get the stretcher."

"I didn't think we'd have to use a tranquilizer dart on him."

"He could have done this the easy way, but he refused to come with us."

"It's always the ones who think they can operate outside of the law who fall the hardest."

"Isn't that the truth."

The two officers called for backup. It was going to take more than the two of them to carry the President from the Quilt Club.

⁌

"Triden, Triden, Triden!"

The chanting could be heard in stereo on the doctor's home screen and the noise from the street below. Triden had become a hero for the Contagions and assigned a new role in Society to help with the reintroduction of the sequestered people in the Compound.

The doctor shook his head. "The last two months have been a whirlwind. We knew there was someone who was contaminating the food at the Contagion Compound, but I had no idea how far-reaching it went."

Roseleen smiled.

The keyholder can unlock the door.

Mallor had held the key. The case he'd left for Roseleen outlined in extensive detail how Sir William had manipulated the research findings. The initial discovery made by the doctor years ago had effectively curbed the virus. Those in the Compound had been treated and the pathogen eradicated. However, Sir William falsified the data, providing the research team with incorrect information to prevent them from discovering the virus no longer posed a threat."

The doctor continued, "The food supplied to the Compound by Society had been formulated to keep everyone covered with rashes, so no one knew the virus no longer impacted their lives. The rash varied day by day based on how much food had been consumed."

Roseleen smiled. "That explains why I started to get a rash when I ate part of a protein puck."

"You didn't tell me that!" Triden looked at her with

concern.

"It was shortly after we met; I thought it was a rash from a forest plant. It went away and I didn't give it another thought."

"Why did he do it?"

"He has an archaic belief there is a hierarchy within Society. Those of a particular race or social standing are "better" than others. He saw no reason to reintroduce "filth" into Society. The majority of residents in the Compound came from specific precincts. Others were included in the mass terminations. I thought this history was behind us." The doctor sighed. "At least we are aware of it now."

Other information in the case brought forth corruption and greed charges throughout the Society hierarchy. Cabinet members who had abused their budgets and their power were removed from their posts. The two corporations established to harvest wood from the forest and maintain the Compound were also exposed and dismantled.

The residents in the Compound had been released and were free to leave. Many of them didn't know where to go and had stayed at the Compound. To integrate the two groups, the newly appointed president asked Triden to take on the role of Ambassador to bridge the two worlds.

Statecraft monies retrieved from Sir William's Quilt account funded a community project establishing housing for Compound residents in Precinct One. Benjam was scheduled to arrive later in the day. The On Book rules were canceled. Everyone was free to explore relationships with anyone they pleased without the need to scan their barcodes. Triden hadn't been surprised to find his friend had immediately moved in with the beautiful woman he'd seen at The Barcode months earlier.

Triden looked at the screen and saw Jordon Connor reporting the latest findings. He was grateful for the assistance the man had given Roseleen.

All is well, Mother. Roseleen was thankful the Forest Seers were no longer threatened by the clearcutting of trees. Their community opted to stay separate from Society, and the new president, grateful for Roseleen's contribution, did not push her for more information on where she was from. The location of the Forest Seer Communion was considered classified information, and the president assured them they would remain undisturbed and off the grid.

There's more than one place you can call home.

Roseleen looked at Triden and down at the ring on her finger. She had found her home with him.

"Breaking news," Jordon's voice emanated from the screen. "Lilia Newbiggers, former Top Lady of Society, has filed for divorce from Sir William Newbiggers, citing irreconcilable differences. This reporter suspects she had no interest in conjugal visits with her husband."

Pictures of the former Top Lady filled the screen. The large image highlighted her plastic surgery, which had finally reached a tipping point. Her face looked drawn and tight. Roseleen felt a pang of sympathy for the other woman. Mallor's information had included detailed reports of multiple indiscretions and hush money paid by the prior president.

Jordon cut to a camera feed at the Compound. "Here's Sir William getting used to his new daily routine. No Quilt games and extravagant lunches here."

The petulant man glared at the camera. He wore an orange jumpsuit and ankle chains. "I am being punished unfairly. Stop this injustice! I've done the most for Society than any other president."

A small group of protesters was outside the Compound, shrieking, "We need a *will* to have a *way*."

The reporter continued, "The last of his followers don't believe the facts. They will in time. There is still information coming to light."

"We don't have to worry about Sir William again."

Roseleen sighed with relief. She also knew Mallor no longer posed a threat to Society. He had disappeared without a trace. The negative energy she'd felt for months no longer haunted her.

※

Jordon watched the news on the screen in his home office. The story had been bigger and more explosive than he expected, and Society had embraced Triden. The image on the screen showed the young man accepting a position as Ambassador to the Contagions to assist with their assimilation into Society.

Reaching for his satchel, Jordon removed the files he'd taken from the metallic case and secured them in his personal safe. Annabella had been furious when she discovered the Compound would not offer the money-making opportunities for Republic Management as she'd hoped. The files in his safe contained other secrets that would remain hidden for now. When he'd read about the deceit at the Compound, he left the information for Roseleen to discover. Annabella didn't have to know he'd had the chance to bury the information. His conscience wouldn't have let him keep the residents detained illegally in the Compound. His wife's reaction had surprised him. Apparently, she would have made a different decision. She blamed him for not discovering the case contents, and it was putting a strain on their relationship. His discovery would remain his secret.

CHAPTER 63

Triden and Roseleen stood at the archway leading into Memorial Park. Rolling hills of green hid the piles of bodies that had been grouped together into a mass grave over twenty years ago. Triden knew his parents were buried somewhere within the large expanse. Several large trees dotted the landscape. They watched as thousands of pinwheels rotated in the wind. The metallic elements catching the rays of the sun cast star-like glints into view.

Hand in hand, they stepped inside and made their way down the walkway stretching before them. Triden held three pinwheels in his other hand.

"I sense they are over here, by this tree."

Triden didn't question his wife. Her intuition was strong, and the tree was as good as any other location to place the pinwheels.

The first pinwheel had his mother's name, Mira, written on one of the petals. The second pinwheel had his father's name, Dauvit, etched inside. The two pinwheels turned in unison, honoring his parents.

"What is the third one for?" Roseleen watched as her husband pushed the sticks of the pinwheels into the grassy lawn.

"It's for all of those who need to be remembered who have no one to put a pinwheel in the ground for them. So many senseless deaths. So much fear which wiped out a million souls."

"We've been given a chance for a new start. Hopefully, Society has learned from its past and will do better this time."

"What does The Source say?"

Lessons will repeat until the message is received.

"I think the message was received this time."

"I agree, Husband." She still marveled at the word. *Husband.* Never in her wildest dreams would they be standing together, free to walk in the world without restriction; Roseleen freed from the Forest Communion's desire to live secretly and Triden and the others released from the Contagion Compound, free to move without fear of harming anyone.

"I'm still getting used to not having a rash on my body. It was such a part of my daily experience for so many years."

"It helped Society shape a narrative about your place in the world."

"I know there are still some from the Compound who are concerned they'll infect someone. It's a hurdle to accept you're fine after so many years of being told otherwise."

"William Newbiggers will have time to reflect on his role in the matter."

"Do you think he'll ever know the harm he caused?"

"Probably not, but at least Society has a chance to heal, accepting everyone in Society as free and equal."

Triden kissed Roseleen. "Thank you for coming with me. I wish you could have met my parents."

"I feel like I know them by knowing you."

"I didn't know them well."

"You know you were loved by them. You are part of each of them, and they will live on in you as well as in our child."

"Our child?"

"Yes." She took his hand and placed it on her torso. We're going to have a baby."

Tears filled his eyes. "But... but I'm sterile from P3264."

"That's another one of the deceptions from Society. The doctor told me the protein pucks not only had the rash inducing ingredients, but it also served as birth control as well."

Triden lifted her and twirled her around, and then quickly placed her feet back on the ground.

"Oh, I didn't hurt the baby, did I?"

Roseleen laughed. "No, I can be active. Jayr says the baby is healthy and strong."

"The doctor?"

"Yes, he's decided to go back to practicing medicine instead of research in the lab."

"That's perfect. He gave us a life; it makes sense he helps give our child a life, too."

"I love you, Husband."

"I love you, too, Wife."

They kissed once more and then watched the pinwheels spinning.

This time will be different.

ACKNOWLEDGEMENTS

While writing can be a solitary activity, producing a book involves numerous people. First, a bigger than big thank you to my agent, Bill O'Donnell, whose expertise and guidance has gotten this book published. Thank you also to Margaret Beegle and Christina Howell for their copywriting and John M. Thompson for editorial review. Additionally, thank you to everyone in my writing communities, most notably Shut Up and Write groups in Munich, Maine Highlands, Bend and Sacramento. Also, Happy Writing in Munich, Writing with Friends in Los Angeles and Berlin Artists and Creatives.

Thank you to my beta readers and listeners, particularly those who were involved from the beginning when the manuscript was almost 106,000 words: Dr. Angi Orobko, Stephanie Zelin-Wilson, Chris Wilson, Jessica Wright, Rosemarie Balla and Judy Kienle.

Thank you to my friends and family, as well as Jean Berry and the amazing group of people who have supported me each week in our Master Club sessions, too many to list here.

And to bookend this project; thank you, again, Jen Nelson, with love and gratitude. If you hadn't asked for a buddy for NaNoWriMo, I probably wouldn't have written this book.

Eli Wellington, Naxos Island, Greece